IT'S TIME TO BELIEVE . . .

He was alone with Bria. He picked his knife off the floor and brought it close to her face. With his free hand, he pulled out a wave of black hair and sliced it off neatly with the razor sharp blade. He wiped the blade shut against his thigh and replaced the knife in his pocket, then dug a match out. Still holding the lock of hair, he struck the match. He brought the burning match and hair together, moving them both toward Bria. The smell of her own hair being charred was driven up her nostrils. A tiny quiver as she breathed was the only sign of life she betrayed. He drew the smoldering clump of hair closer until it singed the fuzz on her cheek. The muscle beneath the burning hair twitched. He ground the hair into the burn. Bria pulled away. The twitch in her cheek spread. He sat back. It was happening now.

DO EVIL CHEERFULLY

Sarah McCabe Bird

AVON
PUBLISHERS OF BARD, CAMELOT, DISCUS AND FLARE BOOKS

AVON BOOKS
A division of
The Hearst Corporation
959 Eighth Avenue
New York, New York 10019

First Avon Printing, July, 1983

AVON TRADEMARK REG. U. S. PAT. OFF. AND IN OTHER COUNTRIES, MARCA REGISTRADA, HECHO EN U. S. A.

Printed in the U. S. A.

WFH 10 9 8 7 6 5 4 3 2 1

Men never do evil so completely and cheerfully
as when they do it from
religious conviction.

PASCAL: Pensées

CHAPTER 1

The body lolling in the half-filled tub of tepid water was a cliché. Clichéd perhaps because it was the kind of body that casting directors and sculptors have always used to define muscular male perfection.

Six feet, three inches tall, it could have served as the model for Michelangelo's *David*. The large, leonine head, crowned with curly, bourbon-colored hair, rested face-up on the curling lip of the old tub. His legs, long and sinewy, were bracketed around both knees by shiny scars, the trademark of a high school quarterback. A silver scar sliced along the top of the pelvic ridge, then buried itself in the pubic thatch; an appendectomy at fourteen. The navel was a neat burrow in a tight landscape of corrugated muscles. His hands, large enough to palm a basketball, floated beside the body like twin escorts cruising alongside a carrier. The waterlogged thumb and forefinger nearly touched, as if he had been caught chanting "om" in the tub. His broad chest was a pampa of springy hair the same color as the ringlets that steam from the rapidly cooling water had plastered to his forehead. One fact, of course, marred all the glories of this bit of flesh—the body was, irrevocably, dead.

"Pull the damned thing out, Kirby." The Lieutenant, a compact officer in his late forties wearing a black uniform and a nimbus of vague anger, gestured toward the tan plastic hair dryer sunk in the bathwater just below the corpse's scrotum.

"Yessir." Kirby, twenty years younger and nearly a foot taller than the Lieutenant, moved in long, athletic strides across the wide expanse of white tiles that lay between

7

them and the old porcelain tub. It was the middle tub in a row of seven. They were on the fifth floor of what had once been a lunatic asylum. In the 1930s, when hydrotherapy had been the rage at this particular institution, the communal bathroom had been built for the patients. For hours they would sit side by side, the seven tubs filled with cold water, ice, and naked bodies. All were calmed by hours of submersion in near-freezing water; some even found the peace that surpasses all others. There had been corpses in these tubs before. Along the adjacent wall were half a dozen commodes sprouting straight out of the tile with not so much as a dishcloth between them to provide privacy. Patients had been herded through by the dozens to perform before their keepers, or to wait for the next scheduled opportunity. A steam radiator sat, unused for almost three decades, in the corner. Nearby was an ornate grill covering the opening to a ventilator shaft.

Kirby paused a moment at the edge of the center tub, the only one to hold an occupant in thirty years, since the showers had been installed downstairs. He bent over, ready to plunge in after the submerged appliance.

"Kirby." The Lieutenant's voice froze the younger man. "Yessir."

"You might want to unplug the cord first."

Kirby didn't speak as he yanked out the cord draped between the tub and an outlet near its clawfoot.

"It's probably already shorted out. But you wouldn't want to be the one to find out otherwise, would you, Kirby?"

Kirby stood over the corpse, staring. It was his first time on an assignment like this, but not his first time out with the Lieutenant. Either first might have unnerved him; the combination most certainly did. He took a deep breath, slowly unbuttoned his right shirt sleeve, rolled it up, bent over, and grabbed the hair dryer by its handle, taking care to avoid contact with the dead man's genitals. He held the small appliance above the tub and let the water run out of its mesh-covered vents. It fell in a stream on the scarred knees. The moment all the water had been drained out, the Lieutenant spoke again.

"On second thought, Kirby, better leave it there. The photographer hasn't been here yet, has he?"

Kirby tightened his grip on the hair dryer. His fingers clenched spasmodically around the handle.

"Nuh-nuh-nuh . . ." Kirby stopped, his face flushed from the effort of forcing out a word that wouldn't come. That damned stutter. He'd been rid of it for fifteen years; only the Lieutenant had the power to make his own tongue betray him.

"Calm down, Kirby." The Lieutenant laid a bony hand on his subordinate's back. "You're going to have many more assignments like this if you remain in this division. You'd better get used to them. We have a job to do here, so let's get it done with a minimum of histrionics, shall we?" He glanced sideways at Kirby's contorted face.

Kirby stiffened against the hand on his back and turned just in time to see a smile flicker out before his superior's face was once again immobilized behind its chilly barricade. The Lieutenant returned his gaze to the waterlogged corpse. The irises of the Lieutenant's eyes were a light hazel, almost yellow. They looked at the body with the amber emptiness of some unfeeling bird of prey, a void that could stare down death without a blink. It was those eyes combined with the black uniform and the way the Lieutenant hunched forward that summoned an image to Kirby's mind: a crow, thought Kirby, the Lieutenant looks like a goddamned crow.

"Here, give that to me." The dripping hair dryer was snatched from Kirby's frozen hand. Without a second's hesitation, the Lieutenant dropped it back into the tub. Kirby winced as it landed squarely on the dead man's penis, before settling on the porcelain bottom.

"All right now, let's get moving. Have you radioed the Captain?"

"Nuh-nuh-nuh . . ." Kirby stopped, defeated, and shook his head in a wordless, negative answer.

"Do that, ASAP. Also, have a print sent to HQ when the photographer gets finished. Make out the usual report. Get me a set of dupes, and that should do it."

Kirby managed a crisp "Yessir," pivoted, and headed for the door, eager to leave. He was halfway across the tiled floor when the Lieutenant stopped him.

"No, wait," he said, still examining the corpse, "that dryer isn't where it was before you fished it out. It's too far down. It should be farther up, closer to his crotch. Get it out, will you?"

Kirby rotated slowly, like a chunk of granite on a sculptor's wheel. He tried not to look at the body, to see the blue eyes locked open in glazed astonishment. He fixed his gaze on the green stain dribbling out from under the water tap. The Lieutenant watched Kirby's labored return. He watched him take several quick, shallow breaths, roll his sleeve back up, and reach his hand down until the tip of his middle finger broke the water. Only then did he speak.

"If you're going to make an ordeal out of this, Kirby, I'll do it myself. Step aside." He edged Kirby away from the tub. "You know, you really ought to decide whether or not you're right for this division. Have you thought about a transfer? I could talk to the Captain about it."

Kirby made no reply.

With one motion, quick as a bird's peck, the Lieutenant dipped his hand into the water and grabbed the dryer. He jammed the nozzle end of the apparatus firmly against the dead man's scrotal bulge. The remorseless yellow eyes then traced every inch of the body, violating its magnificence with their emptiness. His motions had been so brisk that the top two buttons of his black shirt had popped open. Now, as he lingered over the corpse, a small, gold, X-shaped medallion hanging from a chain around his neck was released to swing free. Attached to the chain at the intersection of the two legs of the X, it twirled and danced, almost to mock the dead man below with its endless, deathless spiral.

CHAPTER 2

Bria Delgado lay in bed, her eyes squeezed shut; she needed another few minutes to reconcile herself to the reality she would find when she opened them. Of all the mornings in the two years since Dom had left, these were the ones she hated most—the tail ends of nights when she had dreamed they had talked everything out and somehow she had managed to say the right words, the words that had persuaded him to stay with her, not to go off with them. The dream had been so real. He had been with her; she had felt him, felt his presence. It would be a jolt now to open her eyes and find the other half of the bed as empty as it had been for the past two years.

"Shit," she breathed. It wasn't fair, she was on guard every waking hour against thoughts that plowed open the hurt. It wasn't fair to be betrayed in your sleep. Awake, she fought to keep every moment occupied. At her job with the paper, she did the work of three people. She had stopped seeing all her friends because they were really his friends anyway. She had learned she couldn't date. The few attempts she'd made had been depressing evenings that had served only to make her even more aware of how far short of Dominic Xavier Cavanagh other men fell.

The dream, intact and unbidden, returned to her. It had begun with her telling him the news about the two UPI awards she'd won for her photography—Features and Spot News, in the 100,000-and-under circulation category. After she had brought the news of her two awards to him, like a kid with teacher's stars on her fingerpainting, they'd talked a long time in the dreamer's telepathic way. There were no words for her to remember, only the strong impression that he had been right. For the first time, she understood why he'd left. That's when it had happened, when she'd known that everything was going to be all right: now that she understood, she and Dom could be together again. He'd told her how much he needed her, that he'd never stopped loving her and all he had been waiting for was her understanding. Her relief had been unutterable; after two long years she was whole again.

Bria opened her eyes and lay motionless, watching her breath freeze into tiny smoke signals. She envied people who had incredible, escapist dreams. Hers were a drearily accurate reflection of what obsessed her waking hours— Dom Cavanagh. She wondered how long it would take before she'd stop living her life as if it were some drama that he was continuously monitoring. Dom was the invisible, omnipresent audience to whom she played her every scene. Sometimes, at work, she managed to forget him for hours at a time. But her editor had practically chased her out of the office yesterday. Two years without a vacation strained even the sweatshop employment practices of the *Santa Fe Sentinel.* She'd been ordered to stay away for at least a week.

She glanced around the small adobe cabin. As usual, it was cluttered with jeans, turtlenecks, sweaters, camera bodies, lenses, flash attachments, prints needing to be mounted, and mounted prints needing to be hung on the mud walls. She slid back under the covers. It was cold for so early in the year, even for nine thousand feet high in the Sangre de Cristo mountains. Dom was warm; it was still hot down there in Texas in November.

Her father thought she was crazy, living up here with only a wood-burning stove for warmth. She hadn't been able to make the Senator understand why she'd *had* to move up to what they had always called the Homestead. The old adobe cabin and the piece of mountain it stood on had come to be called the Homestead because they were all that remained of the five hundred sections of land that Polonia and Balthasar Delgado, founders of the Delgado dynasty in the New World, had been granted in 1719 by the Spanish crown. The gringos got the rest in 1895 when the government sent out agents to confirm all the private grants. Unfortunately, the Delgado charter, like most

Spanish grants, was of a lyrical bent, describing the parcel of land as extending "from this rock to that creek to that hill." The government surveyors confirmed less than a hundred acres. The rest reverted to the Territory.

Bria knew that her father worried about her living alone in the mountains. It was such a long time since Dom had left, and still her psychic resources were so depleted that she couldn't bear living in town—seeing the people they had known together, the restaurants where they had eaten, the arroyos they had walked beside. She'd tried and discovered that it would have to be either the Homestead, far from all those reminders, or some special place for battered human spirits, complete with mind pacifiers and a few years of beading moccasins and making plant hangers from old cleaning bags.

She snuggled farther under the covers and considered retreating behind them and her memories for the day. But that desire rang in her mind like the alarm that vaults a veteran fireman out of bed before he's fully awake. The tile floor chilled her even through the thick pair of ski socks she'd slept in. She jumped into the first few articles of clothing she encountered among those strewn about the floor. She had trained herself like Pavlov's dog in reverse to act in direct and immediate opposition to her natural inclinations, which tended toward the passive, the indecisive, the timid.

At the end of a drive too fast for safety down the twisting mountain road, Bria parked her Jeep on Burro Alley, off Santa Fe's main plaza. The plaza was deserted now, unlike that night six years ago when it had all started with Dom. She consciously deflected the memory and headed for her favorite restaurant. Raul's was around the corner, and she needed sustenance. A hot bowl of menudo, that's what her father invariably prescribed for any morning ailments.

She had missed the breakfast crowd. Thankfully, Raul's had never tried to make it as one of the trendy eateries where tourists lined up patiently to pay exorbitant prices for enchiladas made with tortillas ground from blue Indian corn. She slid into a booth. Ignacio Trujillo, the cook, came out of the kitchen to take her order himself.

"Gabriellana, cómo estás, huisa?" Ignacio was a thick-set man in his seventies, a butcher's apron was tucked un-

der his armpits. He always called her by her full name, Gabriellana. Perhaps because it had been Grandmother Delgado's name. It was rumored that the old cook had loved her. Bria had been told she resembled her grandmother, with her small, finely made body and a bone structure that lent her face the aristocratic look of one of those Spanish duchesses crowned with a high comb and mantilla. Bria remembered how shocking her grandmother's eyes had seemed to her as a little girl, the surprising light green, the exact color of the finest turquoise from the Cerrillos mine, contrasting vividly with her onyx-black hair. She wondered if her own similarly colored hair and eyes had the same effect.

"Una orden de menudo, por favor." Ignacio carefully wrote down her order of a bowl of tripe and hominy stew with his stub of a pencil.

"Ahorita, Gabriellana," he said, then disappeared into the kitchen.

Gabriellana. Airy, lacy, delicate. Bria decided it sounded like the perfect name for a fragile lady who wore combs and mantillas and needed to be protected. It really suited her much better than the shortened version, Bria, she had been stuck with growing up. The nickname had always made her uncomfortable. It sounded too much like *brio,* the Spanish word for "courage," which, when applied to her, sounded too much like mockery. Like the fat man called Tiny.

Bria thumbed a dime and a nickel into a machine and pulled out a copy of the *Sentinel.* The prospect of seeing how poorly the paper was faring photographically in her absence warmed her. If they have one piece of art in here, Bria thought, that didn't come straight off one of the wires, I'll hang up the Nikons forever. She crackled the paper shut with satisfaction as Ignacio slid a steaming bowl in front of her. Not one local photo. She'd worked to make herself indispensable and had succeeded.

When she had been hired three and a half years ago, Bria hadn't harbored any illusions about how she had managed to snag the best photojournalism job in the capital. All she had to recommend her were a spanking new BA from the University of New Mexico, a few semesters experience with the *LOBO,* the campus newspaper, and her name. It was the name that had nailed down the job. She was Frank Delgado's daughter—Senator Frank Delgado.

She'd had a lot to prove and, with Dom cheering her on, she had proved it. She brought in assignments that had been classed as write-offs, impossible. In a hard-charging, aggressive profession, she'd made a name for herself as one photographer who never backed off. She went for a picture and got it, if necessary with her camera crammed right up the subject's nostril.

That first year had been glorious, coming home each night to the four-room adobe she and Dom shared, savoring each new triumph, planning strategies for each new challenge. Dom had been happy too, running his own passive-solar-energy design consultancy. Even though it consisted only of a pad of paper by the phone and Dom's own indefatigable energy supply, the business was his, with no help from *his* famous father, either. His enthusiasm often bubbled over into long evenings when Dom would educate her about various alternate modes for heating and cooling. She was always anxious to move on to her own recounting of the day's events.

"Don't take shit off of anybody, *querida,*" he'd told her over and over. It was a standard part of the pep talk he was constantly pumping her up with. "The meek inherit nothing but ulcers and spastic colons. Your name means 'courage'; don't forget it."

"Brio means 'courage,' " she'd countered.

"Close enough."

It had been Dom, the golden blond Anglo, who had awakened in her a sense of her own racial identity. Her mother, a model of assimilation, had forbidden her to speak Spanish at home. Particularly offensive to the first Mrs. Delgado had been the rough dialect her husband and his compadres spoke, the dialect of northern New Mexico, in which *v*'s turned to *b*'s, *w*'s were added arbitrarily, and consonants were swallowed regularly. Francisco Delgado, engrossed in making the transformation to Frank Delgado, had readily acceded. Bria, a shy child, grew up on the periphery of both groups, neither Chicano nor Anglo. It was Dom who had persuaded her to learn her language at the university. However her name translated, if Dom wanted it to mean courage, that would be what she would strive for. Thus the conditioning, which had turned her timid responses inside out, had begun.

Bria tried to remember one tough assignment she had tackled in the past two years when she hadn't thought: if only Dom could see me now. She'd earned the ire of most of Santa Fe's celebrities, the politicos and cultural mavens. High on the list of the disgruntled was John Ehrlichman. She had appointed herself his personal paparazzo. Had Dom seen any of her shots of the glowering Watergate alumnus? A couple of them had been picked up by the wire services.

"Hey, the menudo's no good?" Ignacio asked the question with a grin. He had teased her since she was a girl for eating so little of the platters heaped with flautas and green chile enchiladas he had served to her and her parents at the café after Mass on Sundays. She had never had an appetite. One look at Dominic Cavanagh sitting in the front row of St. Francis Cathedral between his mother, the redoubtable Mary Margaret Cavanagh, and his father, the venerated former governor, always tightened her stomach into a hard knot that repelled food.

"Ignacio, you know you make the best menudo in the state."

Pleased, the old cook pointed to the newspaper. "That rag's not worth buying when they don't have any of your pictures," he said, by way of returning the compliment. "I don't know how you get those pictures, *huisa.* You got . . ." Ignacio clenched his fist lightly and shook it. Bria smiled as she mentally supplied the word he had pantomimed, *cojones*—in English, "balls." He waved at the bowl as he left, "Eat up, *flaca,* you got no meat on your bones."

Bria slid the paper out again and held it up as she dipped her spoon into the stew glistening with a sheen of melted fat. The spoon never reached her mouth. A small item near the bottom of the last page caught her eye and froze her hand. A drop of grease dribbled off the spoon and splattered up onto the paper. A translucent gray halo spread across the short article, but the words remained shatteringly unchanged:

Dominic Xavier Cavanagh, 28, son of the late Governor William Cavanagh, died November 1 near Aura Lee, Texas, 60 miles north of Houston. Cavanagh was found dead of accidental electrocution in the bathtub of a boarding house operated by a religious group Cavanagh had been affiliated with for the past three years.

A memorial service will be held today at 3:30 P.M. at Rosario Cemetery.

Cavanagh is survived by his mother, Mary Margaret Cavanagh.

Bria noticed that a multitude of tiny cracks fissured the black vinyl of the booth she sat in. Pasted on the walls were paintings of ghosts and pirates left over from Halloween. She wondered if Ignacio's grandchildren had done them. Their use of color was really quite good.

She reread the three paragraphs. This time a thudding nausea broke through the shock insulating her.

"No." Her lips formed the word that was cannonading hollowly through her. Not Dominic Cavanagh. Not the Governor's son. Her eyes skittered back over the page, like a mountain climber slipping down an icy face; she couldn't get a grip on the words. The paper crumpled beneath her hand. Mechanically, she fished a couple of dollars out of her parka pocket and laid them on the scarred tabletop.

"Hey, *flaca*," Ignacio called after her as she burst through the door. "Someday I want you to tell me why, all these years, you've been paying me for food you never eat."

CHAPTER 3

Bria was the last one up the hill to the graveyard outside Rosario church. She passed the low wrought-iron fence that blocked off the Cavanagh family plot. The Delgado plot was farther up the hill; it had been the third one staked out, a couple of hundred years before any Cavanaghs found their final rest in New Mexican soil.

The sky behind Mary Margaret Cavanagh was the extraordinary blue of an intensity found only in high mountain areas where moisture and pollution don't dilute the vividness of the late autumn sky. The panorama of miles of windswept mesa spreading out behind her was no more magnificent than the widow of New Mexico's most popular governor.

She stopped and watched the woman. Her hair had softened from iron gray to silver in the years since Bria had seen her last. She calculated that Mrs. Cavanagh must be in her seventies now, but her eyes were still animated by an intelligence that had helped the Governor form most of his better decisions. Standing erect beside the priest, she was every bit as intimidating as she had been fourteen years earlier when Bria had first begun her scrutiny of the Cavanagh family. Even then the Cavanaghs had seemed too old to be the parents of a boy Dom's age. It was only later that Bria heard the story of the first Mrs. Cavanagh, a beauty, adored by her husband, who had died of Rocky Mountain spotted fever, leaving Will Cavanagh alone with his Santa Fe law practice and his circle of friends, which was enlarged annually by his uncommon honesty and innumerable kindnesses. He was well into his forties when he met Mary Margaret, who was not much younger.

18

They were married the next year. To everyone's surprise, and the Cavanaghs' stupefied delight, a son was born nine months later.

"In the name of the Father, and of the Son, and of the Holy Spirit." Father Olivarez intoned the final words of the memorial service and flagged the Sign of the Cross over a freshly dug hollow.

Bria edged through the silent, humped figures until she could peek over the lip of the grave. She was as little prepared for what she found as she had been for the death notice. An urn, decorated with every religious symbol from an ankh to the Star of David, along with some she couldn't identify, nestled in the excavation. Cremation? she wondered wildly. Could the hideous vase contain what was left of Dom? Mrs. Cavanagh wouldn't have allowed it.

A staggering sense of unreality paralyzed Bria. Eyes that no longer seemed wired to her brain watched important faces swirl around Mary Margaret Cavanagh, cooing soft words of sympathy. Dom's mother looked away from them and caught Bria's searching gaze. Instantly she went toward Bria. In a gesture that had nothing to do with the years she had spent as the Governor's hostess, she gripped both of Bria's hands in her own.

"Come with me. We must talk." For the first time since Bria had known her, those eyes, which had always presented such an impenetrable shield against public scrutiny, were not a sunlit sea of calm and control; they were confused and haunted. The overwrought woman spoke little on the drive home.

The Cavanagh house was a fortress in adobe. Bria imagined it as it had been that Christmas six years ago when Dom had first taken her to his home. Hundreds of luminarias, nickel candles in bags of sand, had lined the driveway and sidewalks. The brown paper-bag lanterns had winked from the edges of the flat roof and along the chimney.

"Gabriellana." The Governor, tall as his son, had met her on the porch, his hand outstretched, before unneeded introductions could be made. They both knew only too well who she was, the socially backward daughter of an upstart Chicano contractor who had maneuvered his way onto Capitol Hill using the Delgado name and legacy to collect Chicano votes and a culturally assimilated wife to win

Anglo approval. A wife, Bria had thought bitterly, who had been discarded when she had become a political liability. The Governor wrapped her small brown hand between both of his.

"What's the word from your father?" the Governor had asked, pouring a generous slug of bourbon into her eggnog.

"He's supposed to be home for Christmas."

Frank Delgado hadn't come home to Santa Fe that year. Instead he'd remarried, and Bria had acquired her stridently Latina stepmother, Concepcion. Bria's own mother had left Santa Fe, a notoriously cliquish town, shortly after the divorce to live with a sister in Denver.

"Good," the Governor had boomed out. It was no mystery why he'd been New Mexico's most beloved governor. William Cavanagh projected warmth and integrity. He was the man you'd want for your grandfather, lawyer, barber, confessor, and any other position you could work him into. He had the politician's gift for making each person he met feel as if he were the most important individual in the world.

Bria had felt that way that Christmas six years ago. Today the living room was exactly as it had been then. Massive pieces of leather-and-wood furniture in the colonial style of old Spain set the tone of the room. Paintings by Georgia O'Keeffe and "Los Cinco Pintores," the five painters who had established Santa Fe as an art colony in the twenties, were interspersed with more contemporary classics like the raw slashes of the Indian artist Fritz Scholder. There were the same shelves filled with the black pottery of the San Ildefonso pueblo. Priceless Navajo rugs, woven in patterns now lost, were draped over the furniture. *Santos,* crudely carved representations of the saints, occupied niches dug into the sixteen-inch-thick adobe walls. The room was a collection of the finest of New Mexicana.

"Forgive me for not calling on you," Mrs. Cavanagh began, retreating in her uncertainty behind the wall of formality that had protected her for so many years. Her hands fluttered in front of her, pale, slender birds that she managed to control only enough to gesture toward the leather couch studded with heavy black brads. Bria sat down, and Mrs. Cavanagh perched at the other end.

"I really gave no one any notice other than what was in

the paper. I assume that's where you learned of the memorial service."

"Yes," Bria answered. The finely wrought balance of power that had always separated her from Dom's mother was teetering.

Mrs. Cavanagh closed her eyes. Bria sensed the strength the older woman was trying to gather from the dark room—from all the Christmases, victory celebrations, political parties, and gala events she and her husband had hosted over the years in this room.

"You know that I didn't approve of your relationship with . . ." She stumbled and stopped short of saying her son's name.

Bria's heart gave a sudden, violent stroke. She prayed that Mrs. Cavanagh had not invited her here to make some merciless confession.

". . . with Dominic," she finished decisively, straightening her spine, as if she had indulged herself long enough. "He is dead now, or has been reported dead, so none of that matters. None of it ever really did, though, did it? You loved him and he loved you. If only I had known then how badly everything would go. What Dom was going to do. I would have encouraged instead of—"

"You're right," Bria cut in. "It doesn't matter anymore."

"What does matter is this." Again that haunted, scared look clouded Mrs. Cavanagh's proud gray eyes. Bria wondered what earthly power could have put such fear into the indomitable Mary Margaret Cavanagh. She leaned closer to Bria and almost whispered. "Something is wrong, dreadfully wrong, about Dom's death."

Bria listened to the accelerated thud of her heart. More than her words, the insensate pleading in Mrs. Cavanagh's eyes frightened her, because it was to Bria they were appealing. She wanted to leave; instead Bria listened as her own voice asked with the assurance and authority she had learned to counterfeit so well, "What exactly was wrong about it?"

"It's so hard to put into words. I wish you and I had kept in touch over these past two years since . . ." Her voice faltered and Bria realized she was on the slippery edge of control. "First the Governor died, then Dom left, less than a year later. It was more than I could deal with, him going off with those . . . those Louies. I couldn't understand it. I can't accept it."

Bria immediately saw the truth in that admission. Mrs. Cavanagh now jumped the track onto a completely different subject.

"Did Dominic ever tell you what his name meant?"

Bria shook her head. She would have begun weeping had she spoken. Dom had always meant, would always mean, simply Dom. An elemental sound, a cluck of the tongue that could stand for nothing other than that one singular person. Dom.

"Belonging to the Lord," Mrs. Cavanagh announced, just as she had on the day twenty-nine years ago, during her third month of pregnancy, when she had unearthed the meaning in a dictionary of names. "I blame myself in a way for his taking up with those Life Unlimited people. I raised him the way my mother raised me, on old-fashioned Irish Catholicism. I think Dom was terribly hurt, disillusioned when he discovered that what he had been taught in catechism—the miracles of the saints, the Immaculate Conception, limbo, purgatory, heaven, hell—that it all wasn't literally true. He felt he had been lied to and came to despise the church for tricking him. So he declared himself an atheist.

"But he was left with this spiritual void, wasn't he?" Mrs. Cavanagh asked. "This great need to believe, which I'd dug into him. He had to find something to fill it, didn't he?"

Bria knew that she wasn't expected to answer. She was an eavesdropper on a dialogue that Mrs. Cavanagh had been having with herself for two years.

"It's heartbreaking that the religion—if Life Unlimited can be called that—he finally did embrace is so vastly more dogmatic and rigid than the church would ever have dreamed of being after Vatican II. So much of what we once were taught as literal truth is now seen as allegory. So much is left to an individual's own moral judgment—"

"Mrs. Cavanagh," Bria gently interrupted the monologue, "you were saying . . . about something being wrong about Dom's death."

Mrs. Cavanagh looked old and adrift. "Yes," she began,

pausing to reorder the events in her mind. "Well, I got the phone call—let me see, today is the fifth. They called Saturday, the first. The call was so abrupt, so unfeeling. As if telling me that my son had—" she stumbled over the word—"died that morning were merely some bureaucratic formality to be dispensed with as quickly as possible. But what I found even more disturbing was what they reported to me as the cause of death. It was absolutely not to be countenanced." Mrs. Cavanagh looked sternly to Bria for approval of her firm stand although she had yet to tell Bria what it was.

"What did they tell you had caused . . ." Bria finished with a vague wave to prompt Mrs. Cavanagh in her faltering narrative.

"Accidental electrocution. Said he'd dropped a hair dryer in his bath."

Bria's expression mirrored Mrs. Cavanagh's. They stared at one another in stunned incredulity.

"A hair dryer in his bath?" Bria protested. The two women shared the same basis for their disbelief. They both knew that Dom had been forced to bathe in a tub for the four years he'd attended military school and that, along with everything else associated with the school, he hated tub bathing.

What overrode even that reason, though, was the sheer impossibility of Dom ever doing anything by accident.

"He was always so aware," Mrs. Cavanagh echoed Bria's thought. "Even as a young boy, Dominic never missed a detail. He could never have done anything so . . . so foolish as take an electrical appliance into a bathtub." Bria shook her head in agreement, anxious for Mrs. Cavanagh to pick up the thread of her story.

"I was too shocked to question the person who called. When I'd calmed myself I said, 'What would the Governor do?' The answer was that he would have gotten in touch with whomever he knew in Houston with enough power to rip that Louie camp to shreds with a thorough investigation." Her voice sagged. "Unfortunately, one of the sad facts of being the widow of a powerful man is that, unless you've cultivated some power of your own, you find that your influence dies with your husband. So I did the next best thing and got on the earliest flight for Houston. I was determined that I would get some answers out of someone. The trip was an utter failure.

"They, these Louies," Mrs. Cavanagh enunciated the popular name for members of the Church of Life Unlimited as if it were the foulest of expletives, "held the upper hand from the moment I arrived. They side-stepped me, and put me off, and avoided me, and generally did everything they could to block my getting any real information. They were terrible. To start off, it was a nightmare trying to find their so-called Academy out in the middle of an overgrown forest. Then, when I finally arrived, some strutting martinet stuck a form in front of my face. It was a request for cremation that Dominic had signed. As next of kin, I had to authorize it. I was in such a state that I did sign. Then I had to receive special permission from the Archbishop to have the memorial service." Frustration, rage, and bewilderment burst the dam of Mrs. Cavanagh's resolve. Tears filled the cross-hatched furrows beneath her eyes.

Bria forbade her own tears to fall. Not now. "Had the police been called in?"

"Yes. Some country buffoon of a sheriff from the one-horse town nearby, a godforsaken place called Aura Lee, Texas. Obviously the Louies have not endeared themselves to the local townspeople. The sheriff, a most disagreeable little man, and his sidekick, a tall, gangly kid, were openly hostile and uncooperative. They allowed me to read the official report. Accidental death it had been ruled, no marks on the body, no indication of a struggle. He made quite sure I understood that he considered the case closed and would waste no further time on it. They even had a ghastly photograph, taken in the bathroom, they—" Mrs. Cavanagh slapped her hand to her mouth as if she could shove back the horror of that photo.

Because she had been avoiding it, Bria forced herself to ask, "Did you actually see the body?"

"No," Mrs. Cavanagh mumbled through her white fingers. "No, the next day after I paid the three hundred dollars for the cremation and signed the authorization, they gave me an urn, decorated with all sorts of symbols, and said his ashes were sealed in it."

She never saw the body! The inchoate jumble of emotions howling through Bria's mind were funneled into one

deafening gale that shrieked out her hope: Dom is not
dead. Bria looked around the room, searching for an an-
chor on which to fasten her storm-tossed thoughts. Her
gaze stopped at a picture of Dom taken in front of St.
Francis Cathedral on his First Communion day. He was
seven years old in a miniature suit with short pants, knee
socks, and lace-up Buster Browns.

"Have you thought about hiring a private investigator?"

"Bria." It was the first time she had called her by her
name. Ever. "You don't understand, a private investigator
would be worthless. Some paunchy, middle-aged man
smoking a cigar wouldn't be able to learn any more than I
did. You know enough about them to know that they have
a whole lexicon of jargon, their own system of impenetrable rituals. In order to even get past the front door, a person would have to be somewhat familiar with the group,
would have to be young, perceptive, dauntless. . . ."

The description dribbled off into silence, the final word
ringing synonyms in Bria's head: brave, gutsy, courageous.

"You weren't thinking about me?"

"I thought we could talk about it," Mrs. Cavanagh said
hurriedly. "See how you felt, what you thought we needed
to do. I've been following your work in the *Sentinel*. I've
heard the stories about you, about your . . . daring."

"Insolent brassiness" was probably closer to the words
her informants had used, Bria thought, to recount the escapades of the *Sentinel*'s girl photographer. Bria wondered
how she could tell Dom's mother that she had turned to the
wrong person for help. That, even in her shattered state,
Mrs. Cavanagh had more natural courage in her little finger than Bria would ever be able to fake in a lifetime, that
all her escapades were nothing more than charades for an
audience missing and now declared dead.

"I'm really not all that familiar with LU. Dom took me
to a couple of introductory meetings at what they call the
depot here in town, but that's all. I never got into any of
the more obscure, advanced stuff."

"But even that puts you far ahead of any private investigator. You at least know how they act, how they talk,"
Mrs. Cavanagh looked away, "that strange demeanor they

all have." Bria knew what she meant: the "Louie Eye-lock," a newsmagazine had dubbed it. Once you'd seen it, you never forgot it.

"I was utterly agog when I first walked into that place, that Academy. I couldn't think, couldn't function. At least it wouldn't shock you as much as it did me. I never got past the lobby.

"Bria," the tone in her voice matched the pleading in her eyes, "I heard about how you slipped into the dress rehearsal of the new opera pretending to be the wardrobe mistress's assistant and took that fantastic series of photos they ran in the paper. Your publisher himself told me the story of how you haunted John Ehrlichman until he agreed to an exclusive photo session. And how you disguised yourself as a caterer to gain access to the backstage area during a rock concert. That's the sort of adaptability and resourcefulness that it would require to outwit those people. To find out what really happened."

Bria found herself staring into the face of a carved saint sunk into a niche. Dusk had dug deep shadows into the wooden face of the *santo* until it had become a grotesque caricature of mute suffering and bleeding wounds. The smell of forty winters of piñon fires saturated the room like incense at High Mass.

"Even if I could get in," Bria's voice sounded thin as it broke the silence that had gathered in the darkening room. "What could I find out?" Bria was playing devil's advocate, not for Mrs. Cavanagh, but for herself. Two opposing desires warred within her: as strongly as she wanted to go to Dom, she dreaded facing the Louies again.

"I don't know, Bria, honestly; I didn't invite you here to lure you into some diabolically clever strategy I had masterminded in advance." A nip of frosty imperiousness had seeped back into Mrs. Cavanagh's voice. "I have to know if my fears are founded, that's all. I wasn't expecting you to produce evidence that would stand up in court. I . . ." The starch went out of her voice and she trailed off miserably, "I wasn't expecting anything. If someone could just visit that Academy, unknown to the Louies, just to have a look around, to see if the potential exists for . . ."

The words neither of the two women in the tenebrous room were speaking darted through the gloom like unlit fireflies. In her mind Bria ran through a quick list of possible alternatives to the Louies' version of Dom's death. Wherever Life Unlimited was concerned, she immediately suspected fraud. "Who was the beneficiary of Dom's life insurance policy?"

Mrs. Cavanagh brightened at the question. "You know, I had that exact thought. That was one of the major questions I wanted answered when I went down there to that wretched place. But the runaround those people gave me was positively Kafkaesque. Would you believe that I wasn't able to learn if Dominic even *had* a policy, much less who the beneficiary was? I called some insurance regulation board and was told that there are seventeen hundred companies in Texas and, if I didn't know the name of Dom's company, I would have to call them all to find out if he had a life insurance policy and who the beneficiary was. So, I suppose, that bit of information will have to remain an unknown quantity."

She went on after a long pause. "Bria, I am a proud woman, too proud. I would never ask this of you, never even suggest it, but I have to know what happened to Dominic. I *have* to."

Bria didn't answer; their common need spoke for itself.

"Even if those people are as malevolent as I fear in my wildest imaginings, they would stand to profit nothing from harming you. They don't even know who you are, do they?"

Bria nodded no, but she was thinking of the next seven days—her vacation. It stretched out in front of her like three hundred miles of desert populated by snakes, scorpions, and dead memories, all equally venomous. Stay or go, either way, she knew she would end up chasing Dominic Cavanagh. At least at this Louie Academy there was the slim chance that the ghosts would be alive.

"Of course, I'd pay for your flight and all your expenses."

Bria wished she could make a genteel refusal, but her bank account hovered, as usual, at a trim two-figure sum.

"I can't promise I'll accomplish much more than to spend your money."

Mrs. Cavanagh smiled.

CHAPTER 4

The late morning flight from Albuquerque to Houston started off badly. Her seatmate, a turquoise salesman from Los Angeles, dominated it with a monologue about his trade.

"I know the whole Indian thing is passé," he confided. He was a wiry man with skin tanned to the color and consistency of shoe leather; he had made himself into a brown showcase for the bracelets, rings, and squash-blossom necklace draped on his frame. "But I'm going to be short-circuiting that gig. I'm dealing strictly in Zuñi needlepoint, strictly class stuff, know what I mean?"

Bria didn't have a clue, nor any desire to hear more.

"I've just cut a deal with a designer, see," the man went on, unprompted, a self-fueling selling machine, "and he's worked out some radical new setting concepts that are as different from the usual Indian thing as Picasso is from Grandma Moses. Turquoise without the schlock. The schmucks in Houston will kill themselves to spend their petrodollars on stuff like that."

The man unwound slightly. It was Bria's turn to comment. Instead she wondered if his hair, tortured into dull, crispy frizzes, had been permanented. The man coiled forward again, rewound by her silence.

"This is the first scam, and there have been a few, believe me"—Bria didn't doubt that there had been—"but this is the first one I feel really good about, really comfortable with. Like I was reading in *Newsweek* the other day how there's this whole new trend back toward classiness, prestige, elegance. That's just the kind of project this is. I get indications like that all the time. The national mood, the time, everything is right for this project. It's going to happen in a really big way."

Bria wondered why so many Californians felt they were perpetually on the verge of the big break, reading cosmic signs everywhere, all pointing their way to colossal success. Maybe I should have spent more time in California, Bria thought, it would probably make the Church of Life Unlimited seem less bizarre. A shiver of something resembling stage fright shimmied through Bria's belly. She was already nervous and the manicky stranger next to her was compounding her anxiety by contributing his own permanent allotment. She reached into the overnight case at her feet and pulled out the copy of *Life Unlimited: A Science for Personal Survival,* that Dom had given her. She'd already read it three times. The first because she was curious. The second time, after Dom announced that he'd signed up for classes at the Santa Fe depot, because she loved him and didn't want to be left out of any part of his life. And a third time, last year, as a part of her continuing search for a reason why, a way to understand.

J. Louis Comfort, founder of Life Unlimited, was on the first page. Bria's temples pounded as she looked at the photo. The porcine man was turned in profile to the camera, his head, blunt as a mole's, tilted upward in a visionary pose. The wide gap of naked forehead between his eroded hairline and his eyebrows had been powdered so that it wouldn't shine. His eyes glistened wetly. His puckery jowls and chin were tucked into a brilliantly white aviator's scarf. Bria snorted. They must have glopped a pound of Vaseline on the lens to give the glamour shot the shimmery radiance favored by silent movie stars. In it, Lou, as he was called by his followers in friendly reverence, looked an overfed fifty. Bria turned to the biography that began the book to find out his age. She didn't have to read far to remember that the book wasn't long on factual data.

Lou was a boy to the sky born. The first inhabitant of this planet to take the gift of flight that man has so recently wrested from the creatures of the air, and extend it beyond the materialistic boundaries imposed by the limited minds that struggle always to control men's destinies.

J. Louis Comfort, Senior, was one of that heroic group of barnstormers who toured our country after World War I, where Lou, Sr., had distinguished himself as one of America's legendary flying aces. Young Lou, Jr., learned to fly while still a toddler sitting on his father's lap. His father would operate the rudder while his astonishingly precocious son handled the stick with the technical virtuosity of an old veteran.

Barely into his teens, Lou answered an instinctual call to arms when the soul-shackling forces of Hitler massed in Europe to pose the latest in a historically long line of threats to the survival of spirituality on Earth. Before our country had even considered becoming engaged in this struggle, Lou led America into the fray by enlisting with England's plucky Royal Air Force.

His ferocity in battle against the Huns flabbergasted the brave Britishers. Time and time again, they had to rewrite the record book as Lou scored hit after hit. Then, one foggy night, on a mission over North Africa, Lou's navigational equipment broke down. He would have been able to fly using dead reckoning except that a sandstorm blew in and knocked out all his points of reference. For the first, and only, time in his life, Lou was forced down.

He was found, close to death, by a tribe of nomadic Bedouins wandering through the desert. Though fierce enemies of the despised white man, they recognized in Lou an invincible spiritual presence and, rather than butchering him as was their customary manner of receiving white visitors, they cared for him as they would a young god fallen from the heavens.

The injuries Lou had sustained in the blind crash landing would have killed ten men. They severely inconvenienced Lou. It was in focusing his life forces to heal his battered body that Lou first gained mastery over the physical being. Confined for months to the princely pallet the primitive tribesmen had arranged for him, Lou's spirit took to the etheric realms even as his body lay mending. He became a self-taught adept at the ancient art, unknown to Western man, of soul travel. Lou was Airborne once more!

Bria skipped over the succeeding paragraphs, which detailed Lou's subsequent wanderings throughout the East and his mastery of "all the arcane mysteries of the soul, systematically hidden from Western man by the forces of materialism that have conspired against spiritual freedom since the time of the Greeks and are now massing for a final conquest."

"Jesus, you a Louie?"

Bria jerked up from the hyperbolic prose. The turquoise tycoon was glaring at the book in her lap.

"What . . ." Bria stammered, caught off guard.

"Had a friend once that went that way. You know, got On the Grid, or whatever you call it. Excuse me if I don't get the lingo just perfect; it's pretty technical, isn't it?"

Bria nodded noncommittally. The edge of hostility on the man's question was unmistakable.

"It's been a while since my friend dragged me to some of your introductory meetings. You people can be pretty pushy when you want to." His smile was a transparent veneer over hardened layers of acrimony.

"Stuh-range group, I'll tell you that. Hey, you people are in a lot of hot water with the feds, aren't you? Indictments for conspiracy to steal government documents, suits, countersuits. That federal judge is supposed to pass sentence early next week. Probably find them all guilty." His eyes gleamed at the mention of LU's current legal entanglements.

"What are you planning to do? That's a shitload of bad PR, isn't it? Ruin your image. Cut down on new recruits. Maybe 'Lou' won't get a new jet this year, huh?"

"I really couldn't say," Bria answered. "I'm not a member of the group."

"Oh, sorry." The hostility dissolved. "The book, and everything. I jump to conclusions about people. You have to in my business. Selling, it's like . . ."

Bria had no interest in what selling was like. "You had a friend in LU?"

"Stu? Stuie the Louie, that's what I started calling him. He never laughed, though. Would have before. After he got heavily into the Life Unlimited trip his sense of humor sort of dried up. We were pretty close at one time. Had a pool-cleaning service together for a few years. Did all right with it. Worked mostly in the Westwood/Beverly Hills area. Customized jobs only. Pool cleaning to the client's specifications. I don't know, Stu, he must have always been looking for something, someone. Was always what I'd call a dependent personality type. Full of insecurities, questions. Somehow he stumbled into LU, and they are only too glad to answer any and all questions. He went around acting like he had personally discovered the orgasm or something. It was a real pain. The guy thought he had all the answers and he started force-feeding them to me.

"At first he was very hot to get me into the group. I thought, what the hell? Stu may have his problems, but he was always intelligent, knew a good thing when it came along. So, I went with him to this introductory meeting. Out of respect for Stu, I really, honestly, gave the thing a fair try, and, let me tell you, it was stuh-range."

"Strange?"

"You've got the book, tell me that shit isn't weird. And the money they charge for those 'levels.' Holy Christ, where do the kids get that kind of scratch?" A film of sweat had broken on the man's high, domed forehead and his eyes were straining at their sockets. "Sorry," he breathed, rubbing the back of his hand across his forehead. "I got so used to going ten rounds whenever this subject came up that I still expect the Great Debate. Let's talk about something else, anything else."

Bria sensed that she had somehow unlocked this brittle man's personal Pandora's box. Still, she did not want to, could not, talk about anything else.

"What happened to your friend, to Stu?"

The salesman answered in a monotone. "I don't know. Once it was clear that I had no plans to buy into LU, I just kind of stopped existing for Stu. First he stopped talking about it; then he informed me that we didn't 'share the same reality,' and proceeded to cash in his share of the partnership. Period. End of a great friendship. He walked out and never phoned, wrote, nothing. It was like I never knew the guy. Unbelievable, isn't it?"

"Yes," Bria agreed, "unbelievable." The absoluteness with which Dom had disappeared from her life, from being her lover, her closest friend, her confidant, her life, to being nothing, a death notice in the paper, *was* unbelievable. It couldn't be true. Dom had promised. He'd said he would be back, and Dom was so much like his father. His word, his integrity, was everything to him, the Governor had taught him that. Bria became aware of the man next to her. His stare was softened by concern. She saw the change and felt exposed, vulnerable. His sympathy drew her tears as surely as his hype had deflected them.

"You lost someone too, didn't you?" His question hung between them. Lost? Bria bit the inside of her mouth and concentrated on the pain. She wasn't going to cry in front of him.

"That why you're going down there, to try and find him? Is he at the Training Academy?"

Bria nodded.

"Hey, look, don't be embarrassed, I did the same thing. After I hadn't heard from Stu for six months, I mean not a word, I really started scaring myself. Jesus, the stuff you read about the Louies would scare anyone. Plus, I really cared about the guy, know what I mean?" Bria glanced over. The man's face told her what he couldn't put in words: his feelings for the vanished Stu had gone beyond simple friendship.

"So I stormed down to the Academy—it was the last place I'd heard Stu mention—and burst in demanding to speak to him. See him with my own eyes, talk to him." In a softer voice he added, "Make sure he was all right. That what you planning to do?"

Bria didn't answer.

"If you are, forget it. That demand stuff cuts no slack with the Louies. They got a freeze-dried process that puts Folger's to shame. I mean, they put you on hold and you are in suspended animation. I went in there raving, threatening to call the police, the governor; the louder *I* got, the quieter *they* got. It was very stuh-range. I started shouting and slobbering in the desk clerk's face and he acted like I wasn't there. Everyone did. It was like there was some cue and everyone had withdrawn into themselves, or more like they had left themselves. Their bodies were still walking around but they, you know, themselves, inside, they weren't there anymore. After a few minutes of raving and stomping and no one even blinking an eye at me, I was afraid that if I went up to a mirror it would be blank." The man sank back into his seat.

Bria knew now what had happened to derail Mrs. Cavanagh.

"So you're what, tracking down a boyfriend?"

"Yes," Bria whispered, hoping for more information.

"Well, ditch the direct approach. If you want to see him, you're going to have to fake it."

"How do I do that?"

"Before he split, didn't your old man drag you to some of those introductory meetings?" Bria nodded. "Okay, so you know pretty much how they act—that stare, no emotions, no doubts, no loose ends showing anywhere."

Bria knew. She looked at the jewelry salesman, but all she saw were Dom's eyes, unblinking, absolutely fixed. Focused concentration, he'd explained. It certainly hadn't done much to help hers, though, watching his eyes burn into her during one of the increasingly long and increasingly painful "discussions" they'd had toward the end.

"Listen, if you are planning to do some sleuthing, could you kind of keep an eye open for Stuie, Stuart Benninger? Tell him Jake would really like to hear from him. Tell him to call, collect, anytime, okay?"

"Sure," Bria agreed, but her mind was elsewhere. It was riveted by the memory of her first Life Unlimited class. She had been met by a room full of unswerving gazes, glistening, piercing eyes; they had disturbed her. Yes, she knew that stare. The question was, could she face it again?

CHAPTER 5

The Houston air seemed to cling to Bria as if each molecule were encased in its own private oil slick, compliments of the refineries that ringed the city. It was an unpleasant change from Santa Fe's clean, weightless air. She tried to confine her breathing to shallow inhalations. Each one was tainted with the petrochemical industry's signature scent—rotten eggs.

She spotted the car-rental stands, and found that the only model they had left was a Nova. It was suitably nondescript, and Bria picked one from a lot containing at least two dozen identical to it. She pulled out the map Mrs. Cavanagh had marked for her and headed into Houston's miasmic atmosphere. Aura Lee, Texas, sixty miles to the north, was circled in red. A star some twenty miles east of the small town indicated the Training Academy.

On the freeway, Bria discovered that, as a health hazard, Houston's air was outdone only by its drivers. Rodeoing maniacs in supercharged pickup trucks roared past her, weaving in and out of her lane. She clicked the knob that should have activated the air conditioner. Hot air belched out. She switched it off and cracked her window for an asphalt-heated blast. She was sticky and greasy by the time she shook free of the tentacles of Houston. Finally the massage parlors and feed stores at the city's outskirts gave way to patches of pine that gradually thickened into a full forest, and Bria had time to think.

She eased her foot off the gas pedal and slowed down as her thoughts deadened at the prospect of facing an entire academy full of consecrated Louies. She knew that she wasn't prepared to pull off any elaborate masquerade. But she had watched Dom closely enough, seen how he had been transformed, to attempt a superficial charade. Isn't that all she had promised his mother she would do? Look around, stay long enough to pick up a couple of leads, take a reading of the place. Should only take a few hours, a day at the most. Once outside again, she could pursue whatever leads she had managed to unearth, possibly with her father's help.

Anchored by the strategy she had just worked out for herself, Bria relaxed and began to notice the scenery. A dense growth of pine, sycamore, and mimosa sprang from earth colored a deep rust by iron deposits. No wonder Texans affect the country-boy style, she thought; their countryside is so superior to their cities. Before she had even the millisecond it would have taken to censor the thought, Bria imagined herself amusing Dom with her insights about country-boy Texans. At least the old Dom would have been amused. Like the jewelry salesman's friend, Stuie the Louie, Dom's sense of humor had dried up as his involvement with the Church of Life Unlimited deepened. Commitment and integrity had still mattered, though, maybe even more than before.

Aura Lee, Texas, consisted of a U.S. Post Office, two gas stations—one of them, its doors and windows boarded over, had a sign reading: REGULAR 31.9, ETHYL 33.9—and the Busy Bee Café, which advertised the Rancher's Special, sixteen-ounce steak, Texas toast, biscuits and gravy, choice of three vegetables.

Bria stopped at the gas station that was still in business. While the attendant, a sullen sixteen-year-old in a T-shirt cut off just below his nipples and a cap that advertised cattle feed, filled up the Nova, Bria pulled out her overnight case and retreated to what passed for a woman's restroom. After stuffing toilet paper into a few of the larger holes in the wall opening into the station, Bria stripped off her jeans and top and dug out the designer skirt and silk blouse she had bought yesterday with Mrs. Cavanagh's charge card. The outfit was as close as Bria could come to approximating the expensively chic clothes she had remembered seeing the hard-core Louie women wearing when they had come to the Santa Fe depot to deliver the introductory lectures. Bria tugged the clothes over her sweat-sticky body.

The attendant was waiting in the office. "Looks like you're all set to meet someone special. Your husband? Boyfriend?" He pressed Mrs. Cavanagh's charge card down into the small machine and jammed the roller across it.

Bria gave a curt smile.

"No hablas inglés?" the boy asked with a grin calculated to be sultry and dangerously sensual.

"Yes, I speak English," Bria answered frostily. "When the circumstances warrant it."

"No offense, ma'am," the attendant blurted out. "I didn't really think you was Meskin. Where you headed?"

"I need to ask you about that," Bria said, stepping toward the county map mounted on the station wall. She wanted to be sure about the turnoff.

The boy moved forward eagerly. The girls in his junior class had declared him "town hunk."

"I'm looking for a place," she said, tracing her finger along the road Mrs. Cavanagh had marked, "called the Life Unlimited Training Academy."

Sullenness dropped back over the boy's features and his hormones stopped rioting. He backed away.

"It's supposed to be right here."

"Yeah, that's where it is." The "town hunk" mashed his lips together in disgust. "Just get back on Highway 59. Go up two miles and take the old Spur 357 off to the right." He looked out the window as if he were alone in the office. Bria stuffed her wallet back into her purse and started to leave. As she pushed open the door, the boy spoke, still staring out the window as if he were alone.

"Used to be a crazy house, you know. Some folks say it still is. Only worse now. That's what some folks say."

Bria pushed out. It was like walking into a greenhouse. Driving was a little better: at least moving air was forced past her body. Expecting the turnoff to be marked, Bria was five miles past it before she realized she'd overshot her mark. The muscles at the base of her neck knotted up as she swung the car around, skidding close to the ditches lining the road. She tried not to think about that attendant's parting words. A dull headache began to pound as her tight neck muscles drew in surrounding nerves. She back-tracked to the spur road she had missed on the first pass. It bumped and curved, winding far back into a countryside thickly overgrown with vines drooping in the heat. The only sound was the dull droning of insects in the hot autumn sun. The stretch of road was so forsaken that Bria had nearly concluded that she had taken the wrong turn, when she crested a sudden rise and looked down on the other side.

She felt like an explorer in Mexico at the turn of the century stumbling onto the awesome stone monoliths the Mayans had constructed in the middle of tropical jungles so dense they blocked the light from the sky. The Training Academy appeared to be a small village with buildings from at least three distinctly different architectural eras. Bria pulled the car off the road, backing it behind the overgrowth of foliage where she could see and not be seen.

Looking more closely, she realized that what she had taken to be many individual buildings were actually the rambling offspring of one mother structure, a huge limestone monster. Appended to either side were wings constructed during the thirties in a heavy-handed mishmash of Tudor and Gothic styles complete with rounded turrets at all the corners. They extended for, Bria counted, the space of eighteen windows and two more turrets, until they smacked up against another wing done in the style of a fifties factory. Several other buildings were huddled behind the main one, connected to it by an elaborate system of catwalks. The only structures not somehow raveling out of the old limestone core were a power plant and a large airplane hangar with AERODROME spelled out in orange letters. Beside it was an airstrip.

Bria was dumbstruck. Apprehension prickled through her. For several minutes she stared at the sprawling Academy. Sweat trickled down her neck and pooled in the cup between her clavicles before it rolled down the ravine between her breasts. The lengthening shadows did little to make the disturbing architectural conglomeration any more appealing. The schizophrenic scramble was perfectly suited to what it had once been—a mental institution. Bria had difficulty imagining any sane person voluntarily entering. She had an even harder time imagining Dom living there for two years. Dying there. The more Bria stared at the bizarre jumble of buildings and thought about their remote location, the more convinced she became that anything could, and probably had, happened there. Had happened to Dom, could happen to herself. She focused on the main building. For five stories up, the windows were dark. Could Dom be behind one of them? No matter how many times she tamped down the hope that Dom might still be alive, like an unruly cowlick it kept springing back up.

So what if he is still alive? a voice within her asked. It was her mother's voice, the one that had always told her to be careful, to watch out, not to do this, to stay away from that. Now it asked, so what if Dom *is* up there right now, hiding behind one of those windows? For all you know, he might be a willing accomplice. Maybe it is all some insurance fraud. Maybe he staged the whole thing so that he could permanently disconnect from his past life, be literally reborn in a new life as a Louie.

Her mother's voice faded as Bria picked out a lone window high up on the fifth floor to focus on. Dom had always liked lots of windows. That was one of the main reasons they had chosen their house above Canyon Road. For an adobe, it had had an unusual number of high, airy windows. She thought of how Dom had looked with the morning mountain light washing over him in golden pools as he lay sleeping beside her.

A drone, deeper and more mechanical than that of insects, shattered her reverie. It hummed in the distance, growing louder. Bria slid down, pressing herself against the upholstery. A bus bounced to the top of the rise and bore down on the valley below. It whisked past Bria, the words LIFE UNLIMITED TRAINING ACADEMY blurring on its side. All forty-six seats were filled. It was eerie to see that number of people rocket past in air-conditioned isolation on an utterly deserted, one-lane country road.

Trailing behind the bus came six rental cars carrying the overflow.

Bria turned the ignition key and waited for the last one to sweep down the hill and around the first turn in the road. The lead car was slipping through the gate when she nosed out of the trees that had hidden her and spurted down the long hill toward the Academy. The decision to go had been made for her. All six cars behind the bus had been Novas.

CHAPTER 6

The limestone building was as pitted as a face full of acne scars. Where copper drainpipes pierced the foot-and-a-half-thick walls, they wept green tears that stained all five floors from just beneath the shingled roof clear down to where the foundation met the roots of the magnolias and pine trees. The state of Texas had built the Lunatic Asylum for the Soldiers of the Confederacy for all the gallant Johnny Rebs who came home but couldn't stop the blast of minié balls from ricocheting around in their heads. They came, or more often were sent, from all over the defeated South. The huge wards filled quickly after the asylum opened in 1875 on the edge of a remote forest, far removed from the society casting out its damaged men.

In 1968, after a succession of agency overseers, the soggy white dinosaur was abandoned and the old asylum slid into the rest it had earned. Silence replaced the screams and endless shuffling of sad feet. For nine years no one disturbed the old building's rest. In 1977 the silence ended. Two men bought the complex outright for four and a half million in cash. The good folk of Aura Lee buzzed about the transaction. They buzzed even louder when a high arching sign of black wrought iron was erected over the entrance. It proclaimed the former madhouse's new identity: The Training Academy of the Church of Life Unlimited.

In spite of the temperature, a chill shivered down Bria's spine as the shadow of that sign fell across her car. She pulled up beside the row of Novas. Both the rented cars and the bus were disgorging their loads. Close to eighty travelers milled around, waiting to collect their luggage. Bria grabbed her purse and overnight bag. Her hand on the door handle, she paused. The Louies were just as she had remembered them—few older than thirty-five or younger than eighteen, most in their mid-twenties. There were enough three-piece suits, forty-dollar haircuts, and gold jewelry to outfit a legal firm. For a few, the accoutrements of affluence were nothing more than expensive costuming; their faces had the anonymous look of street corners and bus stations. They were understandable. For them LU was a way out, a way up. But the others, a solid majority, were gilded with the special patina of America's golden children. Like Dom, they had been born for the success they accepted as rightfully theirs. They were the ones who ripped open the perpetual question: Why? They didn't fit. What drew them here? The question slicked Bria's palm with nervous sweat. She unsnapped the door handle.

As she approached the group, Bria fought the unsettling feeling of being minutely, yet irretrievably, out of place. But no one evinced the slightest interest in her. Or each other. There wasn't even the superficial chitchat that strangers exchange at a bus stop.

The only persons speaking were the two Louies at the head of the cluster who were reading names off luggage tags from the stack of bags at their feet. The young man and woman could have been Disneyland guides except for their stern demeanor, which would have been more appropriate to the cadres of an urban-guerrilla unit. The owners of the announced baggage stepped forward, wordlessly claiming their bags, then marched briskly toward the main building. Bria edged toward the point farthest from the group and closest to the building, and waited for the inevitable, a mix-up. A momentary dispute about the ownership of two identical pieces of Vuitton luggage bottlenecked the claiming process. When it was flushed out, a clump of half a dozen Louies flowed through at once. Bria slid in with them. No one in the group glanced her way. It was like being in a herd where each horse is totally intent upon taking the lead.

They mounted the stairs leading up to the column-lined porch that stretched across the entire front of the limestone asylum. The instant the first foot hit the porch landing the heavy oak double doors swung open and two young men, both looking like they were ready to pose for a Marine recruitment poster, stepped out to brace each door with their military rigid bodies. Bria's heartbeat accelerated as she saw the guards greet each entrant with a Louie Eyelock. Heads swiveled to meet and return the laser gaze the guards directed on each person passing the door. Bria took a step up. So did her adrenaline level and the nervous pressure constricting her breathing. It was enough to trigger the self-conditioning she had used to train herself to react to fear by doing precisely what it was she least wanted to do: she took the next step, and the next. The other new arrivals surged past her. The guard's eyes seared her with a stare of inhuman intensity. She bit down on the soft tissue inside her mouth and returned the stare with an equal ferocity. On legs that seemed to be operating by remote control, Bria entered the Academy of Life Unlimited. Both guards pivoted in unison, and the oak doors boomed shut behind her.

Inside was a world as far removed from Aura Lee, Texas, as any Bria could conceive of. Counters manned by uniformed Louies ringed an enormous lobby. Bria figured that the Louies wearing uniforms rather than designer clothes must be the Academy's working class, paying for coursework with their labor. Across from the entrance were panels of windows extending from the floor and soaring nearly twenty feet up to the ceiling. One of the panels had been replaced by the largest piece of stained glass Bria had ever seen. It depicted J. Louis Comfort, complete with white aviator's scarf, striking a heroic pose. Wheeling about his sloping, mole's head was a constellation of religious symbols—a cross, a Star of David, the Buddhist's eight-spoked wheel, a Shinto torii, an ankh, the yin and yang of the Tao—disturbing reminders of Dom's alleged cremation. A sense of urgency charged the air as tangibly as the cloud of cigarette smoke that hung in the still air of the poorly ventilated lobby.

Although no one spoke, everyone seemed to be on a mission of the utmost importance. Louies whisked past one another, crisscrossing like travelers at an airport rushing to catch flights. Bria clipped along with her group to a counter that spanned the length of the far end of the lobby. Five groups of new arrivals were queued up in front of it. A sign overhead read: VERIFICATIONS. A computer terminal sat beside the uniformed person at the head of each line. A soft buzz near the front of the lines became audible. Bria could distinguish a polyglot of accents. She remembered that the church claimed to have five million members in the United States and ten million around the world.

At the head of her line, a calfskin-jacketed devotee spoke with the attendant, who simultaneously nodded and typed out the information on the terminal in front of him. Apparently satisfied with the man's answers, the attendant issued him a tidy sheaf of papers bundled up in a folder like an airline ticket. With no further instructions, the man took the folder and melded with the stream of Louies funneling toward the main stairway.

At its base were two more militaristic guards extruded from the chin-tucked Marine mold. Guns bulged at their hips. The man in the calfskin jacket emptied his pockets on a table in front of them and presented the folder he had just received. A guard examined the folder, then motioned the fellow on. He stepped through an arc of steel extending over the stairway, while the contents of his pockets were shuttled through a tiny, curtained doorway via conveyor belt.

With a jolt, Bria realized what she was seeing—an airport security system complete with metal detector and X-ray machine. If she had been unsure before about how seriously Life Unlimited took itself, all doubts were erased now. Louies wearing plastic identification badges were waved on past the security system. Bria guessed that only new arrivals on their first trip upstairs were scrutinized.

"Pattern deformation."

For a second, Bria had difficulty determining where the high-pitched, mechanical-sounding voice had originated. She turned around to face the speaker, a petite woman tottering on high heels, who jerked her chin forward to indicate the area in front of Bria. A gap had opened up while Bria had been gawking—the "pattern deformation" the woman had referred to in her atonal voice. Bria choked back her instinct to smile apologetically. It didn't appear that Louies did such things. She skittered forward. Only two people now stood between her and the counter. She strained to overhear the exchange, and failed.

For a split second, Bria remembered the last time she'd

attended Mass. To appease her mother, she'd joined those
receiving Communion. It had been years since she'd performed the ritual and, as she neared the altar, she had realized that during those years the entire process had
changed. No more kneeling as the priest shuffled down the
line of communicants distributing hosts on outstretched
tongues while an altar boy slipped a golden paten under
the uptilted chins to catch any sanctified crumbs. Now the
priest stood at the foot of the altar and dispensed the wa-
fers. Bria had experienced then a mild form of the panic
that seized her now as she inched toward the indecipher-
able administrative ritual ahead.

When the Louie directly in front of her, a young man in a
corduroy jacket with leather patches, who looked like a
teaching assistant in anthropology, stepped up to the counter, Bria was able to make out what they were saying. The
words, at any rate, were clear; their meaning was still unfathomable.

"Code Eighty-five," the counter attendant, a handsome,
meticulously groomed man, snapped.

"AXR-twelve hundred," the young man machine-
gunned back.

"Level Assignment."

"Grade Eight. Unexpanded."

"Home base."

"Madison, Wisconsin."

"Sponsor's name."

"Danfers, Matthew."

The only part of the exchange that made any sense to
Bria was when the young man delivered his Visa number.
Then he switched his briefcase to his left hand and extended his right one a mere second before the attendant
had verified his answers and account number, and pulled
out a folder, which he initialed and handed over.

"Elevate," the attendant said as the young man took the
folder. Bria tried to decide if the word were an order or a
blessing.

The man's reply, "I intend to," as he strode off toward
the stairway, didn't supply many clues. Nor did Bria have
any clue as to what she was going to say, what she was *supposed* to say. At the last second, it occurred to her that it
might be best to say as little as possible.

"Code Eighty-five," the handsome attendant said, for what must have been the hundredth time that day.

"¿Hablas español?" Bria asked.

"Spanish?" the attendant echoed. His carefully manicured hands, poised over the terminal, dropped abruptly.

"Sí, español," Bria repeated.

"No, no speak Spanish." The attendant looked around. "Glenda," he addressed the attendant at the next station, "you don't speak Spanish, do you?"

"No. Where's the Spanish interp?"

"I don't know," he answered, sounding considerably more jangled than Bria would have expected. "We didn't show any monolingual Spanish arrivals today." He turned again to Bria. "Do you speak *any* English?"

"Inglés? No." Bria shook her head forcefully.

"Code Eighty-five?" he tried again, drawing out the syllables as if that would make them comprehensible.

Bria pursed her lips with annoyance, then rattled off in Spanish, "Where is your interpreter? I've been traveling since yesterday and made arrangements before I left the depot for an interpreter." The only word Bria left in English was "depot."

The attendant scanned the lobby, his lips pressed into a tight line of annoyance. Seeing no source of aid, and the line behind Bria growing longer, he relented. "Okay, I'll issue a provisional pass. It has your room number on it. The interpreter will be here tomorrow and we can get this all sorted out."

Bria mixed some puzzlement in with her own look of annoyance.

"Room number," he repeated, gesturing with his pen at the number he had circled on the folder, then waving it toward the upstairs area. To hammer home his meaning, the attendant joined his hands in prayer fashion and tucked them under his head as he inclined it to the side to suggest slumber.

Bria nodded and took the pass. *"Elevase."* She translated the blessing/order into Spanish.

"Elevate," the attendant answered automatically. *"Mañana.* Here," he called after her, stabbing at the air above his desk.

Tomorrow, Bria thought. She had won only one night's

reprieve with her cleverness and she still had no more idea of what to do with it than she'd had when she walked in. She handed the guard at the stairway her provisional pass and hesitated a moment before stepping through the metal detector. What if it weren't a security gate? What if this strange crew had developed an apparatus that could detect elements infinitely subtler than metal, like alliances. Her negative attitude would surely set off a huge alarm.

"Step through," the guard ordered. Bria did. Nothing happened. She was handed her pass and ascended the stairs. What a farce, she thought: codes, security guards, metal scanners. How could Dom have put up with all of this?

CHAPTER 7

The upstairs was as great a shock as the lobby had been, in precisely the opposite way. Unlike the first floor, which had been renovated, the upper floors still looked like a lunatic asylum. And smelled like one. The odor of urine and disinfectant had lingered on long after the last incontinent patient had departed. Bria added another cause for disgust to her growing list: LU chose to put its money into glamorizing the more public entry hall and had neglected the areas where followers actually lived.

The high vaulted ceilings and walls were still coated in a dreary hospital green. Continent-shaped watermarks stained them. The linoleum on the long, dark corridor was pitted and cracked. Bare concrete showed through in several patches where the tile was worn away completely. A dark spot on the floor ahead of her suddenly came to life and slithered along the baseboard, disappearing where the wood cracked away from the floor. A cockroach, a large one.

After the first floor, the grand staircase was replaced by a rickety series of metal stairways that looked as if they had been torn out of a lighthouse. On the fourth floor Bria consulted the folder in her hand again. The number 478 was circled on the back. She followed the numbers stenciled on the close-set doors and was standing in front of 478 when she realized that she didn't have a key.

She turned the knob; the door opened. The dank little room was as depressing as the outer hall and approximately the same shape—long and narrow. It was a hall that had a door at one end and a section of mesh-covered window at the other. The cot-sized bed was pressed lengthwise against the wall and still there was barely enough room for Bria to squeeze past it. The flimsy door and thin sheetrock walls told Bria that her room had once been part of a large open ward that the Louies had sliced into a series of wafer-thin rooms. The two walls cut into a window larger than the room. It hadn't been converted; it was still a mental-hospital window, reinforced with a web of wire and sealed permanently shut. It had been designed to prevent escapes and would still serve that purpose, Bria thought grimly. A window that wouldn't open and a door she couldn't lock did little to ease the hard nervous knot clumped in her stomach.

She tossed her purse and overnight case on the bed. The pass fluttered down after them. Okay, gutsy girl photographer, she asked herself, exactly what have you gotten yourself into? She slumped onto the edge of the bed. Metal springs creaked beneath the thin mattress. She wondered how many others had perched where she was. How many lunatics, sitting motionless, buried in catatonia? How many screaming wildly to be let out? How many voluntarily incarcerated—the true believers, young Louies who had pillaged trust funds or the first financial blossomings of a professional career to pay exorbitant sums to confine themselves in this piss-smelling madhouse and have Louie dogma drilled into them? Had Dom spent his last days in a hole like this? Was he somewhere in the old asylum even now? Bria knew that she'd never uncover any answers if she allowed her disgust to deaden her perceptions.

A sound like a gong being struck next to her ear jerked Bria to attention. Chimes continued to ring out on an ascending scale. Bria spotted the source—a speaker planted high in the corner of the room.

"Attention, cadets; attention, cadets: dinner is now being served in the Main Mess. Service terminates in one hour at nineteen hundred hours."

The message echoed and reechoed the length of the hall. Bria wondered if the PA system were two-way, if the rooms could be monitored as well as broadcast into. The chimes bonged again. Before the last note had faded, Bria heard doors opening, a clicking symphony of knobs being turned up and down the hall. Bria looked out. Well-dressed young people were streaming out of rooms that Bria had assumed were empty. They looked like all the others, young professionals dressed for success. Bria stopped only to pick up her provisional pass before she channeled out to join the stream.

Marching with that particular parade gave Bria an eerie sensation. She had expected a mindlessness. She'd read about it so many times, how Louies join up to surrender themselves, to turn over all of life's hard decisions to J. Louis Comfort. But it wasn't so; Bria felt it. The second she stepped in with the crowd, she sensed again the urgency she had felt in the lobby animating each person around her as they all moved toward the stairs. Everyone was headed for the same destination, but even now, even if it were just for dinner, she could feel the individual purposes pulsing around her.

At the stairway, Bria pivoted and flowed down with the rest. At each landing they merged with a larger group. By the time they had reached the first floor the sound of heels pounding on the old floors and echoing off of the high ceilings was thunderous. At the lobby they poured off the stairs and surged through toward a back wing. Bria looked back. The huge lobby was engorged with bodies. As far back as she could see the stairs were choked too. Still, there wasn't the slightest hint of disorder in the throng. No one pushed or shoved, or even nudged. The movement ceased and no one broke synch, the halt rippled back flawlessly. Bria was awed by the silence of that many people. It wasn't like the quiet of church where there are always coughs, and babies' cries, and pages rustling to break the silence. Here it was complete. Complete and disciplined and utterly without effort.

The doors marked MAIN MESS opened. As if that were a cue, a drone of low, pleasant voices started and the crowd entered the dining room. Inside, a larger-than-life bronze bust of J. Louis Comfort greeted the diners as they filed past. Comfort had been cast in a smiling pose, a smile compassionate and omniscient, as if he knew all, accepted all, then knew some more. A cap with four stars sat jauntily on his head.

Like a current hitting a log buried in a riverbed, the group broke in two and eddied around the bust, moving to one side or the other of the mammoth dining hall. Bria

tried to blend in with the group diverging to the left. She
moved with them up the length of the hall. At each row of
tables a seemingly arbitrary number broke off, with people seating themselves according to a predetermined order
Bria could not comprehend. She continued moving uncer-
tainly forward, aware that she was approaching another
danger point. She was nearing the last row of tables and
had no idea how to prevent exposing herself as hopelessly
lost, an outsider.

All the tables behind her had filled up with an implacable precision. There was no chance that she could simply
slip in somewhere. She began to feel that she was being noticed. That her indecision, a quality alien to true Louies,
was being observed. She came to the end of the dining
room. The last table was filled. Far down at the other end
of the hall, the bronze eyes of J. Louis Comfort seemed to
track her. She heard a buzz begin and imagined that the
heads leaning together were whispering about her, about
the intruder . . .

"You a Level Five, Technicals?"

Bria jerked toward the unexpected voice and stared into
the first distinctly brown face she had seen since arriving.

"Yes." Her startled response was reflexive. Instantly,
she regretted it. She had blown her Spanish-speaking
cover.

"Your tables were expunged for the evening. All the
Level Five Techs were to have been diverted to Auxiliary
Mess, but obviously not all of you got the word. Come over
to my table. We had a debarkation this morning."

Bria followed her rescuer, grateful for his intervention
and whatever interpretation he had given her situation.
She sat down opposite him at the end of a banquet-length
table covered with a white linen tablecloth and set with
crystal and fine silver. Twenty-two others sat around the
table. Not one of them glanced over or broke his muted
conversation to acknowledge the arrival of a person who,
Bria figured, must eat with them every night. She and her
rescuer were the last ones seated. The instant they pulled
their chairs under the table, a small army of waiters in
white jackets materialized, pushing carts loaded with
trays. Each one maneuvered to a table, stopped at its head,

and began passing around plates to the diners. The plate's contents made the elegant table settings seem to be an elaborate bit of black humor. Bria passed along plates heaped with a blob of bready dressing studded with some anemic peas, accompanied by a scoop of cranberry sauce in a pinkish puddle. Two cookies sat at the edge of the plate sopping up the cranberry runoff.

Bria began to understand why Louies were, without exception, stylishly thin. She had never sat down in front of such unappetizing slop. All around her, however, the bready glop was being devoured. She forced some down. At the same time she tried to examine the Louie who had saved her. He was Chicano, in his mid-twenties. Bria had already noted that he was short, close to her own height of five foot four. His height, combined with a headful of thick, straight, brown hair, and coppery-brown complexion, told Bria that he had a lot more Indian than Spanish blood in his veins. Amid all the trendy WASP types around him, he looked like a cook's helper who had strayed out of the kitchen. Bria wondered how he had found his way into this cult of overachievers. The question made her realize that, in spite of her pale skin and fine features, some Anglo Louie could very well be asking the same thing about her.

"Good evening, cadets!" A male voice boomed out. Heads lifted and swiveled toward the bust of Comfort, source of the broadcast voice.

"Good evening, Lou!" hundreds of voices called back in unison.

Bria had to struggle to keep her mouth from gaping open.

"I'm cruising now in the new Sabre Liner at an altitude of thirty-three thousand feet." The voice had a faintly British accent lightly varnished over a solidly Midwestern undertone. "But I am with you!" Applause broke out at the curiously emphatic statement. With a blend of chatty joviality and unwavering certitude, Comfort continued.

"Good news to report tonight, cadets. As of this moment 15,134,876 beings across the planet have gotten On the Grid! Of that total, 1,989,493 have dropped all Drag Factors, become permanently Airborne, and gone UNLIMITED!"

Wild cheering erupted. Bria felt she was at a convention of vacuum-cleaner salesmen priming themselves to go out and sell.

"Okay, cadets, that's what you're here for. Either to get permanently Airborne yourselves, or to Upgrid a trainee. It's that simple. If you cannot accomplish that mission, leave immediately. Right now. Put down your fork, go to your Tower, and leave. Do not hesitate. We don't want you here."

A silence, more alarming than the cheering had been, blanketed the hall. No one stirred. Breathing had become shallow. Even if a Louie were disgruntled enough to want to leave, Bria thought, it would take more nerve than the average well-socialized human being possessed to stand up before hundreds of coreligionists and announce his disenfranchisement. The effect for those sitting silently around her was a nightly renewal of loyalty and reinforcement of a shared reality in which people cheered statues.

"Good, then everyone still remaining is with us and with the Mission. Is that correct?"

"Yes, Lou!" hundreds answered, their faces lit with an unearthly radiance. A quality emanated from them that Bria had only read about before—pure joy. Formerly stony faces were transformed by the emotion; they all looked like new mothers gazing at the miracle of their firstborn child.

"Altitudinal!" J. Louis exclaimed, audibly returning the waves of adoration being beamed at him.

"Altitudinal!" the crowd roared back as the connection crackled, then went dead. It was replaced by a low-throated hum that grew and crescendoed at an ear-shattering volume. Bria would have sworn that a plane was taking off right in the dining hall. The sound had an even odder source. Across the table she saw her Aztec-faced friend's throat vibrate. Everyone in the hall was humming a perfect imitation of a plane taking off. As abruptly as the chorus started, it stopped.

"Wow." The brown face across the table was split by a grin mirrored on faces around the hall. "I think I just dropped about a dozen Drag Factors just listening to that."

"Really," Bria answered, using the one rejoinder she'd found appropriate to any declaration. She glanced away, hoping that he wouldn't pursue the conversation. Her gaze traveled to a dim corner.

Removed from the rest was one table occupied by a group of twelve. Not one of the occupants was smiling or reveling in the Comfort broadcast. There were no plates in front of them. On the wall next to the table was mounted a grimy plaque that read: TRAITORS' CORNER. The men were unshaven. They wore shirts that hung in limp, dirty creases from scrawny necks. The women were just as filthy, their hair clumped into greasy ropes. Misery was stamped into their faces. All were a pallid, unhealthy shade that approached the light gray of an overcast day. Bria wondered what the dozen had done to merit such treatment.

As she watched, a particularly haggard man began coughing. He quickly bent his head and buried his mouth in a napkin. A vivid red stain spread over the white linen. No one at any of the surrounding tables so much as glanced as the man crumpled over, still keeping up a rattling hack. Two waiters appeared beside him and yanked him out of his chair. He was hauled from the dining room. Bria searched for a reaction. There was none.

Someone could die here, Bria thought, forbidding the emotions rioting within her to alter her expression, and no one would turn a hair. Without moving her head, she unsuccessfully studied the endless rows for a trace of concern. The faces were all pale, a tribute to the hours spent indoors studying Comfort's theology. Here and there, she recognized a famous face, one of the celebrity Louies who occasionally turned up on some late-night TV commercial to tell how LU had helped their movie/recording/professional-football careers. White was by far the dominant hue among the diners, with Orientals first in number in the miscellaneous section. Black and brown faces were notable exceptions. It could have been a ten-year reunion for National Merit Scholars.

A stack of empty plates appeared in front of Bria. She passed them to the same waiter who had served the meal. When all the tables had been cleared and the carts of dirty dishes wheeled away, hundreds of rear ends lifted off of hundreds of chairs. Bria stumbled to her feet and was swept out. Echoing tinnily through her mind were the jewelry salesman's words: "Stuh-range, very stuh-range."

CHAPTER 8

"How about a coffee in my room?" Bria's short friend had materialized beside her.

She nodded her head enthusiastically. "That'd be great."

"Name's Leonard," he murmured, pleased by her acceptance. "Leonard Davila."

"Mine's Bria, Gabriellana Delgado." She threw out the full Spanish name, hoping to solder the connection between them.

"Stay close." Bria managed to follow the command as the crowd buffeted them gently upstairs. At the first floor above the lobby, they glided away.

"It's just down here." Leonard stopped in front of a door close to the lobby stairway. The door opened without a key. It was a facsimile of Bria's emaciated room minus the window and the PA speaker. With her suspicions about the surveillance capabilities of the speaker, she was glad there wasn't one in the room. As Leonard motioned her to take a seat on the bed, she reviewed her strategy—it was pathetically thin. She was there to gather information, yet she had to obtain it using an identity she knew nothing about. She couldn't even remember what Level Leonard had thought she was studying. Leonard, however, proved to be much more helpful than she could have ever hoped for.

"So, how's Level Five Techs going?"

"Well, you know," Bria hedged, "it's difficult, undoubtedly the most difficult of the five levels I've worked on so far. But it's been incredible. Really altitudinal."

"So I hear. I'm not that far Up the Grid yet. I'm having to work to pay off my Levels and earn Grid time, so I'm not gaining altitude as quickly as I'd like. I can't wait to get to the Tech Levels. Even the unclassified data on the Techs is so, well, you know . . . if it weren't classified, I'm sure we trainees would go snow-blind just from seeing Lou's brilliance on paper!"

Bria tried to fake a smile of blissful radiance like the one Leonard beamed at her. It wasn't a complete counterfeit; she'd been let off the hook. She wasn't going to have to grope her way through a conversation about "Techs." Whatever level Leonard assumed she was studying was obviously confidential.

"Where's your PDS?" Before Bria could begin fishing for an answer, he added, "I'm based at the Houston depot right near here."

"Mine is in New Mexico: Albuquerque." She hoped there was a depot there.

"New Mexico. Beautiful country. At least that's what I've heard. I had a Tower from there. Well, not Albuquerque; he was from Santa Fe. I guess they're fairly close."

"You did." Her vocal cords clenched, strangling the casual tone she was striving for. From the introductory lecture she had attended, Bria knew that a "Tower" was an LU counselor. From what little Dom had told her before leaving, she knew he'd come to the Academy to become one. "New Mexico is pretty sparsely populated, maybe I knew him, or her. Your Tower, I mean."

"Him. Definitely him. He was a big guy."

Bria's heart lunged. She scrutinized Leonard's face. His pupils blended into the irises in one dark pool. She braced herself, like a patient in a dental chair when he hears the drill being switched on.

"His name was Dominic Cavanagh. Did you know him?"

Even knowing in advance that it was coming, the name still slammed like a fist. She shrugged her shoulders in an uncertain reply.

"He wasn't really my Tower, but I considered him a high-magnitude terminal. I guess nearly everyone who met him did. He was one fully exteriorized essence. Maybe you heard of his father, William Cavanagh. Used to be governor."

"Oh, right," Bria said offhandedly. "New Mexico's favorite governor, sure I remember. Everyone loved him. Honest, fair—"

"I don't doubt that," Leonard cut in. "Just from knowing Dom, I'd guarantee that he would have chosen a father loaded with integrity. I guess that's why it's funny." Leonard stopped. His face lost its cheery animation and slipped back into a blunted ancestral mask, an Aztec carved in stone.

"What's funny?" Her voice was too high, too eager.

"I guess the New Mexico papers didn't pick this up, or maybe you were already in transit, but Dom debarked the physical plane early this week."

Bria didn't know if it were proper for a Louie to offer condolences. She tried to remain impassive.

The stone face crumbled. Tears pooled in his eyes, and Leonard whipped his head to the side. Several moments passed before he spoke again. "I realize that I'm dragloading on this. I plan to run it through with my Tower during my next session, but I just can't get over the way Dom chose to go supradimensional. I mean, I didn't know him real well, but he spoke Spanish and was more attuned to our culture than anyone else down here. Don't misunderstand me," he added hurriedly. "I'm here at the Academy to get Airborne, just like you, but I still miss the joking around, speaking in Spanish. Dom and I did those things, he appreciated them. I think he kind of liked taking time off from being an adjutant and just having a few laughs. But it was more than that. I got to know him, knew what he would do. I can't believe that Dom Cavanagh would accidentally drop a hair dryer in the bathtub." Leonard stopped as if he expected Bria to say something. His dark eyes carried an unresolved load of grief. It was a burden she understood well.

"That was how he was supposed to have debarked. I wish you could have known him. You'd know that Dom was too elevated, had too much control over his externals, to ever let something that stupid happen. He wouldn't have allowed it." Abruptly Leonard got up and went to a card table set up at the end of the room. A pan, a bag of coffee, and a hot plate sat on it.

"Yeah, I'm drag-loading on this, all right. How about the coffee I promised?" His question trailed off in a husky blur. He picked up the pan and disappeared into the tiny bathroom. Water ran for much longer than it should have taken to fill the small pan. Leonard came out, his eyes red, and placed the pan on the hot plate. He measured two scoops of coffee into a filter cone and placed it on a chrome pot. His fingers were short and strong, his hands squared off, like her father's, the Senator's. They trembled slightly as Leonard poured the boiling water over the grounds. The tremor made her decision.

"I don't believe it either," she stated flatly.

When Leonard turned toward her his face had that stone hardness again. It reminded Bria that, of all the pre-Conquest Indians, the Aztecs were the most feared, for they demanded heavy tribute, not only of gold and silver, but of sacrificial victims by the thousands. Bria was afraid she had made a terrible mistake.

"What don't you believe?" Leonard's face was open and vulnerable again.

Bria scolded herself for being so twitchy. She couldn't completely read Leonard, but one undeniable quality came through—his feeling for Dom. It was easy to understand when she thought about it. She recalled that no one in the dining hall had spoken to Leonard, not even a polite greeting. Dom's friendship, his appreciation of Hispanic culture had probably meant a great deal to this lonely brown Louie.

"I don't believe that Dom Cavanagh would sit in a bathtub, much less with a hair dryer in his hand." Bria made her assertion with an authority she could only wish for and pretend to have.

The steaming pan of water in Leonard's hand stopped, motionless, in midair. The hand had stopped trembling. "You knew Dom?"

"Yes. We lived together for two years."

He placed the pan gently on the table. "Lived with him," he echoed. "Then you know what I'm talking about, how impossible it was."

Bria nodded.

"Did he Tower for you?"

Shreds of possible answers ground through Bria's mind. In one snap decision she discarded them all. "I'm not one of you. I'm not a Louie." What she feared happened. At first disbelief clouded Leonard's face. She knew that what rapport she had established was in danger, and she scrambled to shore it up.

"Look, Leonard, I'm not sure what I'm doing here. I didn't come with any plan. The only reason I came is that, like you, I don't believe the official version of Dom's death. I haven't been able to make the questions stop since he left two years ago, and now this. It's more than I can absorb. I have to understand." Bria felt a sudden, sharp empathy for Mrs. Cavanagh.

"I don't know how you managed to breach security," Leonard said, ignoring Bria's plea. "We've really tightened things up since we found out how many enemies Lou has. I don't see what you expect to accomplish. You're a Limited. The Protectorate will find you out. They find out everything that happens here. You'll be out as soon as you leave this room. It's just dumb luck that you've made it this far. That and my mistaking you for a Level Five. There's no way you can possibly get any information."

"Yes, there is, Leonard."

"How's that?"

"With your help."

"My help? You don't seem to understand, I *am* what you refer to as a 'Louie,' a disciple of the teachings, not the man, the teachings of J. Louis Comfort. I have given my first allegiance to them and to the group promulgating them. Helping you would be counter to that allegiance." The softness had disappeared from Leonard's voice. It had the canned quality of someone delivering a memorized spiel.

"I'm not asking you to betray any allegiances, Leonard. Just give me enough information so that I can stay for a few hours, a day at the most, and see for myself what Dom's life was like here. See what Life Unlimited is all about."

"You mean, see if LU could have warped Dom badly enough that he'd fry himself in a bathtub? Well, save yourself the trouble, it couldn't have. I can tell you that right now. But why are we even discussing this? I have to report you. There's a security leak somewhere we need to plug." Leonard headed for the door.

"No, wait, Leonard, please. You said yourself that you

have some doubts about how Dom died. Give us both a chance to put them to rest. I have to know. I loved Dom; can you imagine what this is like for me?"

Leonard pivoted slowly to face her.

"All I need is for you to prep me on some of your practices and procedures. Just enough so that I can survive here for a day. That's all, Leonard. Just let me look at Life Unlimited for myself."

"*Chingao,*" Leonard cursed softly. "I don't know."

"Please, Leonard. I have to know."

"You just want some basic information, right?"

"Nothing more than you'd tell any potential recruit."

"All right, but just basics, okay?"

The "basics" of Life Unlimited's complicated belief system took several hours to explain. By her fourth hour and sixth cup of Leonard's coffee, dark as furniture stain and potent as amphetamines, Bria felt more jittery than enlightened. Drag Factors, Lift, Altitude, Vectors—the terminology sounded as if it had come from a pilot's training manual rather than the catechism of what was represented as the world's fastest-growing religion.

"Why is there such an obsession with planes and aeronautics?" Bria asked, feeling not one inch closer to understanding what Dom could possibly have found so compelling about LU. "Like that unearthly noise everyone was making after dinner. I thought a DC-10 was taking off in the kitchen."

"That's what it's supposed to sound like," Leonard said enthusiastically, ignoring the acerbic edge on her remark. "It focuses us on the Mission, becoming Airborne and staying that way."

"But doesn't it strike you as a bit bizarre? Absolutely everything fixates on some aspect of air travel. Don't you ever feel that you might be living out J. Louis Comfort's RAF fantasy?"

"I wouldn't call it a fantasy." Leonard strained to inject a civil tone into his answer. "Since the moment Homo sapiens evolved into a cognitive being, he has looked up, skyward, to the etheric realms, to express his spiritual longings." Again Leonard's voice lost its natural cadence and took on the unnatural enthusiasm of a speaker trying to pump life into memorized words. "The early Greeks placed their gods high on Mount Olympus. Later priests placed theirs in a heaven in the sky. Christian believers press their hands together in a gesture that shoots prayers upward. Cathedral spires cut high into the sky. It's all a device to focus attention and energy, to put both where you want them to go, like the Buddhist's gong, or the sound of om, or bells at Mass. Our chant calls forth an airplane's unstoppable upward thrust. Psychically, that's where we want to be, where we want our energy and attention to flow. The plane has more meaning for today's man than some chant out of the Bhagavad Gita."

"Yes, but don't you think it gets carried to an illogical extreme? All this aeronautics jargon, the uniforms, the robot communications—I feel like I've stepped into some Buck Rogers fantasy gone berserk."

"For centuries now on this planet, we've had materialists and power-mongers running things, and look where it's gotten us," Leonard continued, impervious to Bria's sniping. "The planet is acting out a mass death wish. Even the disciplines that have been developed to help man understand himself—psychology, sociology, all those 'ologies'—haven't contributed anything other than shock treatments, aversion therapy, lobotomies, hellholes like this." Leonard gestured at the pitiful room.

"But mostly these great 'ologists' have come up with drugs, chemicals. They treat man like an animal, like the white rat they are so fond of. They deny man his soul, his spiritual essence. Only one man, J. Louis Comfort, has been able to come up with the technology to do what psychology purports to do—to predict and control human behavior. But that was child's play for Lou. His real goal is liberation. Liberating man from the world of matter, energy, space, and time and returning him to his original state of perfect spiritual power."

Bria listened, stimulated by the extra-strength doses of caffeine she'd downed and by the emotional power Leonard was punching into his words.

"Soul travel is nothing new. Lou acknowledges all his debts to past adepts. But what this planet had never seen before was the precision of Lou's technology. When he first invented the Grid in the late forties, he tried to share it with the world. But the human mind, encrusted in centuries of materialism, could no longer accept its true nature. Lou was ridiculed, mocked, just as you have mocked him. His technology was ignored. That was why he developed the aeronautic packaging, to make the Grid accessible to a world of Limiteds. All the great teachers have used parables: Jesus, Lao-tzu, Gautama Buddha. That's what Lou is doing with what you call his Buck Rogers/RAF fantasies."

Bria didn't interrupt.

"Like I said, at first I was a little turned off, but . . . You probably expect me to say that I was searching for something when I got into LU. I wasn't. I had no idea three years ago how empty my life was. I'd just gotten out of school. Had a BA in bilingual education. My choice of jobs. Didn't even have any debts to pay back. I'd had a full scholarship for the whole four years. I figured I had it made. I was dating a girl my family liked. They couldn't have been happier. We were close. My father had come over the river from Mexico and now he had a son with a degree, a schoolteacher.

"I never questioned any of it until our principal started bringing me some of Lou's literature. I probably never would have even read it except that I really respected the man. He'd shaken up that school. For the first time, every kid there was learning to read, to behave, to learn. His methods were unorthodox, controversial, but no one could argue with his success. To make a long story short, the more I read, the more sense it all made to me. Still, I was resistant, even more resistant than you. But I applied Lou's technology, put it on trial, in my life, in the classroom, and it worked. It made a good life even better. I started wanting more. I took the Beginner Levels at night at the Houston depot. Then I Exteriorized." Leonard stopped and Bria watched that radiance she had seen in the dining room burst across his face.

"After that my life has not been the same." He shook his head in amusement at the feeble understatement. "I won't even attempt to explain that part of it to you. I don't mean this as a put-down, but there is simply no way to describe Exteriorization to a Limited. You have to be On the Grid to even begin to understand. All I can tell you is that I feel closer to God here than I ever have in my life."

After a silence, Bria said, "I'm almost convinced just by the look on your face."

Leonard laughed, breaking the tension.

"I don't know about Unlimiteds," Bria said as she stood up, "but six cups of coffee have a definite effect upon the Limited bladder. May I avail myself of the facilities?"

With a mock courtly swing of his arm, he gestured Bria into the bathroom. It was on a par with the rest of the upstairs. When Bria flushed the commode, it filled slowly with water, then seemed to choke before swirling out of the bowl in a lazy whirlpool.

"I'd like to apologize for my attitude earlier," Bria said, reentering the room. "You've been very kind. Please don't take this as an insult, but everyone else here acts like an android. It's almost spooky."

"That's funny, my family thinks *I* act like an android. I guess it's all relative. I used to feel the same way about Unlimiteds until I Exteriorized. Then . . ." Leonard paused, searching for words. "I wish I could explain this better, but my life just suddenly seemed so much more crucial after I got On the Grid. I realized how vital every second is, how much time I had wasted. I saw how much I had to accomplish, to learn, while I was on this plane, and how short my time here is."

Bria was submerged in a familiar emotion. She felt Leonard straining to reach her, just as Dom had. She realized that she had never really listened, never actually heard what he had wanted so badly to share with her. Perhaps if she *had* listened, understood . . .

"You need a handkerchief?"

Bria ducked her head and wiped the back of her hand across her cheeks. "Sorry. It's late, I haven't slept much for the past few nights."

"It's all right." Leonard wrapped an arm around her shoulders. "It is late, nearly two."

"I'd better let you get some sleep." Halfway to the door, she halted abruptly. "I just remembered, I have to check in tomorrow at Verifications. You'll have to tell me those codes; they're going to have a Spanish interpreter."

"Don't worry," Leonard said, herding her toward the

door. "Just go, get some sleep, and come down to the counter tomorrow around seven. You'll get your permanent pass." Leonard pressed his forefinger into his chest. "I am the Spanish interpreter."

CHAPTER 9

Bria woke the next morning with a dull headache, a sort of caffeine/information overload hangover. Her eyes stung from lack of sleep. The headache pounded further into her skull as she made her way down the four winding flights of stairs to the lobby. Already, at seven o'clock in the morning, the lobby was clotted with single-minded Louies and cigarette smoke. Through the fetid haze, she made out Leonard's form bent over a pile of papers. He barely glanced up at her. She passed his counter and made her way to the one marked Verifications.

The attendant who had issued her provisional pass the day before gestured for her to follow as he headed for Leonard's station.

"Leonard, this cadet is mono-Spanish. Get her stats so I can verify them and issue a pass if they check out."

"Acknowledged." Leonard turned toward Bria and fired off a series of questions in rapid Spanish.

"Say five-three-four-two," he ordered.

Bria complied, answering sternly in her university Spanish though there was no one close enough to hear more than a Spanish-tinged garble. Leonard continued dictating answers to her, which he dutifully recorded. When the form had been completed, Leonard, with Bria at his heels, marched it over to the attendant, who punched the numbers into his terminal. Bria tensed as she watched the bogus responses being fed into the computer.

"Don't look so worried," Leonard said to her in Spanish, "I took all those codes from a cancellation I intercepted this morning. They're all bona fide. You'll have at least twenty-four hours before they contact the desk about cancellation vouchers. Will that be enough time?"

"It will have to be."

"Leonard," the attendant said peevishly, "this readout calls for a mono-interp for the cadet. None of the Towers on call now are Spanish-speaking."

"I guess I'll have to co-Tower then."

The attendant pursed his lips in annoyance, as if this were a matter of enormous inconvenience to him personally. Bria was pleased to see that LU was afflicted with at least one exemplar of the bureaucratic mentality. "Take the cadet to Flight Control and file a Flight Plan." He surrendered Bria's pass. Leonard took it and strode across the lobby, with Bria trying to keep pace. "Then come right back," the attendant called after him. "We've got a huge stack of vouchers to process."

"Acknowledged, Stu," Leonard called over his shoulder.

Halfway up the first flight of stairs, Bria stopped Leonard. "What was that attendant's name?" she asked.

"Stu. Stuart Benninger. Why?"

"For a moment he looked familiar, like someone I know," Bria lied. She'd found Stuie the Louie but knew she'd never pass on the turquoise salesman's message. It was pointless. Stu appeared to be one of the rare Louies who are born, not made. Bria changed the subject. "Thanks for getting me up here."

Leonard shrugged. "I just want you to see LU for what it really is, not what *Newsweek* and the *National Enquirer* make it out to be."

"Where is everybody now? It's so quiet up here."

"Either studying in their rooms, running Grid sessions, or in class. Want to check one out? Take your first peek at the 'Cult that Skyjacks Minds'?" Leonard mimicked a headline Bria recalled having seen splashed across the front of a tabloid on a rack next to the checkout counter at her grocery store. He was galloping down the hall before Bria had a chance to agree.

"Classes are in the far wings." In the space of a few hundred yards, they covered nearly a century of institutional architecture. Their destination was the wing added in the fifties, when patient populations at mental hospitals around the country were reaching their peak.

"All the Discipline classes are conducted in this area," Leonard whispered. He gestured for Bria to join him at the window of one of the classroom doors. Inside she saw an instructor and a class of about thirty Louies.

"Stand on your chairs," the instructor commanded. Obedience was instantaneous. All thirty unsmiling Louies climbed up on their chairs.

"Touch your head to your right knee."

Again the response was immediate, the class turning into a flock of crazed flamingos.

Bria could barely pull herself away from the door when Leonard tugged at her sleeve.

"That's an elementary class."

"Why? What's it for?"

"To shorten reaction times when a trainee is On the Grid. It's for the cadet's own safety. Here, this is an advanced class."

Bria peeked into another room. The instructor's back was to her. Two dozen Louies were seated in student desks in front of him, all with their eyes tightly shut. The instructor patrolled the rows of students whispering in their ears. Their faces twitched and flinched, reflecting the mental efforts they were making in response.

"Pretty lightweight so far, huh?" Leonard asked, backing away from the window. "I wish I had time to show you more, but I have to get back to the desk."

Bria stifled her questions about the puzzling display she'd witnessed; she had a much more critical inquiry in mind.

"Leonard, I have one more favor to ask of you. I have to see Dom's room."

"Bria, you're pushing me. Do you know what will happen to me if what I've already done is discovered? And now you want me to sneak into a dematerialized Tower's room. I thought you just wanted to see LU in action. You never said anything about breaking and entering."

"Leonard, none of the rooms have locks."

"That's what makes it so bad. Crashing down a door, picking a lock, all that would be unheard of here. There's no need for locks. That's for the Limited world. If a person has made it this far in LU, he would rather dematerialize than intrude on another cadet's physical integrity."

"I'm not asking you to intrude on anyone's integrity. Just tell me what his room number is. I'll commit the sacrilege."

Leonard glanced nervously up and down the hall. "All the Towers have rooms on the fifth floor, in the main building. I'll have to go with you. If you're stopped up there, you'd better have a damned good excuse or we'll both be hitchhiking out of Aura Lee."

The fifth floor was magnificent, the reception area furnished like the executive suite of a multinational corporation. It exuded the kind of understated power that would have prompted Dom to pick up a picket sign in years past. The entire area was bathed in diffuse golden light. Instead of the pitted linoleum of the lower floors, thick cream wall-to-wall carpeting was everywhere. Even the odor of urine had been banished. A guard sat behind a large console equipped with closed-circuit television monitors and a battery of security instruments. A phone beeped discreetly as they stepped up to the security station. The guard answered it. After a few crisp *acknowledged*s, the conversation ended, and he hung up.

"Wait here. I'll be right back," the guard ordered, then left.

Bria looked around the reception area. Artwork was scattered tastefully throughout. She thought she recognized a Chagall, one of his delightful airborne fantasies, and moved in closer to see if it could possibly be an original. It seemed to be. Leonard, still standing stiffly in front of the security station, hissed for her to return, but, on the adjacent wall, she spotted one of Blake's Winged Figures. Bria had thought both pieces of art were part of some museum's permanent collection. Intrigued, she explored further.

On a pedestal, spotlit by the track lighting system overhead, was a primitive-looking terra cotta figure with both stubby arms upraised. A plaque beneath it read: Egyptian, c. 400 B.C., Praying Figure. A potbellied stone carving claimed another pedestal. Its plaque identified the little troll as: Mayan, c. 600 A.D., Corn God. Bria took a brief survey of the rest of the pieces on display: Etruscan, 500 B.C., Mother Goddess; Cretan, 1500 B.C., Minoan Snake Goddess; Aztec, 1500 A.D., Goddess of Earth; Chinese, T'ang

Dynasty, 700 A.D., Burial Urn; Assyrian, 880 B.C., Winged Deity; Egyptian XXVI Dynasty, 663 B.C., The God Thoth. On the walls were more paintings: Adorations of the Magi, Visitations, tonsured monks in postures of divine ecstasy, winged archangels wielding swords. The room was a museum of mankind's spiritual aspirations. Bria had the unsettling feeling that the pieces had been collected, by whatever means, at a cost of millions, for the express purpose of documenting humanity's "progress" toward Life Unlimited.

"Purpose," the guard barked, resuming his position behind the control panel.

"Orienting a new Tower," Leonard barked back. Bria scurried back to his side. "She's taking over Tower Eighteen, Dom Cavanagh's former post."

"Why isn't the new Tower orienting herself?" the guard asked, glaring at the laminated badge pinned to Leonard's shirt pocket. "She outgrades you, cadet."

"She's mono-Spanish."

"Mono-Spanish. I don't remember that qual in the posting specs."

"It wasn't. Counterdirective from GHQ."

Bria didn't have to pretend that she didn't understand most of the exchange. Out of the corner of her eye, she saw that Leonard's forehead was lightly beaded with sweat. She recalled the tableful of "traitors" she had seen yesterday and wondered if that would be where Leonard would end up sitting if she were discovered. She truly believed that Leonard was sincerely and deeply committed to LU, but the more she learned about the Grid, the more frightened she became of the power it conferred on LU.

The guard initialed her pass and handed it back.

"I'll show the Tower her new quarters before she reports to her duty station."

"Negative, cadet," the guard said. "HQ ordered Cavanagh's room sealed off until his belongings have been catalogued and shipped to next of kin. The room's not ready for inspection yet."

Leonard leaned close to the scowling guard. "Towers are not diverted by material objects, you know that, cadet. The Tower wants to inspect her new quarters. I don't have to remind you that she is filling a Grade Eighteen, Expanded, position?" He straightened back up. "Have to keep our Towers elevated, right?"

The admonished guard gave a curt nod. "Right," he affirmed.

As they whisked down the hall, Bria noticed that the doors were not cramped together as they were on the lower floors. Rank obviously had its privileges. That became even clearer when Leonard opened the door marked 508.

"Dom was a Grade Eighteen, Expanded," Leonard said as they walked into a room as sumptuous as the reception area had been. "LU is run strictly on a rewards-for-results basis. As you can tell, Dom was one of our most successful Towers. His record was . . ."

But Bria had stopped listening. The moment she'd opened the door, everything other than Dom Cavanagh had stopped existing.

If certain special belongings, smells, and a characteristic kind of messiness can evoke a person, then Dom was there, in that high-ceilinged room, just as surely as he was in the chambers of Bria's mind.

"I'd like to be alone."

Even after Leonard left, closing the door softly behind him, Bria felt less alone than she had at any time during the past two years. She stood absolutely still in the center of the room and drank it in with her eyes. A racquetball racquet hung from a peg on the back of the closet door, its handle ringed in salty white circles. A bath sheet lay crumpled on the floor. No ordinary towel was ever big enough for Dom, so he favored those terry-cloth monstrosities. A pile of corduroy pants in muted colors, browns and grays, lay heaped next to the giant towel. A moat of books and papers surrounded the bed. On the nightstand beside it sat a pocket watch. Dom had called it "Biscuit" just as his father had for the fifty years he'd carried it before his death. Two quarters, three pennies, a squeeze bottle of nose spray, and a nail clipper waited mutely beside the watch. Bria slipped the watch into the pocket of her skirt. Mrs. Cavanagh would want it.

She sank onto the bed and wondered who Dom might have shared it with. Had LU been his only passion for the two years they were apart? It was hard to imagine any of the militaristic automatons she'd encountered doing anything as spontaneous as making love. She buried her head in his pillow. His smell—a cross between baking bread and musk—saturated it. She ran her hand over the crumpled sheet. It snagged on something. She picked up a horny yellow paring of nail, hard as a dog's claw, and thought of all the nights when Dom, rolled into a fetal ball, had snuggled up against her and dug those toenails into the backs of her calves.

A huge rolltop desk hung open at the other side of the room. Papers spilled out like a gaping mouth clogged with unchewed food. Bria dislodged a wad of papers and began sifting through them. Most were embossed with LU's logo, a stylized jet taking off in a swirl of graphically exciting exhaust blasts. They were printed with announcements, personalized with Dom's name at the top, which unveiled yet another new level. The glories of the latest level ("brought to us through Lou's unstinting research and masterful control of the technology") were extolled along with effusive testimonials about the radical changes the new level had wrought in devotees' lives. Price lists, carefully labeled as "donations," were given at the end of each hyperbolic announcement. Each new level cost a few thousand more than the previously announced "ultimate breakthrough."

Bria wondered why Dom hadn't discarded them long before. They made it so obvious that the courses were an upward spiral that had no end. Just when a Louie had put every cent he could scrape together, or work off, for a "donation" for the latest level, J. Louis's "unstinting" efforts would produce yet another one, and the money-grubbing began again. Bria figured that the generous trust fund Governor Cavanagh had left to his only son must have been exhausted, squandered on these ridiculous courses.

Bria was angrily stuffing another handful of paper into the trash when she noticed a piece of lined notebook paper. It wasn't emblazoned with the flamboyant Louie logo and it didn't bear the printed signature of J. Louis Comfort. It carried her own. She pulled the wrinkled paper out of the bunch she was consigning to the trash, searched through the desk, and found the pile it had come from. There, in a neat stack, were all the letters she'd written to

Dom over the past two years. All the letters he had never answered. Letters she had come to believe he'd never received, or been allowed to receive.

It tore at her to realize that Dom *had* gotten them. All of them, the bright bouncy ones she'd written at first, filling him in on Santa Fe gossip, asking when he was coming back, and saying that she couldn't wait to see him again. Then the questioning ones. "Why aren't you writing?" "Are you getting my letters?" "What are they doing to you there?" Finally, toward the end, the entreaties, growing more and more desperate. "Please write." "I can't go on without hearing from you." "Dom, please." They were all there, carefully preserved, and stored in the exact order in which she had sent them. And they had been read. Many times. The paper was limp in her hand, the creases fuzzy where it had been folded and refolded. Certain sections were underlined, as if Dom had studied them.

"I'll die before I let what we have be stolen by them." The phrase was one of the ones that had been underlined. A little dramatic, Bria thought, but she had meant every word of it; still did. Why had Dom underlined it and all the similar protestations? Had he been testing her? She leafed through the rest of the letters. All the sections that had been meticulously underlined repeated that same thought: Bria would never abandon him or their love, she would do whatever she had to to regain him. In one of the last letters she sent, she had even threatened to use her father's influence to investigate LU. She promised that her father had all the necessary connections to unearth any secret he cared to. The threat too was underlined. It almost seemed that Dom had been searching for proof of her devotion. How could he have ever doubted it? She clutched the letters. The hope and despair that weighted them pulled her down into a dark swamp of memories. A long time later, she shook herself free and continued rummaging.

The middle drawer contained photos of Governor and Mrs. Cavanagh. Bria sifted through the photographs and found a large number of pictures of herself and many she had taken of Dom. They had the soft, technically inexpert look that had characterized her work in the days when photography was only a hobby and Dominic Cavanagh had been the career she was really working at. It hurt to see herself back then: her hair long, trailing almost down to her waist, a misty, innocent look on her face—a Chicana Alice in Wonderland. She slammed the drawer shut. All her search had accomplished so far was to intensify her doubts.

She rifled through the remaining drawers and became aware of an odd feature of all the papers she'd gone through—not a single one bore Dom's handwriting. Nowhere had she seen his familiar, sloping hand that galloped across the page at a scrawling, downhill tilt. At least there should be a list. Dom was an inveterate listmaker. She remembered them tacked all over their small house: Restring RQB racquet. Return lib bks. Call Carl. Cancel dent. appt. Take staple gun to Mary Marg.

Bria tried to imagine what his lists here would have looked like: Study. Eat. Withdraw money. But there wasn't even that. The desk had been scoured clean. Too clean. What Bria really wanted to find was some evidence of the existence of an insurance policy, a receipt, a bill, any scrap of paper with the name of one of the 1,700 insurance companies in Texas on it.

A long legal pad, the kind Dom always wrote letters on, sat on the desk top. It was blank. Bria fingered the shreds of yellow paper still clinging to the pad's binding. Half the paper had been stripped away. On the top sheet were a series of faint indentations, all sloping downhill. Bria grabbed a pencil and did precisely what she'd seen the clever heroes in countless thrillers do—she shaded lightly over the top sheet. The familiar scrawl jumped off the page:

Cont. of Notes   Oct. 31

less certain is how much they already know about the Recon Squad. Can almost guarantee though that they've infiltrated us. Almost sure that they have an operative in place here at the Acad. Have id'd a suspect. Caution is paramount. We already know that they have no ethical restraints. Will confer with Tower 11 before taking action. All can be trusted with him, no matter how dangerous. And this is. Will see him tomorrow. Feel it is imperative to

The shaded words dribbled off the end of the page. Bria's eyes raced back upward. Recon Squad? Operative? Suspect? Dangerous?

"Find anything?"

Bria jumped at the sound of Leonard's voice, yet still she couldn't tear her eyes from the date at the top of the page. October 31. The "tomorrow" in which Dom was to have seen Tower 11 had never come.

CHAPTER 10

"Leonard, what do you know about a Recon Squad?"
His face snapped into an expression of studied casualness. "Recon Squad? What are you talking about?" He sounded like a child actor trying to simulate surprise.

"You heard my question, Leonard. I'd like to have it answered."

"Jeez, Bria, I don't know. Sounds like something out of WW Two or that RAF fantasy you were talking about."

"Read this." She handed Leonard the pad.

"Hey, good trick," he said, pointing to the shading Bria had done. She didn't return his determinedly guileless grin. He read in silence, then gave a low whistle. "Sounds like Dom was into some heavy shit."

"No, Leonard, sounds like *LU* is into some heavy shit. Want to tell me about it?"

Leonard did an impression of bewilderment complete with shoulder shrugging and baffled silence. Bria decided she had overplayed her hand. That, even if Leonard did know anything, he wouldn't, or couldn't, tell her. Then unexpectedly he spoke.

"Look, I'd like to help you, but you've got to understand, Dom was a Grade Eighteen, Expanded. I'm only a Grade Seven. That's like the difference between a lieutenant and a three-star general in the military. He was in on missions that I only read about in the papers."

"Did these 'missions' involve, by any chance, breaking into government offices and stealing documents?"

"I would hardly call recovering your own stolen property breaking in and stealing, but, yes, those kinds of operations. Maybe I do know a little bit more than you do,

76

but not much. It doesn't make any difference though, because I'm under an integrity constraint not to discuss sensitive church affairs with Limiteds."

Elyse Morgan, a twenty-five-going-on-forty-year-old investigative reporter with the *Sentinel*, came to Bria's mind. Bria had been out on a number of tough stories with the tenacious reporter when she was confronted by a recalcitrant source. Elyse's most devastating weapon had been a few well-worded questions followed by silence in which the interviewee was allowed enough rope to hang himself. Bria followed this tack, not saying another word. Finally Leonard blurted out:

"Okay, I'm sure you've read in the papers how the government has been harassing us since 1952 when they raided our base in Kansas City and confiscated a lot of Grid Screens."

"Sure, back then Comfort was claiming all sorts of miraculous powers for his little invention, including cancer cures. The FDA stepped in and announced that the mythical Grid was nothing more than a galvanic-skin-response device, and not a very sophisticated one at that."

"That's what they said." Leonard's scorn was genuine. "Anyway, we complied."

"Complied?" Bria echoed the word, edging it with incredulity. "You just switched from claiming physical cures to saying that LU and the Grid would cure psychic ills. That's when Comfort went into big-time religion."

"First you endanger me and my allegiances, now you're insulting them. We could go round and round all day with you spouting the kind of twisted propaganda we've come to expect from the media. Do you want information or just to have all your prejudices confirmed?"

Bria gestured for Leonard to continue.

"Anyway, after the first attack failed to cripple the Church—we actually got a federal judge who wasn't under the control of our enemies and he ruled that the raid on the Kansas City base and the confiscation of Church property were unconstitutional—the government changed its strategy, or rather those controlling the government changed their strategy. The campaign was taken over by the IRS. They tried to crush us by challenging the tax-exempt status of each individual depot, base, and academy around the country. As soon as we would win one judgment, the IRS would attack somewhere else. Their object was to exhaust our resources fighting an endless round of legal brushfires. Even the IRS, though, is no more than the hired lackey of the real forces trying to destroy the Church."

"And who might they be?"

"You wouldn't comprehend, much less believe, even if I told you. The point here is that the government has been persecuting us for nearly a quarter of a century. When it became clear to Lou that we were dealing with vultures and that, if we didn't repel them, the bureaucratic scavengers would strip our bones bare, he formed the Protectorate to ensure the security of the Church while under attack. The Reconnaissance Squadron, Recon Squad, is our intelligence arm. It was instituted after we learned that the government and their agents were posing as serious searchers after a fuller spiritual reality in order to infiltrate the Church and steal confidential documents."

"And Dom was a member of this 'intelligence arm'?"

Leonard shook his head.

"Was he one of the Louies who broke into the office of an attorney for the Justice Department to copy his files on LU?"

"We never broke into any government offices."

"Okay, so you forged ID cards. Was Dom a part of that?"

"If he was, I wouldn't know."

"Leonard, why do I get the distinct impression that you know a lot more than you're telling me? Jesus, how could Dom have gotten involved in all this third-rate intrigue? One more question. Does any of this have anything to do with Agent Wilkers?"

"Who's he?"

"Come on, Leonard, you're proving that you're not being honest with me. Anyone who reads a newspaper knows that he was an IRS agent who worked his way up to the top rungs of the LU hierarchy. Even made a few transatlantic flights with Comfort himself."

"All I remember about Agent Wilkers is that even the papers admitted that officials would only speculate about what happened to him. Nothing was ever proved."

"No, nothing was ever proved. He never even became a hard-news item. The speculation was that Wilkers had been found out by the Protectorate. He'd reported as much to his superiors. Odd that a hit-and-run driver should have killed him not long afterward."

Bria watched Leonard's face harden. "That *was* odd."

"Leonard, can't you see?" Bria felt a barely controlled rage rise within her as Leonard withdrew further and further into cool detachment. "I mean, this whole charade you're playing out is nothing more than a sacrilegious farce masquerading beneath a silly mask of aeronautics jargon. It's a ridiculous game you all are playing at, spying on the government, but don't you think the stakes have gotten dangerously high?"

"Lou was right again," Leonard said, his tone expressionless. "Limiteds perceive only what fits in with their own limited perceptions. It's not your fault, Bria. Just remember, you can change. You're not doomed to your limitations. Not since Lou's research has made it possible for everyone on the planet to achieve Life Unlimited. Obviously, part of our problem here is that I gave you too much unrefined data. You've balked at processing it. I can understand that and I accept responsibility for it."

An unnerving glimpse at the borderlands of that shared reality that passes for sanity compelled Bria to take a more placating tone. When she spoke again her voice was low and plaintive. "Our problem here, Leonard, is the—" Bria made herself say the word—"death of the man I love. *That* is the problem here."

"My Tower keeps telling me that I'm drag-loaded on the compulsion to help. That's how you got to me. You reeled in my compulsion. I should listen more to my Tower. I keep overloading, picking up Parasite Drags that keep me from staying Airborne. My Tower could handle you, Bria. Let me schedule a session."

"No, Leonard, seriously, no one should know that I'm here." Bria spoke in a studiedly calm voice. She was suddenly frightened of upsetting Leonard. "I explained all that to you, remember? You promised you'd help."

"I've tried, Bria, but it's beyond me. You're a lot more drag-loaded than I thought. I'll just report that you're here and my Tower will start you out on the Levels. That's what I should have done last night."

Bria started to protest, then Leonard's eyes found her

own. She met an unblinking stare radiating from a mind animated by a single, unswerving purpose.

"Right," she agreed feebly, knowing that further argument would only crystallize his determination more solidly. "I'll just go on down to my room and you can make whatever arrangements need to be made."

"Altitudinal!" Leonard's enthusiasm was curiously hollow. "Confine yourself to quarters until a Tower from the Protectorate contacts you. Do not attempt to call anyone." Leonard's words marched to a robotlike cadence that chilled Bria as much as his mechanical gaze.

"Acknowledged," she answered. Leonard had sealed her out of his mind as surely as if he had never met her. He opened the door of Dom's room and Bria reluctantly left. After delivering her to her room, Leonard pivoted and returned upstairs, back to Protectorate Headquarters.

Bria forced herself to wait until his footsteps had faded before she raced back outside the room, carrying only her purse. She ran down the hall, her heels clicking on the worn linoleum. A couple turned the corner. Bria slowed to a brisk walk, knowing that Leonard was probably already talking to some Protectorate strong-arm. The couple turned another corner, and Bria dashed for the stairway. She paused. Overhead, from the fifth floor, came the sound of footsteps. She took the stairs two at a time. Over the sound of her breathing and the frantic tattoo she was beating out on the stairs, she heard the footsteps coming down the stairs, coming rapidly. She hurtled down the rest of the flight.

The smell of cigarettes overpowered the odor of urine as she descended into the lobby, slowing again to a brisk walk. The two guards, guns at their hips, were at their stations at the foot of the stairs. A walkie-talkie crackled as Bria neared them. She sucked in a deep breath, quickened her pace, and slipped behind the guard as he put the apparatus to his ear.

"Code Thirty-eight," he barked at his partner, then motioned for one of the two door guards to come to him. Bria and the door guard crossed paths. She knew that if she allowed the guards time to exchange messages, the heavy oak doors to the outside would be sealed shut. She even glance at the remaining door guard. She twisted the knob. The massive door opened.

Her purse slapped her thigh as she ran, full out, to the Nova. Pebbles from the crushed-stone parking lot jumped into her shoes. She thought of Agent Wilkers and kept on running. At the car, she couldn't find her keys. She glanced back. The big doors were swinging open. She plunged her hand back down into her purse. A sharpened pencil dug deep under the nail of her middle finger. Her hand jerked away in pain. At the bottom of the bag the keys jangled. On the porch the guard with the walkie-talkie was pointing toward her. Bria dumped her purse out onto the parking lot. Hairbrush, cosmetics, wallet, coins, and finally keys tumbled out. She grabbed them and opened the door. The guards were streaming down the porch steps. She jumped in and locked the door.

Bria's mouth went dry when she turned the key in the ignition and the Nova produced only a feeble whir. In the distance, she could hear the guards' feet crunch over the parking-lot pebbles. She stomped on the accelerator and tried again. The engine turned over. She threw the car into reverse. A spray of gravel shot out from under her tires as she wrenched them around and gunned the motor.

Only when the wrought-iron arc proclaiming the Training Academy of the Church of Life Unlimited had passed over her head, did Bria dare to look back. It was hard to see much because her rearview mirror jerked wildly as the car careened out onto the lonely road. But she did catch a glimpse of one guard's face. Bria knew then just how upset she was; she would have sworn that the man's face was split by a huge, howling laugh.

CHAPTER 11

Bria had already put Aura Lee, Texas, and the piney woods far behind her by the time her pulse dropped down to anything approaching a normal rate. It also took her that long to realize that, in addition to the used tissues and dried-up Chapstick she had dumped on the Academy parking lot, she had also abandoned her wallet. It contained every cent she had, the credit cards Mrs. Cavanagh had given her, as well as her driving license and all her identification.

Bria checked the gas gauge. The needle was snuggling up against E. She checked the map and figured that thirty miles stood between her and the airport. If she coasted down the hills, she might make it. Her strategy would have worked except for the inevitable search for an airport parking place. She failed to find one on her first pass. On her second approach, the fuel-starved Nova coughed to an unyielding stop. Bria left the rented car on the street it had chosen as its resting place and hiked in to the terminal area.

As she entered the Houston Airport with its high, vaulted ceiling, Bria wondered why Texans would build an airport to look like a cathedral. Or why Louies would run a "church" as if it were an airport. It was all too bizarre to think about anymore.

At the car-rental counter, Bria briefly considered telling the girl about the undernourished Nova outside. The girl's uniform, however, a yellow-and-green affair in shades of an intensity achievable only in polyester, wilted Bria's resolve. She was sure that the company would send a bill with towing, and any other charges they felt they could get away with, tacked on.

A cluster of phones was grouped in the center of the main terminal area. Bria was automatically digging through her purse for some change, when it dawned on her that she didn't have even a quarter to place a collect call to her father. She looked around for a kind face. Businessmen bustled past her. Their computerized drive was too reminiscent of the Louies for Bria's taste. She spotted a young woman about her own age with two children in tow and decided to approach her. As she did, one of the children, for no apparent reason, burst into a piercing wail. Bria stopped. In a far corner she saw a young man dressed in an airport security uniform. His round face clouded with genuine concern as he watched the tears run down the youngster's cheek. Bria changed her course and headed for him.

"Excuse me," she said unnecessarily—the husky guard had been staring at her from the moment she had started toward him. "I was wondering if you could help me out." Up close, she saw that the guard was no more than nineteen. He crossed his bulky arms in front of his chest, making a barricade between himself and Bria. His face impassive, he nodded for her to go ahead and make her request.

"My wallet was stolen and I need to use a quarter to get the operator to make a collect phone call. I'll bring it right back."

His biceps barricade crumbled and he shook his straight blond hair as if ashamed of himself for suspecting her. "Sure. A quarter," he mumbled, digging into his pocket. "Sure. Here. Don't worry about bringing it back. Keep it. Sorry I was so mean. You get that way after working here a while. Folks you meet here, you don't know what to expect after a while."

"I'll bet," Bria said, taking the coin.

"Like them two there." The guard nodded toward two young women with shoulder bags. They darted like terriers after the travelers hustling past them, especially the young male ones.

"When I first started working here," the guard went on with an easy, country volubility, "those two hit me up for ten bucks. Said they was raising money for a church proj-

ect, a camp for crippled kids. Sounded good to me. Hell, I
didn't know nothing. Then I heard them going after folks,
telling this one they were raising money for a senior-
citizens' activity center, and that one that they were col-
lecting for a home for stray animals. A different deal for
everyone who came along. Then, one day, I saw them two
getting out of a big van. There was a whole damned army
of them inside." Bria returned the look of angry amazement on the young man's face.

"That same week the paper had an article on them. I
never would have given no ten dollars to some crook to go
drive around in his damned Rolls-Royce and live in some
damned mansion."

The young guard's outraged pride flared again as he saw
that the two women were double-teaming a gangly youth
wearing a tall cowboy hat and crisply pressed jeans held
up by a chrome belt buckle the size of a saucer. The second
that the cowboy stopped, the girls began pressing very
close to him, talking rapidly, and smiling into his face as
if his presence had rendered them both goofy. He looked
around nervously at the travelers streaming past him,
smiled awkwardly, and shook his head. The girls upped
the wattage they were shining on him in dazzling smiles.
The long feather in his hat danced in the air as he looked
around for an escape. He began slowly backing away from
the pair. They pressed in closer. His smile was locked in a
rictus of embarrassment. He dug his hand into his tight
jeans and pulled out a wad of bills and coins. Without even
glancing at them, he held out the crumpled notes and as-
sorted coins. The girls whisked them from his hand, and he
escaped. The money disappeared into the shoulder bags,
and the pair leaned close together, squeezing each other
like two sorority sisters sharing a secret.

"Bitches," the guard said. "Bad as they are, they ain't
half as bad as that outfit over there."

"Which one?" Bria looked around for other panhan-
dlers. All she saw in the direction the guard pointed out
were the backs of an expensively tailored couple. "Them?"
As soon as her question was out of her mouth, a distant
danger signal began to flash at the edge of her mind.

"Never notice them, would you? They're what you call
Louies. You heard about the Louies?"

Bria nodded her head. The couple turned around and she saw that they were the Disneyland guides with the urban-guerrilla demeanor.

"It takes a while to spot them, but they're Louies. What's weird about them is that they meet flights and the other Louies always know them. Didn't really know much about them until all that stuff started coming out about them being on trial for stealing government documents and such. Not that I think them government boys are a band of angels or . . ."

A voice over the loudspeaker, announcing the arrival of a flight from New Orleans at Gate 11A, interrupted the guard.

"This is the flight they're meeting," he said. "Watch this. You're not going to believe it."

Bria wouldn't have if she had never visited the Training Academy of the Church of Life Unlimited. The flight from New Orleans carried a mixed planeload of passengers, except for one strikingly homogeneous group that surged to the front of the crowd. Without a word or gesture being exchanged, the group veered over to the waiting couple.

"Transit visas," the male demanded in a low, commanding voice. Hands rustled through coat pockets and purses. The newcomers produced packets of papers, which the man examined. On the periphery was a slight man in a plaid sports coat who arrived, out of breath, after the others. When the Louie guide reached him, the man was empty-handed.

"Cog up, cadet," the guide hissed. The man glanced around him, saw all the proffered visas, and dove into his jacket's inner pocket, fishing out his packet. At that moment another group of about a dozen drifted in through a gate on the far side of the terminal. The same inexplicable instinct guided them to the New Orleans group. Their transit visas were inspected, and the entire group moved swiftly toward the baggage-collection area. Bria turned her back to them as they passed.

"Like a goddamned bunch of robots, ain't they?"

"Pretty close," Bria whispered. The quarter slid around in her sweating palm. Her reason for being there had come sharply back into focus.

"I'd better go try to make my phone call."

* * *

"Where the hell are you?" The heat from Senator Frank Delgado's question was hot enough to singe the receiver Bria held away from her ear. But she had weathered her father's anger before and learned to use it to her advantage. The louder he yelled, the worse he felt later on, and the harder he would try to make amends for the outburst.

Bria had few illusions about the path her father had trod to Capitol Hill or, at least, few that had survived her years with the *Sentinel.* Even if they hadn't published everything they had on Senator Frank, she was made privy to most of it. None of it was of the stuff that topples governments. Francisco Delgado had simply traded a lot of favors in his time and had somehow always managed to come out with one more favor owed to him than he owed. Or knowing just a bit more than someone would have liked him to know. If there were any seamy undersides to be uncovered, her father was the man who could tell you where to look. After her visit to the Academy, Bria was convinced that Dom's reported death demanded just such an investigation.

Still, she hated turning to her father for anything. She'd avoided most voluntary contact with him since the gossip about his romantic entanglements in Washington had reached Santa Fe. It was partly out of loyalty to her mother, and partly out of her fear of the Senator's ability to dominate anyone he came in contact with, to bend them to his will with his brash charm. But she had no choice now. He was the only person she could turn to who could possibly get her the information she needed.

"Houston," she answered, not liking the whispery, apologetic sound of her voice.

"Where?" her father bellowed incredulously.

"Houston. Texas."

"God, that's what I thought you said. Your mother's hysterical. She called me from Denver, she's been trying to reach you for the past forty-eight hours. She thinks that Dom's death was all you needed to drive you around the bend. Why in God's name would you go to Houston? Are you trying to punish yourself? *Díme, hija?*"

Bria tried to fend off the reflexive anger that overcame her every time her father spoke Spanish. It annoyed her that he hadn't chosen to defy his ex-wife's embargo on the language when she was growing up, when assimilation was in vogue.

"Dad, I've got a very important favor to ask you."

The familiar words of supplication soothed the legislator.

"I need to have all the information you can get on any government investigation of Life Unlimited."

"I knew this all had something to do with that bunch of *bandidos.* Are you conducting a one-woman investigation because they stole your boyfriend? I don't like you having any involvement with them whatsoever, Bria, and I'm telling you that I don't like it."

An angry knot choked Bria's breathing. She swallowed. "What you like and don't like is of no concern here. If you can't, or won't help me, I'll go to someone who can."

"Someone? Like who?"

"Someone who might like to spearhead a courageous fight against cultism and a return to the original meaning of the First Amendment."

"Bria, you're naïve. No one on the Hill wants to touch the cult issue precisely because of the First Amendment. You'll end up like Bob Dole did a couple years back when he conducted his informal hearings into the Moonies, with all these cultists screaming freedom of religion and acting like they're a bunch of Christs come again and you're the second Pontius Pilate. Messing with the First Amendment is a no-win proposition."

"Dad, listen, the First Amendment says that, 'Congress shall make no law respecting an establishment of religion, or prohibiting the free exercise thereof.' "

"Bria, I'm fully aware of what the First Amendment says." A tone of bullying sarcasm entered the Senator's voice.

"Yes, but no one pays much attention to what it means, do they?" Bria wouldn't let her father interrupt. She had rehearsed these words too many times in her mind not to get them out exactly the way she wanted. "According to Justice Hugo Black, they mean that no government, state or federal, can pass laws that—I think he said—that 'aid one religion, aid all religions, or prefer one religion over another.' "

"Been doing some homework."

"Yes, I have a personal interest in the subject," Bria answered dryly. "But the point of it all is that this meaning is ignored. Religion—*all* religions—are aided by the federal government because their revenues are effectively tax-exempt. When the Founding Fathers proposed that church property be tax-exempt, they meant the little white church on the corner, not the twenty-five-billion-dollar portfolio of the Catholic Church."

"Or the millions J. Louis Comfort stashes away each year."

"Or that. Tell me honestly, how long do you think any of these money-making religions would stay in business if they had to open their financial records and pay taxes?"

"Bria, I thank you for these insights into the First Amendment, but you're arguing with yourself. I agree with you. Unfortunately, the Moral Majority doesn't see it that way, and those people vote. They would be very unhappy if their legislators tried to curtail the government's support of religion. And, as you so perceptively pointed out, since government must not prefer one religion over another, these quasi-religious cults get a free ride, becoming more invulnerable than ever."

"Maybe so," Bria conceded, "but I'm certain that one of your colleagues could get some mileage out of the suspicious circumstances surrounding the death of the son of a prominent former governor."

"Come on, Bria. Your mother read me the article in the *Sentinel*. These things are checked out, you know."

"By who? A sheriff from a hick town that hates Louies. I can't imagine that he strained himself in his thoroughness. Dom is missing, that is one certainty. The other is that he would never accidentally electrocute himself in a bathtub. That's the official story. Can you really believe that Dominic Cavanagh would do something that stupid?"

"I wouldn't have predicted what that kid would do if you had put a gun to my head. Anyone who would throw away a future as bright as his, bury the Cavanagh name, do something as stupid as run off and become a Louie. You're a lot better off without—"

"Don't start that again," Bria cut in on the harangue she had heard too many times before. "Dom is either dead or, I don't know what. The only possibility I'm willing to eliminate is that he died trying to dry his hair in a bathtub."

"So what else is there, *hija?*" Her father's voice had the same careful tone she herself had used when she was afraid of upsetting Leonard. Did he think she was that close to the edge? Good, Bria decided, let him think I'm crazy. Let him think anything he likes, just so long as he helps.

"I can't begin to fathom the motives of J. Louis Comfort and his followers," Bria answered. "They're all so utterly convinced of their absolute righteousness that I'm sure they'd feel no qualms about committing any fraud that would further their 'mission' of 'getting the planet On the Grid.' Dom's disappearance could be part of an insurance scam or some publicity ploy. I just don't know. Before I start pumping up theories, I need more information. And that is what you can supply."

"Bria," her father's voice had a soothing tone that was both forced and irritating. "I know I was blunt at the beginning of our conversation, but I worry about you. It's over two years now since you've even seen Dom. You need to start getting over him. This isn't natural, you living up in the mountains in that shack, cut off from any friends you might still have, working yourself to death at the paper. Now this. Whatever wild crusade you're on down there isn't going to bring him back to you, or back to life. Bria, I'm speaking harshly for your own good. I won't help you with this obsession. I'm worried. I don't want you messing around with those people. They're dangerous. You saw what happened to Dom, what's happened to thousands, millions, of other young people. I want you to stay away."

"Dad," Bria answered, her voice softer now too, "I have no intention of becoming involved with Life Unlimited. I agree with you, there is a potential for danger. I'm sure you know that LU is involved in a huge legal wrangle with the government. Both sides have agents and counteragents skulking around like a bad spy novel. The problem is that they're taking it seriously. Anyway, all I plan on doing is getting enough information about LU to raise some doubts about Dom's death, giving it to a contact I have at the *Houston Chronicle*, then leaving. I'll let the investigative reporters at the *Chronicle* smoke out what really happened to Dom."

"But you wouldn't go out there, to that Louie place?"

Bria recognized a bargaining point when she was handed one. "Not if you send me the information I need."

"In Santa Fe?" her father asked hopefully.

"No, better send it here." Her father made a noise of disapproval. "I'm at the Houston Airport. Nothing could happen to me here."

There was a silence as her father considered.

"If I can't get the information I need any other way," Bria said quietly, "I'll have to go out to the Life Unlimited Training Academy."

"Bria," her father said with a sigh of exasperation and defeat, "all right, you win. Now, you want anything I can get on a government investigation of the Louies. Okay, that would be Bill Speratti. He'd head of a special committee that's investigating the Louies. I'm sure he'll have a copy of any material that has been confiscated. Think that would be enough?"

"Terrific. Just what I need. How soon do you think you could get it out here?"

"How soon do you think you could be back in Santa Fe?"

"I'll leave right after I call the *Chronicle*."

"That's a deal."

"I'm really grateful, Dad," Bria said, eager to end the conversation.

"Just get back to Santa Fe. I'll have Jenni pack it up and drive it over to Dulles International. We'll get it out to Houston on the next Continental flight, whenever that is. That should simplify matters." At the mention of Jenni's name, Bria visualized the flirty, Kewpie-doll blonde who was her father's secretary.

"Perfect. One other thing. I lost my wallet. Could you pay for a ticket home for me on your end, and I'll reimburse you?"

"Consider it done. My treat. Pick up your ticket at the Continental counter. Tell the guys at the commuter airline in Albuquerque to put your flight to Santa Fe on the Senator's bill." Senator Delgado's pleasure was audible.

He enjoyed intervening in people's lives and using his power to straighten them out. It had been a long time since Bria had let him do that for her.

"Well, now that that's out of the way, how are you?"

"Good. Been busy at the paper."

"When are you coming for a visit? Concepcion asks about you all the time."

The mention of her stepmother's name didn't irritate Bria as much as it usually did. "Say hello for me. Mom asks about you all the time too. I never have much to tell her that she couldn't read in the papers."

Before the sudden silence could lengthen, Bria finished brightly, "Anyway, I'll go check with Continental and wait for the file and ticket. Thanks again."

"Sure, *cariña.* I'll be back in New Mexico as soon as this session is over. Have to start chewing on the upstarts. I need to keep my job, Concepcion likes it here in D.C. Please do be careful and keep away from those Louies."

"Right, see you in Santa Fe."

"Take care of yourself and try to put Dom to rest, one way or another."

Before she could respond, the receiver went dead in her hand.

At the Continental counter, Bria received the bad news that the last flight in from Dulles had departed one hour ago. The early flight was due in at 8:30 in the morning. It was 4:40. She had fifteen hours and fifty minutes to kill.

Bria had been pumped up, ready for action. The delay deflated her, and she came down hard on an empty stomach. She didn't have enough to buy a package of crackers. Bria decided she'd borrow a few dollars from the friendly guard.

The guard insisted on lending her five dollars, which Bria accepted with profuse thanks and headed toward the nearest coffee shop to order enchiladas and a milk shake. After her meal, she bought a stack of magazines and listlessly thumbed through them.

At midnight, the coffee-shop waitress told her that she would have to leave; they were closing. Eight and a half hours stood between her and the early flight in from D.C. Bria decided to pass a little of it with a tour of the airport. She struck off down one of the long concourses that spoked

off from the main terminal. At the end of the lonely
walkway were a cluster of gates for Arrivals and Depar-
tures. She sat down in one of a line of scooped-out plastic
chairs that sprouted from one leg along a metal bar riveted
to the floor. A placard near the check-in counter announced that a flight was due in from San Francisco at
12:30.

Bria picked up a *Houston Chronicle* which had been left
on the chair beside her and leafed through it briefly. A half
dozen others, greeting the late flight, had joined her.

"Superjet service from San Francisco, Los Angeles, and
Phoenix arriving now at Gate Nine," boomed the loudspeaker.

After the last debarkee had greeted the last of those
waiting in the lounge, and she was alone again, she made
another attempt at the *Chronicle.* A headline suddenly
riveted her attention: LOUIES TO BE SENTENCED. The article
was datelined Washington, D.C.

A U.S. District Court hearing in the criminal-
conspiracy case against six top members of the
Church of Life Unlimited will come to an end tomorrow. A federal grand jury investigating various aspects of the church's activities spent the last three and
a half years working toward the hearing.

Papers filed with U.S. District Judge Alton Hayes
outline the conspiracy in which church members removed thousands of classified documents from government files. The documents show that church officials
wanted to penetrate the government illegally to fight
what the church considered illegal harassment, including numerous tax audits, designed to curtail its
religious freedom.

Judge Hayes will sentence the six defendants next
Monday. Hayes is expected to hand down verdicts of
guilty with sentences ranging from one to five years in
prison and fines of up to $250,000.

Attorneys for the church have filed harassment
suits and are seeking an injunction. Church leaders
have vowed to tie up the courts in "perpetual litigation" if the Justice Department continues what they
term "its attack on religious freedom."

Bria wondered how badly items like that one set back LU's mission to "get the planet On the Grid." Maybe even a few true believers would become disenchanted. Then she remembered Leonard. Probably most Louies had been indoctrinated as thoroughly as he had into believing that "The Media" were out to destroy them through slanderous journalism. The thought brought back Bria's headache. She closed her eyes to ease it and locked all thoughts of Life Unlimited out of her mind. She was through with them.

Half an hour later, she jerked her eyes open again, aware of three things: her heart was pounding, she was a long, long way from the main terminal, and there was someone behind her. The words "Agent Wilkers" shot through her mind. The footsteps came closer.

She spun around. A matronly woman stepped out of the shadows. It was clear from her cheap polyester skirt and blouse that she wasn't a Louie. Such apparel would never have found its way into the upwardly mobile wardrobe of a Church member.

Bria sank back in her seat.

"Are you through with the paper?" Her voice was pleasant.

"Take it." Bria smiled. Relief made her overly congenial.

As the woman bent over to gather up the paper, her maroon blouse gapped open between the top buttons. Bria noted with interest the unusual medallion that dangled within the dark folds. She had never seen one like it before. The medallion's classic simplicity seemed at odds with the woman's discount-store clothing. Bria wondered if the symbol stood for anything. It was just a plain gold X.

CHAPTER 12

Back in the main terminal, Bria found an excruciatingly uncomfortable plastic pod chair and tried to curl up in it. Her exhaustion overcame the chair's contours and she slept. Five hours later, at 6:30, she awoke, cramped and chilled. A norther had blown in, dropping temperatures forty degrees overnight. She was hobbled by kinks as she made her way to the coffee shop to revive herself.

Two hours later, she headed over to the Continental counter. The packet was waiting for her, along with a one-way, first-class ticket to Albuquerque. She checked the schedule. The next departure for Albuquerque was at 10:50, two hours and twenty minutes away. She would have to work fast to sort through the six inches of forms and documents her father had sent, call in enough facts to the *Chronicle* to pique their interest, and still catch her flight. She returned to the coffee shop to start her research.

Clipped to the first page was fifty dollars in cash and a note from her father: "Bill Speratti culled this from his LU material. Most of it was subpoenaed by the grand jury. Some of it was procured by other means. Didn't think you'd want all of it, it covers 18 feet. You're right, the whole thing is like a bad spy novel—Don't get involved. D."

Bria dug into the stack of paper. She was three-quarters of the way through when she realized that LU's secrets were meaningless to her. They were couched in a military-sounding jargon and filled with numerical notations. Because a part of her, the part she had tried to exterminate, wanted so badly to give up and head for home, Bria made herself go through the stack a second time.

That was when she found it. The document had been

xeroxed so many times that the words looked like a half-completed fill-in-the-dots puzzle. The bold handwritten words at the top were clear enough, though: RECONNAISSANCE SQUADRON MEMBERS, PROTECTORATE STAFF EYES ONLY.

It had been stamped: Internal Revenue Service, Intelligence Division, Alfred Rienstahl, Director. Below that was a penciled notation: Submitted, August 27. The document had obviously been procured by the "other means" her father had referred to, which meant that LU's claims weren't all paranoia—the church really had been infiltrated. She backtracked and figured that the agent who had stolen the document she held must have done so shortly after the grand jury indicted the Louies who were to be sentenced next Monday. Bria plunged eagerly into the thirty-six-page series of capsule biographies. In spite of the faintness of the type, the name at the top of the fifth page instantly grabbed her attention: Dominic Xavier Cavanagh. He was number five in the series. The page below his name was filled, single-spaced, with biographical information that started:

Rank: Grade 18, Expanded, Level Ten Augmentation
Service Time: 2 years, 10 months
Squad Time: 9 months, Active Duty

Beneath the esoteric Louie rankings were facts and figures Bria could recite like a Hail Mary. Dom's birth date, places of education, parents' home address, phone number, occupations. Bria thumbed quickly through the pages. This was it! She had found her bomb and didn't care whether it exploded on the government or LU. Just so long as the facts about Dom's disappearance were flushed out. With a little background, a bit of verification, Bria knew she would have a story any decent reporter would kill for. She transferred herself and the pile of papers to one of the terminal's sit-down phone booths.

She turned to the first name on the list, Leslie Aaronson, and dialed "Parents' Home Phone." No one answered. She dialed the next number, the parents of Jerry Besenberg. A recording told her that the number was no longer listed.

Number three, the parents of Theresa Brennan, answered, or, at any rate, a gruff Mr. Brennan did.

"Hello," he said, making the word sound like "yellow."

"Hello, Mr. Brennan, is Theresa in?"

"Who is this?" The voice was hostile and suspicious.

"I'm a friend of Theresa's, Molly Applegate." Bria almost gagged. Out of what remote corner of her mind had that name come from? "Theresa and I went to school together." She skimmed through the paragraphs in front of her and found the few lines headed "Education." "At Stephens, in Missouri," she added quickly.

"Oh," Brennan paused. "So you haven't been in touch with Terry for some time."

"No, I was just passing through town and thought I'd look her up, find out what . . . Terry has been up to."

"I'm sorry to have to tell you this Molly, but . . ." Brennan faltered, "but Terry died three weeks ago."

Bria was stunned, though she didn't know what else she had expected to hear. She hated herself for having to press further, but now, more than ever, she had to.

"My God, what happened?"

"Well," Brennan's voice had already turned from gravel to mush and was getting huskier, "you know how much Terry always loved to sail, learned down there at Stephens. I don't know if you knew this or not, but she'd been living up near Ithaca, New York, for the past two years. Anyhow, she was in with that Life Unlimited crew up there, had a training base or some damned thing. It was near to the Finger Lakes. Beautiful country. She went off a couple of weekends ago—October eighteenth, they told me—and rented a sailboat. Went out by herself. It capsized and Terry . . . Terry didn't make it back."

"I'm really, really sorry, Mr. Brennan. She had so many friends. She was so well liked at school."

"It was just a little Sunfish," Brennan went on, ignoring Bria's mumbled comments. "Terry handled those in all kinds of weather. It just doesn't make any sense. The weekend she went out there was no chop, a gentle breeze; I checked the weather reports all around that area. No heavy weather anywhere. Everyone tells me it was 'just one of those things.' What the hell is that supposed to mean? 'Just one of those things.' She was our only one, you know. Just mother and Terry and I."

"I . . . I," Bria stammered. Knowing there was nothing she could say that would comfort him, she forced herself to ask, "Have you already had the funeral?"

"We had a memorial service. The—her body must have snagged on something under the water, because it hasn't surfaced yet." A choked sob cut off the last word. Finally: "Sorry, it was just so sudden. We'd barely started getting used to the idea of losing her to that Life Unlimited."

"Yeah, I know, it's hard," Bria finished lamely. She replaced the receiver gently and clung to it. She had discovered another suspicious death, or report of a death. Before the scarier implications of that discovery could catch up with her, Bria was reading through the information on the next squad member on the list. If something had happened to one other squad member besides Dom, she'd have a lead on a story that the *Chronicle* couldn't ignore.

Wayne Cahill, Jr., was page four. All the grades and levels he had attained in Life Unlimited meant little to Bria, except for the last one. She remembered reading the overblown announcement about it in Dom's room. She also remembered the price tag, a $5,800 "donation." Where had Wayne Cahill gotten the money for that and all the other ever-increasing fees that had led up to it? Had he bled a trust fund dry like Dom? She read through the biographical data.

Date of Birth: 6-26-45
Place of Birth: Tumble Springs, Wyoming
Education: United States Air Force Academy, 9-63 to 5-67; Air Force Intelligence, 6-67 to 3-68
Military Service: 5-67 to 4-72, Vietnam. Discharged 6-72
Parents' Address: Rte. 3, Box 21, Tumble Springs, Wyoming
Parents' Home Phone: 307-258-4325

Air Force Academy. Tumble Springs, Wyoming. Bria knew that she wasn't going to be able to masquerade as either a friend from school or someone who was just passing through town.

It was 10:05. The Cahills were probably ranchers or farmers. With any luck, Wayne, Sr., would be out of the house.

Bria direct-dialed and the phone rang with the muffled gargling sound peculiar to rural phones.

"Hello." The phone was answered on the second ring by an older woman.

"Mrs. Wayne Cahill?"

"Speaking."

"This is the Veterans' Administration calling. We're terribly sorry to have to disturb you at a time like this." Bria stopped. She'd hoped that just that opening would be enough to prompt some response of either affirmation or negation. "We need some information for our files."

"About Wayne?"

"Yes, Mrs. Cahill. Could you tell us the story?"

There was a long delay before Mrs. Cahill made a hesitant beginning. "Well . . . we got the news about two weeks ago. They called and told us that . . ." Mrs. Cahill's voice surged, then quavered. "Couldn't you get this information from someone in Boulder? The police or someone."

"I'm terribly sorry, Mrs. Cahill, but we are required to make verification before processing benefits."

"I see. This has been so hard on all of us. . . ." Mrs. Cahill collected herself and went on. "I don't know what you need for your records, but Wayne developed his own computer business, Cahill Computronics, after he got out of the service."

Bria already knew where the profits had gone.

"Of course, toward the end, he began to neglect that. He became involved with a sort of religious group. The Church of Life Unlimited. You'll have to ask them, if you have any questions about the last three years. That's how long he was out of touch with the family. I was contacted by someone from that group. He told us that Wayne had died in a climbing accident." Mrs. Cahill couldn't stifle the sob that broke. She continued in a wavery voice. "Wayne always did love getting off by himself. They said he was climbing in the mountains around Boulder and slipped and fell into a crevasse. They almost didn't get him out. Had to use a helicopter. He died on the way to the hospital."

Bria made herself ask the one question that most needed answering and that she least wanted to ask. "Did you see the body?"

"No, the person who called told us that Wayne had signed a form requesting that he be cremated. Had to do with this group's religious beliefs. His father and I, well ever since he got back from Vietnam, we've hardly known him. So we sent in the telegram authorizing them to cremate the . . ." She stumbled again. "To cremate Wayne."

"Thank you, Mrs. Cahill. You've been extremely helpful. Someone else from this office may have to get back to you again. We appreciate your cooperation with our initial inquiry."

A climbing accident. Counting Dom, that made three deaths. None with any witnesses. All three in different parts of the country. All three officially accidents. Accidents that just happened to have occurred to people committed to spying on the government and tying it up in "perpetual litigation."

At first, Bria refused to follow the path being laid out in front of her. It did not lead to the villain she had anticipated: the one she had hated for taking Dom from her. Worse, it looked like LU was the victim. The shaded-over words, written in Dom's sloping hand—"infiltrated," "operative in place," "suspect," "dangerous,"—flashed across her mind as clearly as trail markers urging her toward the conclusion that one of the creepier government agencies was responsible for the three disappearances.

She pulled Dom's pocket watch out of her skirt pocket. It was 10:20. She had been struggling with her own incredulity for fifteen minutes. Not only couldn't she sort out what she had uncovered, she didn't have any more time to try. Her flight to Albuquerque would be boarding in a few minutes. Okay, she reminded herself, all you have to do is to communicate this information to the right people. Let them piece it all together. She knew she had enough to whet the appetite of any reporter, and Todd Samuels, her friend at the *Chronicle,* had a voracious hunger for conspiracies, scandals, and exposés with a particular appetite for IRS abuses. He thrived on rooting out corporate collusion and government malfeasance. He'd dig out all the missing puzzle pieces and put them together on the front page.

Ten twenty-two. She still had time for one more call. If it were positive, she would have an undeniable pattern. Bria hedged. She wasn't up to another gut-wrenching conversation with a grieving parent. She looked down the list. After Wayne Cahill was number five, Dominic Xavier Cavanagh. She flipped the page and located the parents' number for the sixth member of the Recon Squad. The number was local. That clinched the decision. Bria dialed. After half a dozen rings, Bria was on the verge of hanging up, when someone answered.

"Bueno," a sleepy-voiced woman said.

"Bueno," Bria returned the Spanish greeting automatically. Her eyes raced back up the page and came to a dead stop at the name at the top: Leonard Davila.

"I'm sorry, I must have the wrong number." Bria stammered the words. Her mind was whirring so rapidly that it was difficult to think, much less to speak.

Leonard was a Reconnaissance Squadron member. That was how he had known Dom. Bria had felt from the beginning that he and Dom had been more than the casual acquaintances that Leonard had claimed. If they had been fellow members of this intelligence squad, it was reasonable to assume that they had been friends, which would explain the intensity of feeling Bria had detected when Leonard had first talked about Dom. Dom had probably even told Leonard about her, about his Chicana sweetheart, shown him her picture. That would account for their "chance" meeting in the dining room. Leonard had spotted her, guessed why she was there, and decided not to blow her cover. For some reason, he had tried to help her for a while.

"For some reason." Bria's emotions finally caught up with the line of reasoning her mind had raced forward along. Of course Leonard had helped her: he must have been desperate for information about Dom's death—his was the next name on the stolen list.

The word "death" derailed Bria's entire train of thought. For the first time, she realized that, deep in her heart, she had been operating on the suspicion that this whole thing was some incredibly elaborate scam put up by the Church of Life Unlimited, probably for its financial betterment. Being confronted with the proof that the government actually had penetrated LU, that they knew the names of the Louie spies, and that the first five of those spies listed on the government-confiscated document were gone, chilled Bria. Mentally, she scrambled to regain her grip on the notion that she was still dealing with some labyrinthine Louie con, that all five of the missing Louies might still come dancing out of hiding, with Dom leading the way. She clung to that notion and to the increasingly threadbare hope it represented that Dom might still be alive as she reached for the Houston phone directory and looked up the *Chronicle*'s number. Surely they could expose whatever scheme LU had concocted. She thumbed a quarter into the coin slot and started to dial. She was on the seventh digit when she dropped her hand on the receiver cradle. The quarter was spit back out with a clunk. She replaced the receiver and listened to the conclusion that had been brewing at the back of her mind: She no longer had the time to nurse along her hope for a reunion with Dom.

She didn't have the time to bet Leonard's life on that rapidly unraveling hope. What if her gut-level feelings about LU were wrong? What if Dom had been right about LU just as he had been right about so many other things? What if the Louies really were the target of a government hit squad? That would mean that right now the government plant, or whoever was behind the series of "accidents" that seemed to have claimed a total of three victims, and maybe even five, was stalking Leonard, waiting for an opportunity to strike. Perhaps he already had.

Bria looked behind her. The Continental counter beckoned. Her flight to Albuquerque would leave in fifteen minutes. She could simply get on board, nestle into her first-class seat, soak up the free liquor, and call all this in to the *Chronicle* long-distance after she'd showered and had a hot meal. Once the story was out, Leonard would be safe, if he were in any danger to begin with. But how long would it take for the story to come out? No paper would be foolhardy enough to take on the IRS and Life Unlimited without thoroughly checking out its facts.

And if there were an assassin systematically killing the members of the Recon Squad, Leonard wouldn't survive the next day or two until the story was printed. Dom had been reported dead six days ago. Wayne Cahill's mother said she had learned of her son's death about two weeks ago. And Theresa Brennan's father had said his daughter had died three weeks ago. That put an even week between each death report. Today was the seventh day since Dom was supposed to have died. Or had died. Assuming that the two she hadn't been able to verify fit the pattern, it was time for number six.

She could call Leonard. Warn him. Then she could leave, she would be free. She'd have fulfilled any obligations she might have to him.

Unfortunately, it couldn't be that simple, and Bria knew it. She realized that she had about as much chance of reaching Leonard at the Academy as she would of getting through to the President. Maybe less. A bitter memory of the hours she had spent in her fruitless efforts to reach Dom came back. She remembered that awful night a year ago when she had called for the last time.

The same brisk voice had answered the phone with the same "Training Academy. Name and purpose of call" she had heard every time in the past year and a half she'd called. After her initial three failed attempts, using her own name, Bria had tried every ruse she could come up with. She was Dom's friend, cousin, sister, wife. She lowered her voice and claimed to be Mrs. Cavanagh. She told the receptionist that she was sick, dying, leaving for Europe, wanted to join the church. The impersonations changed, but her request was always the same: Let me speak with Dominic Cavanagh. The result was just as invariable. She was put on indefinite hold. That last time she had sat, the phone crushed against her ear, watching the numbers flip over on her digital clock. Tears of frustration rolled down her chin and disappeared into the holes punched into the mouthpiece. She "held" for one hour.

If she were going to warn Leonard, she would have to do it in person. The inevitability of a return to the old insane asylum caused a nauseating clenching in Bria's bowels. As she looked at the file in front of her, however, the queasiness subsided. She realized that she was holding her insurance policy, her passport out of the Training Academy. Knowing what was in the file, what the government had on them, would be invaluable to the Louies. As long as she could trade access to that information for her own safety, Bria knew she'd be all right. She tidied up the papers, replaced them in the manila envelope, and found a vacant luggage locker, number 1328. That number was embossed on a plastic strip glued to the otherwise blank locker key. Twisting the key out of the locker, she tucked it into her shoe, in a spot where it was sure to hurt as it dug into the sole of her foot. Bria wanted to be aware that she had that key every second. She wished fervently that she had a copy to mail to her father. But she didn't. Time was running out. Caution and her cynicism about LU became the ballast she was forced to toss overboard if she was to reach Leonard in time.

Merely thinking of passing beneath that black wrought-iron arc once more nearly caused Bria to bolt for the Continental gate. It was 10:50. Her flight to Albuquerque was leaving without her.

CHAPTER 13

She ground her foot over the key and drummed the plan through her mind. Get out there. Get past the guard. Warn Leonard. Period. From that point on, it won't matter who knows who you are or why you're there. Just tell whatever Louie higher-up you eventually have to talk to in some soundproof office that you have a significant portion of the government's file on Life Unlimited and will be happy to share it with him, with LU, with the world at large, in exchange for a ride back to the airport. Then, once you're safely back in the Houston Airport, you can toss the locker key to the Louies as you walk up the boarding ramp.

The built-in security of the plan calmed Bria enough to allow her to consider another major detail: How do I get out there? Renting a car took too much money. She dismissed hitchhiking. Bria recalled that she hadn't seen any vehicle other than the official bus on the desolate road out to the Academy. She braced herself to face another odious inevitability: sneaking onto the Louie bus from the airport to the Academy. That was her one chance of getting out there and her best chance for getting in.

Bria looked around her. The airport had come to life while she'd been engrossed in her strategies. It was hard to reconcile the frightening urgency that hammered within her with the banality of the airport. People stood in line to buy tickets, check baggage. They leafed through magazines, glanced at watches, adjusted ties, greeted relatives, smoked, waited. Bria studied the comforting familiarity of her surroundings and wondered exactly how she was going to carry out her plan. Surely the Louie guards would recognize her and stop her at the front door. She would have to correct that.

She walked over to a conveyor belt scooting luggage along its little track. She hung back from the crowd until only one small group was left—a man and his wife, both dressed in Western clothes and completely occupied with greeting another couple, who had obviously come to meet them. Bria waited. The security man who had been checking luggage tags moved away to another area. Three lone suitcases were shuttling around the track, unnoticed, behind the two couples—a large leather case, a tartan-plaid canvas bag, and a powder-blue suitcase. Bria stepped forward, not allowing herself to think, to reconsider, and swooped down on the blue suitcase. Without a backward glance, she marched to the exit gate and whisked through, headed for the ladies' room.

The stall for handicapped persons at the end of the row was the one she wanted. She closed the metal door, threw the chrome-plated bolt, propped the blue suitcase on top of the high commode between the railings that sided it, and popped open the clasps. Puffs of frilly garments confirmed the accuracy of her choice. She dug through the stranger's clothes and quickly saw that the woman's wardrobe leaned heavily toward country and western, with a strong emphasis on polyester pantsuits. The best of the bad lot was a pastel-checked affair. The pants drooped in the butt and rode high over Bria's ankles. The whole outfit made her feel like she should be wearing a hair net. The thought of hair prompted Bria to dig deeper, hoping to scavenge a scarf of some sort to hide her hair. What she came up with was even better—a fall, an artificial mane of hair that attached to a cloth band. Bria held it out at arm's length. It glistened in its chestnut-brown Dynel artificiality. She tied the cloth band over her own hairline and stepped out of the stall, pausing only to retrieve Dom's watch from the pocket of the skirt she was abandoning.

Bria barely recognized the matronly reflection in the mirror over the restroom basin. She didn't look like a standard Louie, but she didn't look like Bria Delgado either. As she stepped out of the restroom into the high-domed terminal, she saw the owner of the pantsuit she was wearing standing with her husband in front of the Lost Luggage counter. Bria slipped quickly into a phone booth where she could hide and watch. Only after the couple reported the loss and left the airport did she emerge.

A little after noon, the security guard she had befriended the day before came on duty. Bria's confidence in the modifications she'd made in her appearance was shored up when the young guard walked past her without a blink of recognition.

For the next four hours, she had little to do but experiment with the makeup she had found in the blue suitcase and scratch her scalp beneath the synthetic hair. At least the norther had brought temperatures down to a level Bria found comfortable. At 4:30, the Louie couple who had been greeting new arrivals the day before burst into the terminal. She watched them take up their stations near the far north concourse. A few minutes later, eight Louies deplaned and gravitated toward them. The prickles of nervousness that had turned Bria's back moist with sweat increased. The group of eight was too small. She'd be spotted immediately. The greeting couple split up and worked through the eight, checking the papers they held out to them. It was impossible. Bria knew she needed, at a bare minimum, a group of twenty to lose herself in. I tried, Leonard, she thought, seeing his brown Indian face in her mind as she got up to check on the next flight that would take her anywhere in New Mexico.

On her way to the Continental counter, a dozen travelers, all in their late twenties and early thirties, nearly trampled her as they whisked past, propelled by a sense of urgency usually seen only in persons about to miss planes or go into labor. Bria didn't even need to turn her head to see that they were hurrying to join the other group.

What's the worst they can do to me? Bria asked herself as she left the airline counter and cut across the terminal to the far corner of the baggage-claim area. The group was twenty strong when they wheeled around and headed to pick up their luggage. People backed away and gave the heel-clicking brigade wide berth as they swarmed over the area, efficiently jerking their expensive suitcases off the conveyor belt. When the group reformed outside the fenced-in area, Bria slipped in with her stolen suitcase, trying not to clump with either the original eight or with the twelve new additions. Their leaders herded them toward the exit.

The bus waited outside. The driver jumped out as they approached, and began tossing luggage into the vehicle's belly as soon as the first cadet reached him. Bria handed him the powder-blue suitcase, then attempted to board. The male half of the greeting couple blocked her way.

"I don't remember you being with either group." He scrutinized Bria with the full force of a Louie gaze.

"Cog up, cadet," Bria answered, imitating the imperiously annoyed tone she had heard him use yesterday. "My transit visa was checked outside Gate Eleven-A by your partner."

The man broke the eyelock and glanced around. The woman was already inside, on the bus.

"Altitudinal," he said and stepped aside.

Bria gave a curt nod of tolerant forgiveness and hoisted herself up the steps. She was careful to avoid looking directly at any of the passengers seated on the bus so that it would not become obvious that she knew no one from either group. She wondered how she was going to make it through the hour-and-a-half-long journey without betraying herself. The woman guide solved that problem. As the bus pulled into traffic, she rose and took a position at the head of the aisle. Clinging to the metal framework behind the driver, she began to speak, oblivious to the bus's rocking as the driver jockeyed through Houston traffic.

"I know you've all been in transit for the past few hours and that you've been cut off from Church comm lines. So you haven't been getting any uncensored data on how our defendants are doing."

Bria thought of the item she'd read in the *Chronicle* predicting that the six Louies would be found guilty of criminal conspiracy and wondered why the woman was smiling so hugely.

"In one word," the woman erupted, "stupendous!"

Cheers and applause burst out. A burly man in a three-piece suit in the seat in front of Bria clenched his fist and waved it in the air like an ecstatic football fan celebrating a touchdown. Bria pounded her hands together.

"Today, at oh-nine-hundred hours, Life Unlimited went on public record with a full disclosure of the unethical,

drag-loaded practices the IRS and the Justice Department
have covertly used in their mud-and-blood campaign
against freedom of religion in the United States of America!"

The cheering started again, as on-cue as a sound track.
"In Banner Council Brunches for the Defense of Religious Freedom held yesterday, in every major city
throughout the country, one-quarter of a million dollars
was raised! That's enough to fuel our fight in the courts for
another two months!"

When the cheering and applause stopped, the woman
went on, somber now, "I'm sure most of you are as bewildered and saddened by the government's continuing attack on Life Unlimited and our Mission of returning man
to his true spiritual nature as I am. Lou, for patriotic
reasons—because, in spite of everything, he has remained
a loyal patriot of this country—has not made a full disclosure earlier. However, after observing the dangerous
depths to which his formerly beloved country has sunk in
its attack on religious freedom, Lou has ended his silence.
The truth is out: This latest government attack was
prompted by the results of an intensive investigation
undertaken by the Protectorate into the causes of this harassment. Details are still classified, but Lou has authorized the release of this chunk of data: That investigation
revealed an international drug-trafficking cartel that involves Interpol, the Drug Enforcement Agency, the Justice
Department, a large number of highly respected Congressmen, and, of course, Rienstahl and the IRS. A federal
grand jury handed down a few indictments. And we've
been in court ever since. It doesn't take a criminal master-
mind, like the one Rienstahl's got, to make the connection
between those two events."

The aggrieved silence that was achieved in that bus,
in the middle of Houston traffic, was remarkable. Bria
strained to look out of the corner of her eye for a glimpse of
incredulity on any of the faces around her. All she saw
were expressions of sad, unsurprised resignation to this
latest onslaught of treachery. Surely someone must have
read the paper. Bria was staggered. Even if there was one
question forming in one mind somewhere on this bus, she
knew that the questioner wouldn't express it. Not here,

not now. Instead, the person would make his or her face into a mask of belief, just as Bria was doing, though probably with less effort. How often could the questioner suppress his doubts before they disappeared altogether?

The woman continued. She told of how this drug-trafficking cartel that Lou's special investigative force had uncovered had influences that even the Protectorate had not been able to track down.

The male half of the welcoming team stood and took over. "This revelation makes the Justice Department's charges of obstruction of justice somewhat ludicrous. In order to obstruct justice, you must have it to begin with." His last words drew a flurry of knowing laughs.

"And what do you think Lou's response to these attacks has been? To turn tail and run?" The man worked the crowd like a revival preacher, feeding it the rhetorical question.

"No!" came the pat response.

"Affirmatively not! In U.S. District Court for the District of Columbia at oh-nine-hundred hours, church lawyers filed a seven-hundred-fifty-million-dollar harassment suit against the IRS and a few of its cohort agencies. Rienstahl's grandchildren are going to have to carry on his work of suppressing the forces that seek to liberate mankind. Lou sure isn't acting much like a defendant, is he? No, he's acting like an *oh*-fendant, and it's got the entire United States government shaking in its boots."

Again Bria forced herself to join in the boisterous applause. There had been no mention of the probable prison sentences. No questions about them. Nearly everyone on the bus had at least a college education, and the majority held some graduate degree. There were lawyers, doctors, accountants, teachers applauding the outrageously twisted propaganda. Why?

A perfectly coiffed blonde in a slit skirt and heels stood and took the guide's place at the front of the bus.

"I just want to go on log," she said in a voice that combined a Southern accent with a full-volumed delivery, "with an altitude gain in my own life. I'm with the Atlanta contingent. I own my own investment-consulting firm. I started it five years ago right after I went Unlimited. Before that time, I was as zero-ceiling as all these government lackeys." She beamed as the busload of Louies chuckled appreciatively. "I had limited my world to the one thousand square feet of my home in a blue-collar neighborhood.

"Well," she continued brightly, "thank J. Louis Comfort for expanding *those* horizons!" Chuckles interspersed with applause. "Comfort put a money imperative on me and I had to stretch to meet it. And I've kept stretching to meet each new imperative that's come down. Only I've met and exceeded all of them by a factor of one hundred!" When the uproar created by her monetary marvels had subsided, the woman went on in a hushed, intimate tone.

"I started as a secretary. I was making the coffee and writing the letters and reports that earned my boss a thousand a week. And I was happy with the few hundred I took home each month. Then Lou entered my life." A moment of reverent silence followed. "I started applying his technology at work and quickly maxed-out the potential of that position. The boss stopped coming to work. I was doing my own job and his so much better than he ever had that his income had doubled. Of course, he kept feeding me raises, pittances compared to what I was bringing in for him. I was moving Up the Grid rapidly and finally went Exterior. From the altitude I gained during that first Exteriorization, I achieved a perfect insight into the whole financial game and knew immediately that it was time to start playing it for myself. I left my old job the next day. Within a month, my former boss's business had crumbled and he was being dragged into court by his creditors." She paused and waited for the cheering to stop.

"With each new level that I attained, my worth increased by a factor of ten. Last August three investment firms in Atlanta bottomed out and most of the others showed net losses. I cleared twenty-three thousand dollars in commissions that month and, right now, I am going on log to pledge a donation of that entire sum to the Council for the Defense of Religious Freedom. Because it's this simple—the survival of Life Unlimited is being threatened and I plan to keep myself and Lou Airborne."

The woman retook her seat amid the loudest tumult of approval yet. The man in front of Bria screwed himself around to face her. He was wearing aviator sunglasses set against the florid red of his overheated complexion. "Now *that* is what I call a No-Ceiling Action." His tone was an enthusiastic mixture of awe and admiration.

"Absolutely stratospheric," Bria ad-libbed, trying to duplicate his fervor.

The rest of the ride was devoted to more testimonials to the stunning changes Lou's Levels and the Grid had wrought in the testifiers' lives and bank accounts and how they weren't going to let the government ghouls block their continued progress Up the Grid. Bria was astonished by the exhaustingly high peak of emotion they reached and sustained. Outside of Aura Lee, the bus rocked off the main highway onto the side road, and the male guide stood.

"We're approaching the base. Training Discipline is now in force."

Abruptly, the bus fell silent. The vehicle's straining motor, inaudible before, suddenly sounded like an iron foundry in full operation. The riders stored away the personalities, or whatever force had animated them so brightly only seconds before, and replaced them with LU's remorseless, unswerving purpose. The grim silence made Bria feel as if she were riding in a troop transport filled with soldiers bound for a suicide mission. That impression was strengthened as they entered the darkly overgrown forest surrounding the Academy. Each mile took Bria farther into a world ruled by a bizarre code more distant from her reality than that of a group like the Penitentes of Northern New Mexico, who ritually flog themselves in secret ceremonies.

As the bus crested the rise above the Academy, the driver pulled the hand mike of his two-way radio off its clip and muttered into it. Bria felt a claustrophobic fear well up and stifle her as the bus took its final turn onto the Academy driveway and the shadow of the black wrought-iron arc fell across it. For one last time she tried to calm herself. I'm just going to warn Leonard, then leave; that is all. No matter what happens it couldn't possibly be worse than the mental wringer I'd put myself through if I didn't try, and something did happen to Leonard. Bria clung to that thought as they pulled onto the pebbly parking lot.

CHAPTER 14

Even the second time, Bria was jarred by walking into the Academy lobby. Deep in the middle of an east Texas pine forest, it bustled with fevered activity and a polyglot of foreign accents. Something was different, though. The large hall looked even larger, even more efficient. The unmoving air in the lobby seemed both clearer and staler. Bria sniffed. The hint of an unpleasant odor filled her nostrils. But she didn't have time to puzzle out what it was. Her group veered sharply to the left, toward the Verifications Counter. Bria searched the faces behind it. Leonard was not on duty. To the right were the stairs leading up to the second floor, to Leonard's room. The guard at the foot of the stairs stood with his arms folded across a chestful of swollen pectorals. He examined the passes proffered to him so intensely that he might have been memorizing them.

Bria couldn't pause. No one in the mammoth lobby was still. She moved closer to the Verifications Counter, taking a place at the end of the longest line. She couldn't pretend not to speak English again and the clown mat of a wig on her head wasn't going to conceal her identity from anyone if she came under scrutiny.

She moved reluctantly forward. A man in his mid-thirties, dressed in a plaid shirt and Sansa-belt pants, was in front of her. In front of him was a young woman, a poppet with springy blond curls and obvious dots of rouge on each cheek. Even at that distance, Bria could tell she was drenched in perfume, a floral blend that contrasted sharply with the musty odor Bria had noticed earlier. To her right, at the stairs, Louies were ascending at a steady, carefully monitored rate. Think, damn it, Bria ordered herself. Getting in where you're not wanted is supposed to be your specialty. Some bizarre cult shouldn't be any tougher to sneak past than the backstage guards at a rock concert. Apparently, the IRS and who knows what other agencies have managed it. As Dom's mother had reminded her, she'd pulled off some fairly ingenious stunts during her short career.

The line in front of Bria shortened. Only two people now remained between her and the attendant. The odoriferous young woman was issued a pass and turned toward the stairs. Bria doubted that she was very far out of her teens. Her barely controlled exuberance made her seem even younger. She fairly bounced toward the stairs with her pass. Probably not too long ago she'd done the same thing with a high school diploma clutched in her hand as she waltzed across some auditorium stage. Bria was curious how such a perky type could have been lured into Life Unlimited with its grim militarism. She thought of the overdone makeup and perfume and decided that a boyfriend might have encouraged her "enlistment." Maybe he was waiting upstairs for her right now. Bria could understand a reason like that. Perhaps if she could have persuaded herself to become involved with LU when Dom did, he too would be waiting for her upstairs.

The line stepped forward. Only one body now stood between Bria and the counter attendant. Her scalp itched. She worked one finger underneath the fall for a surreptitious scratch. The attendant and Sansa-belt were yelping codes at one another. Bria's temples began to throb, pounding out the rhythm of the conflict between the possibility that Leonard's life was in danger and the impossibility of warning him. She wondered if a fit of screaming hysterics, demanding to see Leonard, would bring him down. She remembered the jewelry salesman and the failure of his raving demands.

She scanned the lobby, searching for a possible opportunity. The young woman Bria had imagined to be on her way to a rendezvous was approaching the stairs with her newly issued pass. Just as she reached them, a pair of Louies, engrossed in a conversation, intersected her path. The collision of two single-minded purposes, one of them locomoting on high heels, was as effective as a clip in football. The woman, knocked to the shiny, slick floor, clutched her ankle. The guard launched himself out of his arms-locked position at the foot of the stairs and knelt beside her.

It only knocks once, Bria told herself. She left the counter just as the attendant asked for her code, and hurried to the young woman's side.

"I think it's sprained," announced the guard, bent over the young woman.

"You're right," Bria answered as if he had been speaking to her. "I'll go for the Flight Surgeon." The guard nodded without looking up. Bria slipped through the metal detector.

She loped up the stairs, two at a time, driven by an emergency far greater than a sprained ankle. On the first floor, directly above the lobby, Bria allowed herself a sigh of relief. The odor she'd noticed downstairs was even stronger. Again Bria dismissed it. The hardest part was over—she'd gotten upstairs. All that was left was to warn Leonard. If he wasn't in his room, she could leave him a note, then get the hell out of this spook house, forever. At the room beside the head of the stairs, she knocked on the flimsy door. There was no answer.

"Leonard," she hissed, "it's Bria. I have to talk to you."

Silence. Maybe he thought she had betrayed him and was not answering. Probably he had been ordered to break communication with her, just as she suspected Dom had been ordered.

"Come on, Leonard, open up." She put her ear to the thin door. No sound met it. She decided a note would have to fulfill any lingering obligation she might have to Leonard Davila. She turned the cheap doorknob. Of course the room was unlocked. She shot a glance up and down the long hall. It was abandoned. She backed into the room, making sure no one was coming down the hall, and quickly closed the door.

The windowless room was dark. Once inside, Bria was overwhelmed both by the odor she'd twice dismissed and by the terrifying suspicion of what it was—leaking gas. Her hand trembled as she felt inside the door for a light switch, then remembered that the makeshift rooms hadn't been wired for overhead lighting. She walked forward, her arms outstretched in the blackness like antennae, feeling for the lamp at the head of Leonard's bed. Her knee bumped something in the dark. It gave as she brushed against it. She reached down and grabbed Leonard Davila's cold hand.

Her own hand recoiled. She stuffed it in her mouth to bottle up the scream unwinding at the back of her throat. Her other hand flew out and found the lamp, knocking it to the floor. She groped for it and switched it on where it lay. The forty-watt bulb cast a naked drizzle of light upward on Leonard's dead face. His corpse was tucked tidily beneath a blanket and a sheet on the iron cot.

"Leonard." Bria's whisper was involuntary. She didn't have to touch the hand that jutted out from beneath the covers again to know that warm blood had not pumped through it for several hours. At the instant her control began to crumble, a jolt of adrenaline shot through her, a physical reminder that she was not staring into the face of ordinary death. She could no longer pretend that this was some monstrous hoax that would turn out like Halloween with everyone ripping off their spooky masks and her dancing away with Dom at the end of the evening. She was staring at a person who hadn't just been reported dead, but one who was, unequivocally, dead. Murdered.

A second realization rose up and obliterated even the horror of the first: the circle of murder she had stumbled into could tighten around her at any moment. Her own survival brought an immediate focus to her thoughts; her senses sharpened. She positively identified the odor saturating the room: gas. She cracked the door open, letting the deprived room flood with oxygen, then turned back to find the deadly element's source. At the head of the cot was a small gas space heater. The rubber tube connecting it to the gas valve in the wall was worn away. Or pulled away. The letal methane gas tainted with its rotten-egg signature scent poured forth as it must have been doing for hours. For long enough, at any rate, for Leonard's body to have gone cold and for the gas to have slithered downstairs, leaving the odor she'd detected in the lobby. Bria was certain that an official investigation, conducted by an unconcerned Aura Lee police force, would rule that Leonard Davila's death was an accident. Just as Theresa Brennan's, Wayne Cahill's, and Dominic Cavanagh's had been.

They weren't. Bria didn't have to see any more corpses to eliminate both the possibilities of accident and of insurance fraud. But murder? The grisliest of explanations emerged as the only plausible explanation.

The killer, for whatever reason he, she, or they had for murdering a select group of the followers of J. Louis Comfort, had undoubtedly been watching Leonard since finishing their last assignment—Dominic Cavanagh. The slight change in the weather, the drop in the temperature brought on by the norther, had been the break the killer had needed.

The murderer, if he'd been clever enough to infiltrate a Louie Academy, knew that the cadets, especially the working ones like Leonard, weren't ever allowed enough time for sleep, and, when they did find a few hours to rest, their deprived bodies lapsed into near comas. Or sleep heavy enough, at any rate, to allow someone to slip into their room, tug open the cracks on a piece of old rubber tubing, and open a gas jet full force. A common enough death. Happens all the time, especially after the first cold snap. Another accident. Another crazy cult member dead with only a few relatives, most of them too long out of touch with the deceased to ask questions. Questions like: Why?

The answer that resonated in Bria's skull contained all the words she had dismissed as Louie propaganda—"government attack," "mud-and-blood campaign against freedom of religion," "the forces trying to destroy the Church."

As quickly as Bria could formulate objections, her mind churned out further amplifications on this theme. She remembered the guide on the bus and her fervent avowal that J. Louis Comfort had uncovered high-level connections between the government and an international drug-trafficking operation. Did Recon Squad members really know some dirty secret that would explode the highest echelons of power? Were the alphabetically ordered deaths a warning to surviving squad members to keep what they knew to themselves? Had Leonard, had Dom, died because some Protectorate commander refused to halt their investigations?

The welter of questions froze. Bria whirled around. The old floorboards outside Leonard's door had creaked. Bria crouched on the floor and grabbed the fallen lamp, gripping it by its base like a bludgeon. She breathed through her mouth and tried to loosen her vocal cords, preparing the bloodcurdling shriek she would utter when the door swung open and she hurled the lamp at the agent who would step in. Poised and ready to strike, Bria felt so close to exploding in a mass of jerks and tremors that, when she heard another creak outside the door, she was halfway to hurling the lamp before she realized that the footsteps were moving away. She dropped the lamp, raced to the door, and flung it open. The hall was empty. She shut the door and collapsed against it.

Suddenly everything had changed. Bria realized that she was trapped; however odious it might be, her fate had just been cast with Life Unlimited. She no longer had the option of simply waltzing out the front door and letting the Louies dredge themselves out of the muck they were mired in. No, it was no longer that simple.

Whoever had stalked Leonard was, undoubtedly, stalking her now. If she tried to hike back to the main road, she was dead. They would trail her—wait until she was alone on that long country road, then obliterate her. A fast-moving car, swerving off the road, would do it. It wouldn't be an accident, but then it wouldn't have to be. There would be no witnesses. All anyone could do would be to speculate and condemn the senseless violence of a hit-and-run driver cutting down a young woman. Then the matter would be dropped.

No, for the time being, Bria knew that her survival was linked to the Church of Life Unlimited. She knotted her hands together to keep them from trembling.

"Don't clutch." It was the same order she always issued to herself when she went out on a tough assignment, when her deepest instincts called for her to chuck it in and find a safe, quiet job in some library somewhere. Only the degree of fear was different now; considerably different. And the cost for not mastering it would not be a slightly disgruntled editor or a hole in a layout if she came back without the photo.

Bria responded in the same way she had responded to

every critical situation she had encountered over the last two years: she asked herself what Dom would have told her to do. At first, as faint as the lines she had penciled over on the yellow legal pad, then just as clear as they had become, came the answer.

"Tower 11. . . . All can be trusted with him." And all would have been trusted with him, if Dom had not been killed first. She knew a Tower was a counselor of sorts, someone who conducted the Exteriorizations LU built its theology around. But who precisely was Tower 11?

Given the altitude-obsession of LU, Bria figured that if he were important enough for Dom to trust, she would find him at the building's highest level, the fifth floor. Still crouched beside Leonard's body, Bria had no intention of stepping out the door unless there were an abundance of witnesses nearby. She picked up Leonard's pass off his nightstand and used a small penknife she found in the drawer to scrape away the last two letters of the first name.

The small room held little to capture Bria's attention and, unwillingly, her gaze returned to Leonard's face. It was an oxygen-starved, cyanotic blue. In death, his face, dark against the stark white of the pillowcase, was serene and dignified. More than ever it had an ancestral look of Aztec nobility.

How ironic, Bria thought, as she noticed a small gold cross trailing a golden chain, resting on the pillow just beside his ear. The last trace of his vestigial Catholicism. But it wasn't a cross at all. All the legs were of an equal length. It was more like the X she had seen around the neck of that woman at the airport. Remembering that Leonard was from Houston, Bria wondered what significance the medallion might have for people in this part of the country.

From far down the hall, the muffled sounds of conversation filtered into the room. Bria picked up the altered pass, pinned it above her breast, and moved to the door. When she was sure the group was near, she slipped out.

The cadets passed. Bria peered down the dimly lit hall. Empty now, it was pocketed by shadows and honeycombed with dumbwaiters and laundry chutes that dropped five stories—an ideal setting for murder.

CHAPTER 15

The fifth floor's magnificence had little impact on Bria on her second trip up. She was locked beneath a bell jar of shock and horror.

"Purpose?" The guard's voice bit through Bria's emotional concussion.

Knowing that Leonard was regularly dispatched all over the Academy, Bria stammered, "Message for Tower Eleven." The guard stared at Leonard's pass. He didn't question the gap between Leona and Davila.

"Proceed to Control Room Eleven."

Bria struck out as if she had visited Tower 11 in his Control Room dozens of times. She prayed she was heading in the right direction. Walking down the carpeted hall lined with closed doors was like tiptoeing through a library. The aura of intense, awesomely silent, mental activity was palpable. On either side she heard muffled mutterings filtering through the closed doors, like Friday-evening confessions at the Cathedral. Midway down the hall, she stopped. The words "Control Room 11" were stamped in lucite on a door. Below them was a professionally lettered sign reading, "Exteriorization in Progress. Do Not Disturb."

Bria glanced back at the guard. He was intent upon monitoring one of the screens on his console. Bria moved close to the door, close enough to hear the muffled sounds from within. Abruptly a deep, low voice picked up volume.

"Attention, cadet, you are experiencing wake turbulence. Repeat, wake turbulence. You are in danger of vortex roll. Institute vortex-avoidance procedures at once!"

The room fell silent again. Then the voice, relieved and

now barely audible, spoke. "Excellent, Gates. You've sta-
bilized. Continue with filed flight plan." Images of a frantic air-traffic controller screaming at a pilot in trouble
flipped through Bria's mind.

A rustling noise coming from the security station propelled Bria's hand forward. Her fingers touched the knob,
she was committed to turning it. She felt the guard's attention sweep over her. She opened the door.

The Control Room was barren except for a pole lamp
that had been turned to face the wall so that its thin illu-
mination was muted even further. A door which Bria assumed led to a bathroom was closed. In front of it two men
were seated across from one another at a table. On the
table rested an apparatus that Bria identified instantly as
the cornerstone of Life Unlimited. The chunky metal device was what adherents turned to reverently to demonstrate the soul's tangibility, to test and measure the force
that animates the physical shell. It was the Grid.

The man facing Bria was a cadet taking one of J. Louis
Comfort's sitting tours of the cosmos. He had his eyes
tightly shut and was sweating with the effort of keeping
his fists clenched around what looked like an airplane
steering wheel sticking out of the backside of the Grid. The
cadet's eyes opened. They had a wild, disoriented glaze
over them. They were seeing only the frightening array of
images being projected by his own mind.

Bria stared at the Grid's heart, the Screen. It resembled
a small, round radar screen, cross-hatched with horizontal
and vertical lines like a sheet of graph paper. Two thicker
markings delineated the ordinate and abscissa. A white
dot blipped erratically in the upper-right-hand corner as
an arm swept past it.

The man behind the screen whirled around to freeze
Bria with an angry glare. Immediately, he spun back to
study the screen. "Fuck," he whispered, "you got my cadet
into a stall." The Tower's anger disappeared as he spoke
reassuringly to the frenzied cadet opposite him.

"Attention, Gates, attention. Repressurize."

The cadet pulled trembling lids over his madman eyes.

"Initiate stall recovery," the Tower ordered in a calm
voice straight out of NASA Mission Control. The white dot
blinking in the upper right quadrant became less er-

ratic. The Tower fiddled with one of the many dials beneath the Grid Screen. "Good. Now get your nose down." The Tower pulled a sweaty hand from the dial and dried it on his khaki pants. "Not so steeply," he cautioned, jerking his hand back to the dial. "That's it. Okay. Open throttle. Smoothly, Gates, smoothly."

Bria was transfixed. She felt as if she were eavesdropping on a Lamaze coach bringing his partner through a difficult delivery.

"You're walking the rudder, Gates, ease up! That's it, that's it. Altitudinal! Great, come on in."

Several minutes passed before the cadet loosened his hands on the metal wheel. The instant he did so, the white dot blinking on the screen disappeared. The cadet slumped back into his chair with a sigh. Gradually, as if he were coming out of a coma, he opened his eyes.

"Thanks." The cadet's voice was dry and shaky. "I was fixing to Zone Out, go Off Grid, wasn't I?"

"Didn't even really come close. You made a nice recovery."

"Thanks to all those Discipline Drills. Hated them while I was on that level, but am I glad my trainer didn't let me off until I got those responses wired."

As the charge from the crisis the two men had just weathered began to dissipate, Bria's presence was noticed again. The Tower swiveled around.

"Why did you ignore the Exteriorization warning on the door? You are aware, of course, that you have incurred a grave Standards Violation."

"No, I'm not. I don't know about any of this. I apologize. Are you Tower Eleven?"

"Let's first establish exactly who you are." His voice was sharp.

"If you are Tower Eleven," Bria insisted, "I have to speak to you. Privately. It's urgent."

The Tower looked at the cadet. "Gates, we'll get you Airborne again later this evening. I have my last scheduled session at twenty-three-hundred hours tonight. We should be through at twenty-three-fifty hours. Want to come back then?"

"You know it." The emphatic answer was delivered with a half-smile and a knowing laugh, as if the Tower had asked the cadet if he could arrange to return that night to take possession of a quarter million in gold bullion. Bria had to step quickly away from the door. The cadet backed out, beaming beatifically at the Tower.

"I was close, you know," he said, his hand on the doorknob.

"Yes, Gates," the Tower answered. "It scanned."

The cadet held up his hand and left.

"Now, what is it?" The Tower's face was long and furrowed. At the moment it was curdled with irritation. It wasn't a peevish kind of irritation, though. The Tower had the same world-weary look that Abraham Lincoln and the early Franciscan missionaries, depicted in woodcuttings, had. They all seemed to dwell in bodies that had been stretched vertically into a pinched angularity that suggested a lifetime of long-suffering. Bria was reassured by the man's annoyance; it was important to know how seriously he took his role as a spiritual guide.

"I take it you're not an Unlimited." Bria was further reassured by the Tower's comment, by the way he stated it, as if it were a fact obvious to him that was neither a condemnation nor a major revelation.

"No, I'm not." Bria slid the stolen fall off her head and shook her own hair out, glad to feel air on her scalp again. "Are you Tower Eleven? Were you Dominic Cavanagh's Tower?"

"Why?"

"Because I'm Bria Delgado. Dom and I lived together for two years. I came here to find out what happened to him. So far I've just uncovered more questions. I want answers." Bria heard the last three words, the way they came out as a desperate plea. She couldn't help it. The Tower responded to her desperation.

"Yes, I was Dom's Tower."

Bria drew in a deep breath. "Leonard Davila is dead."

"The Spanish interp?"

Bria nodded. "He's been murdered. I just found his body in his room."

Without another question, the Tower stood and stepped outside. Quick footsteps and the slap of a holster against thigh announced the guard's rapid approach. In a low voice the Tower issued steady commands.

"Dispatch a provost marshal from the Protectorate to Cadet Leonard Davila's room. This is a classified matter. Have the PM report directly and immediately to me, at my office."

The guard nodded solemnly and pivoted to carry out the order.

"Let's go to my office." Bria trailed him into an office that contrasted sharply with the opulence of the reception area. It was modestly furnished with a battered gray metal desk, a couple of equally dilapidated chairs, and haphazard mounds of files and paperwork. Beside the door was what appeared to be a window with wooden panes.

Bria was pleased; she needed to trust this man and that would have been hard in surroundings reminiscent of an oil-company headquarters. The Tower sank his long frame into the old secretarial chair behind the desk. Bria pulled up a folding chair.

"You're wondering—"

Tower Eleven held up his hand to cut Bria off. "Let's not dive into this until we have as complete a data base as possible to work from."

For several minutes they sat in silence; then the intercom, hidden beneath a stack of papers on the desk, began to buzz. Tower Eleven dug it out, pressed down on a switch, and leaned close to the device so that Bria could hear only his half of the conversation, which consisted of, "Yes, go ahead. . . . Are you sure? . . . Seal off the room. . . . Post a guard. . . . Notify Slako."

Was Slako the one who had told the parents that their children were dead? Would he be calling Mrs. Davila soon? Would he tell her that her son had had an accident, or that he had been murdered? Bria decided that the answer would probably depend heavily upon what she was about to say.

The Tower took his hand from the intercom and glared at Bria. "Why do you think that Davila was murdered?" The tone was harsh. Bria understood why. At that point, she was as likely a suspect as they had. She weighed her options. She had no choice but to enlist the aid of the Louies as rapidly as possible against what had become their common enemy.

"Because he was the sixth member, in alphabetical order, of the Reconnaissance Squadron, and, unless I'm seriously mistaken, he was the sixth member in that same order to meet an accidental death in as many weeks."

"How do you know about—" The Tower stopped himself and studied Bria warily, looking as if he'd just avoided a trap she had set. "Who sent you? Who are you with?"

"As I said before, I sent myself. I'm not 'with' anyone."

Bria envisaged a potentially endless series of proofs and counterproofs stretching out in front of her if she couldn't make the Tower believe who she was.

"I couldn't have been the first to notice this series of 'accidents,'" she said. "I know for sure about Theresa Brennan, a boating accident. Wayne Cahill, a climbing accident. Dominic Cavanagh, a . . . an accident in the bathtub. Now Leonard. Another accident? And what about the first two on the list, Aaronson and Besenberg? I couldn't get hold of their parents."

"Dead," the Tower said, looking more than ever like a weary Abe Lincoln. "Aaronson, a car wreck. Besenberg, some strange illness. Encephalitis. The doctors couldn't say. No, of course you're not the first one to notice. The Protectorate started investigations after the second report. After Besenberg. We know that these deaths aren't coincidental and we have a pretty good idea who's behind them."

"Who? Did Dom talk with you before he . . . died?"

"No," the Tower wagged his drooping face. "Why?"

Bria told him about the note Dom had written, which had been excised from the pad.

"Dom, Dom." The Tower muttered the name softly. Bria felt a link forged between them. Dom was as alive for him as he was for her.

He leaned forward and rested his head on the tips of his outsized fingers. "This is all classified. Even the existence of the squadron is classified. How did you know about it? Did Dom tell you?"

"No." Bria revealed how she had acquired the confidential material from her father.

The Tower listened silently. When she had finished, he creaked far back in his chair and closed his eyes, massaging them with his long fingers. After a defeated moment, he swooped forward again.

"God," he said, seemingly reenergized. "They've been

after Lou for twenty-five years. But I never would have dreamed they'd ever . . . it's hard to believe, even after all the treacherous maneuvers they've pulled, it's still hard to believe that they'd resort to murder."

"They? Who are 'they'? The government? The IRS? Rienstahl?"

"No. Oh, they've used them all. I know that it's hard to picture the IRS acting as anyone's pawn, but that's how powerful these people are. We've known for fifteen years who our enemies are."

He stared at Bria. "They're your enemies too, now, whether you realize they exist or not. They can't run the risk that, someday, you might put together what information you have. For your own protection, you will have to be thoroughly briefed."

"Yes, I'd appreciate that," Bria replied mockingly, trying to defuse the sinister atmosphere that had begun brewing.

The Tower looked up at her with an expression that came close to sadness, as if he were sad about Bria's scorn, and even sadder about the story he was going to have to tell her in spite of it.

"It started more than thirty years ago," he began, his eyes never leaving Bria's, "when Lou first Exteriorized. It would be impossible for me to try and describe to a Limited like yourself what a landmark that event was for mankind. Future generations will recognize it as the watershed point in the evolution of Homo sapiens into a truly cognitive being. It took Lou three years of intensive research after the discovery to perfect the Grid and the technology for guiding soul flight. During those arduous years, Lou stayed Airborne a good part of the time, soaring to etheric realms of which no man had ever conceived of before."

As she listened, Bria consciously had to remind herself that the Tower was spouting the canned Louie line. What made his words so difficult to ignore was the clear fact that he spoke straight from a believing heart harnessed to a sharp mind. His manner forced Bria to the same conclusion Dom had come to: "All can be trusted with Tower Eleven."

"In these unimagined realms," the Tower continued,

"Lou was made privy to masses of truth quadruple the volume of those uncovered here on Earth throughout the combined histories of all cognizing peoples who have made the planet their home. Lou made a sacred pact never to reveal any of these truths until mankind had been pulled far enough out of the spiritual abyss it had sunk into to process the data that would once again return them to their true nature."

Bria was unsettled by the saintly gaze that now lit the long, bony face. He looked more than ever like a sixteenth-century Franciscan missionary who had come with the Spanish conquistadores to enlighten the savages of the New World.

"I'm sorry. I got carried away." The Tower laughed at himself. "I just broke one of Lou's cardinal rules: 'Never throw open the floodgates of knowledge, you'll drown your listener.' The point I'm trying to make is, during those first three years, Lou had his first Fit." The Tower smiled at what Bria figured must be a Louie inside joke.

"Virtually everyone who Exteriorizes now has these Fits. From the objectivity, the removal, the altitude, that one gains during Exteriorization it is quite easy to discern hidden or camouflaged patterns. Pieces fall into place and perplexing conditions in a person's life or a nation's history suddenly 'fit.' Do you follow?"

Bria nodded, impatient for him to get past the propaganda and start explaining the corpse downstairs.

"Okay, so Lou was cruising the stratosphere on September 15, 1951, and he paused to metaphorically 'look back' on Home Planet. He cogged immediately on a pattern that stood out as clearly as the polar ice cap—the increasing role of drugs in man's recent history. It was a Fit all right, and so obvious once he'd seen it."

Bria stared blankly.

"What's the number-one prescription drug today?" the Tower asked didactically. "Valium. A little tranquilizer, often accompanied by a little upper to balance its effect, often accompanied by a whole host of other pharmaceuticals that are absolutely acceptable everywhere—bridge club, church group, everywhere. No one raises an eyebrow. And how about a nationwide addiction program underwritten by our federal government that hooks millions of citizens on a drug far more addictive than heroin? How about the Methadone program?"

The Tower was no longer concerned about the uncomprehending look on Bria's face. He was wound up tight and kept spinning. "How did we get this way? It didn't happen overnight. Maybe if it had, more people would have noticed. No, it was a process that took decades. During that time the American public has been skillfully indoctrinated to view drugs, drugs prescribed by their friendly family physician, as no more dangerous than vitamins. And this process is far from complete. Community psychiatry was the big step toward the second phase. We're already seeing it at work. Increasing numbers of criminals, starting now with crimes like wife beating and child abuse, are delivered, not to a jail cell, but to a mental health center, for 'counseling.' This 'counseling' invariably involves chemicals. More and more citizens every year are walking around in chemical straitjackets—former mental patients, current mental patients, anxious housewives, driven businessmen, overactive schoolchildren, unhappy teenagers."

Bria could control her impatience no longer. "What precisely does all this have to do with Leonard's death? With Dom's? Shouldn't you be on the phone to the police?"

"Let me finish." The Tower held up his hand. Bria almost expected to see a stigmata. "As you know, there cannot be an effect without a cause. And the effect of turning our nation into a pathetic country of addicts tyrannized by the mental-health industry and unaware of their true spiritual nature was a major one. Lou organized a LU investigative task force, which uncovered a conspiracy extending through generations of the richest, most powerful families on earth, all acting through their diverse corporate entities. It is into their pockets that the astronomical profits from psychopharmaceuticals go. You've read the names of those families in your grade-school history books."

"Oh, this is too much." Bria rolled her head away in disgust.

"I know that it's hard to believe. It was hard for me too, at first. That's because we're not used to thinking in terms of unlimited power and unlimited time. You have to put yourself in the frame of mind of the offspring of one of these dynasties. They don't think about this year's net profits. They think about what future generations, about what their grandchildren will be reading about them in history books. Anyway, that was the mentality that, shortly after the Second World War, drove three of the families that still control national economics to conspire to make the United States the largest marketplace ever to exist for drugs. They didn't expect to hit full production for another century, and they didn't care. They would be long dead, but they knew that their heirs would enjoy the profits and the power of their intrigues."

"Look . . ."

"George," the Tower supplied his name.

"All right, George, this is fascinating, I'm sure, and someday I'd love to go into all of it in the depth I'm sure it deserves." Bria struggled to remain civil. "But don't you understand? Six people have been murdered. I could very well be number seven." Bria followed George's eyes as they trailed down to her hands. She had both of them braced on his desk and was leaning over it, straining to reach him both physically and intellectually. She pulled away and sat back in her chair.

"That," George said like a teacher pleased with a slow student who finally catches on, "is precisely why it is imperative for you to understand what we are up against. Because you too must now confront this monstrous evil."

Bria slumped back further in the hard chair.

"All right, where was I?" The Tower began to look less like Abraham Lincoln to Bria and more like Ichabod Crane. She felt a powerless rage well up within her, and fought it down. This ectomorph spewing out a harebrained conspiracy theory was her last, her only chance.

"Lou spent many years after that Fit and the preliminary investigation building up a dossier on these families hiding behind their corporate identities. The criminal connections only grew stronger. He established the Marseilles–Washington connection because it wasn't too long before the families started using their drug know-how and the distribution network they'd set up to push heroin with the help of some highly placed legislators and agency heads as well as—"

"George," Bria cut in hotly, "I have heard sleazy rumors like that weekly since my father took office. They make it sound like everyone from the President on down to the janitor who cleans out the men's room in the Senate chambers is on the take. What I have yet to see is any proof of these nasty innuendos."

"That's where Lou is different. He documents. After one of his first investigators met with an 'accident' during his inquiry into Interpol's role in all of this, Lou knew he had been warned. The families were telling him to get out. Instead, he got tough. That was when those pioneer investigators turned their notebooks and gumshoes in for sophisticated surveillance equipment and were transformed into one of the finest intelligence teams the world has ever seen. And they got the proof, the documentation. We have dozens of bureau chiefs, Congressmen, agency heads, the top men in every corner of government, we've got them on tape in incriminating conversations. On September twenty-ninth, we handed those tapes over to a special Senate subcommittee investigating international drug trafficking. That was Lou's response to the grand-jury indictments. It was a clear message to the families that he was not going to be intimidated by their power plays, their legal threats.

"That following Saturday, Leslie Aaronson's car was forced off the road, into a ditch. The police called it an accident, our agents told us otherwise. A week later Besenberg was in a coma with some disease the doctors still haven't been able to identify. They're saying it's some kind of encephalitis. Our intelligence sources link it with a top-secret project undertaken by the CIA to develop a microbe for which no antibody exists. Then Brennan, Cahill, Cavanagh, now Davila. We don't know how they're identifying squad members. That is information that only Protectorate staff is privy to."

"Jesus," Bria sighed in exasperation. "You are infiltrated, you know that. You plant a few undercover people in government offices, the agencies plant a few of theirs in yours. A list of squad members was stolen by an IRS agent. It's got an IRS Intelligence Division stamp on it. The list went directly to Rienstahl."

"God, not the Protectorate too. How could they have penetrated us too? You can't imagine the screening Protectorate initiates are subjected to."

"I don't know, but they obviously have. What I don't understand," Bria said acidly, "is if Lou had such an inside track on all this Washington skullduggery, why did he expect to find justice there, in the viper's nest?"

"We missed a link, Bria. We thought that subcommittee was clean. No one is more disillusioned about it than Lou."

"Well, besides being disillusioned, what are you doing? Your elite corps is being murdered."

"That's exactly it, what can we do? They want us wiped out. We've gotten too close to the truth. They've used the FDA, the IRS, the CIA, National Security, Military Intelligence, and a couple of deep-cover agencies, along with the media, and the courts to try and eradicate LU. None of it has worked. Now they've gotten blunt, they're using an assassin. He's here, inside the Academy, but we have no clue as to his, or her, identity."

"Call the police, for God's sake. Get fingerprints. Start isolating your suspects. Can't 'one of the finest intelligence teams the world has ever seen' even save their own hides?"

"We've tried the police. Five times we've tried. Each time they rule the deaths accidental and refuse further investigation. Bria, we have begged for a complete investigation. Even if we'd gotten cooperation, how well do you think some police detective could have done against a professional government spook? Even if he didn't start with orders from the top to fluff the assignment?"

"Why," Bria asked, "as soon as you found out that your 'crack counterintelligence' force was being murdered, why the hell didn't Lou, or someone from the Protectorate, order some of this sophisticated surveillance equipment to be used in behalf of keeping those squad members alive? Why weren't they kept under a twenty-four-hour guard? How could you have let Dom be killed?"

"Bria, I understand your bitterness, believe me I do. That's the worst part. We didn't react quickly enough. No one could make themselves believe that this was really happening. Lou has been devastated by the deaths of those so dedicated to him, to our Mission."

"To say nothing of how 'devastated' Mrs. Cavanagh, the Brennans, the Cahills, the Aaronsons, and the Besenbergs are. Oh, and let's not forget, Leonard's mother will be getting the news today, and his father from Mexico. They'll be joining a lot of devastated parents, relatives, friends . . . and lovers.'' The core of anger within Bria dissolved with the last word.

"I know how you feel," George said gently. "I don't expect this to change anything, but Dom meant a great deal to me too. I miss him terribly."

Bria nodded tightly, willing herself not to surrender to the gush of tears that the Tower's tenderness had released within her. She forced herself to continue tearing this demented nightmare apart, to piece together some flimsy bit of coherence.

"I take it my meeting with Leonard in the dining hall was not coincidental. That you knew all along who I was?''

"Half right. No, the meeting wasn't coincidental. All Verifications Counter personnel had been instructed to report immediately any non-reg entries. The entire Academy has been on maximum security procedure ever since . . ."

"Since Dom was killed," Bria completed the sentence George had balked at.

"Right. When your entry was reported, your feigned inability to speak English, it was natural that Leonard be assigned to make contact with you. Apparently, though, when you told him who you were and why you'd come, he chose to make common cause with you. He was desperate to learn what had really happened to Dom, even more desperate than you. Fearing what we now know has happened, that the Protectorate was infiltrated, he didn't report you. He verified your story, and a pass was authorized for you."

"I don't understand why Leonard was even allowed to remain here after you realized you had been infiltrated. His was the next name on the list. He should have been sent into hiding."

"Leonard refused. He thought that by staying, maintaining his usual routine, he could draw out the counteragent. He was overconfident. He had been trained thoroughly in karate and other martial arts as well as having completed Level Nineteen, Sensory Amplification, which had quintupled the acuity of all his senses. He didn't believe that a Limited, or even a traitor Unlimited, could ever gain the upper hand with him. I know that this may be hard for you to grasp, Bria, but for an Unlimited, like Leonard, having your autonomy denied, your integrity restrained, would have been worse than death. So, Command agreed with his decision to stay here and attempt to draw out the agent."

Bria nodded wordlessly, unable to express her feelings about the lethal delusions the son of a wetback had been fueled on. And what of the deluded son of a state governor? Couldn't any of them see that they were children playing with matches on top of a keg of gunpowder? Whoever their enemy was, the Louies were heavily outclassed

But what if they *had* blundered onto some incriminating piece of information? Bria was far from believing in an international drug conspiracy. What was important, though, was that LU did. It was quite possible that, during their investigations, they had stumbled over some rock in Washington and seen a few of the crawly things that slithered out. Then, in their rush to strike back at "government harassment" through the Senate subcommittee, they just might have stepped on some sensitive toes. If the owner of those toes had wanted to kick back, he wouldn't have had much trouble locating the right target. A copy of the list of LU's Recon Squad, complete with home addresses and current duty stations, didn't seem to be much harder for an insider politico to score in D.C. than a handful of Quaaludes in east L.A.

"Listen, George, whether you or Lou, or any of the rest of the LU hierarchy cares to admit it, you are facing a vastly superior enemy and you need help. I agree that the local police may not be the ones to ask. Besides being hostile to LU, they're clearly incompetent. Even if they did investigate the deaths, it would be weeks before they came up with enough evidence to act. By that time, there won't be enough squad members left alive for a game of checkers."

"Now," said George, "you're beginning to understand our position."

What Bria had begun to understand was her own position. The locker key grinding into the sole of her sweaty foot was to have been her ticket out of the Academy and the madness that percolated through it. She'd planned to

relinquish the key and the government files it would unlock only when she was safely removed from all of LU's in-
sanity. Finding Leonard's body had altered her plan to toss
the key to some Louie as she boarded a plane for New Mexico. Bria evaluated her position: she was trapped in a
choice between the lesser of two evils. Though the conclusion was repellent, Bria had to admit that, given the evidence supplied by her father, Life Unlimited was less
menacing than the faceless assassin of a faceless government agency. Along the one avenue of escape from both
that she saw open to her, a premature and very unwelcome
surrender of the locker key loomed unavoidably.

"All I understand," Bria blurted out, "is that you need
to act quickly. Before anyone else is killed, especially since
I seem to be as likely a candidate as the next squad member on the list. As I see it, George, you have one recourse—
the press."

George began sputtering protest. Bria pushed right
through it. "It's your only hope. Shine the bright light of
publicity on these ghouls. They'll run from it like a vam-
pire from a cross. I have a contact at the *Chronicle*, Todd
Samuels. I'll get in touch with him, and we both will turn
over everything we know about the murders, start to finish."

George opened his mouth to argue, then closed it. "You
could be right," he began again. "But it really doesn't matter what I think. I couldn't authorize an action like that
even if I fully agreed. This is a matter for the Protectorate
to handle. You'll have to clear it with Anthony Slako, head
of the Protectorate."

CHAPTER 16

As she waited in George's paper-strewn office while
the gangly Tower went to radio the head of the Protectorate, Bria had plenty of time to pull from her mental files
the odd assortment of facts she'd collected on Anthony
Slako. Most of them were drawn from a *Newsweek* article
she'd read last August on LU's response to the grand-jury
indictments. Anthony Slako's checkered past had rated a
separate sidebar.

Tony Slako, as he was called in his earlier years, the
sidebar revealed, had been educated in the streets of
Chicago's notorious South Side. With special courses in
car theft, pimping, and breaking and entering, Slako had
graduated to Cook County Jail. As soon as he was released, he had finished off some postgrad work in armed
robbery. The last course earned the twenty-one-year-old
street hoodlum a thirty-year fellowship at the Joliet State
Prison. There, through the kind of chemistry that brings
elements like sulphur and potassium nitrate together to
form gunpowder, Anthony Slako found J. Louis Comfort's
best-selling tract, *Life Unlimited: A Science for Personal
Survival*, in the prison library. He was never again the
same. From that point forward his life belonged to J. Louis
Comfort, a man whom he had never met. Tony Slako, vi-
cious punk, became Anthony Slako, model prisoner, and
made parole in six years. He was off probation in one year.
In 1961, Slako was free to move to Washington, D.C., site
of Comfort's first training base. Those were the early
years, before Comfort went into seclusion. He was conducting Exteriorization sessions himself back then. Slako had
no money, so he offered Comfort himself, his life, the one

he was currently living on earth, and any future existences in which he might serve the aims of Life Unlimited, all in exchange for the opportunity to get On the Grid.

Slako's zeal was unmatched and well rewarded. When Comfort began his investigations fifteen years ago, he placed Slako in charge of them, declaring privately that his new director's past uniquely qualified him to deal with the criminals who controlled the planet. As Comfort retreated further and further, Slako became his personal envoy, ready to jet anywhere in the world where Life Unlimited was threatened.

For years, Slako's past had been LU's best-kept secret. It was clear that Comfort's troubleshooter was quite different from the college kids and young professionals who made up the bulk of LU's membership. Even as Comfort's enforcer, Slako was an alien among those born bright and beautiful. But his slightly sinister foreignness had always produced what the organization most desired: results. Since the indictments, however, church leaders were making Slako's past public with, and for, a vengeance. The Protectorate wanted the world, and the government in particular, to know that LU wouldn't be pushed around.

The tone of the article had been half-mocking, with Slako coming off as a two-bit hood who'd gotten religion, albeit of an offbeat strain. Bria decided that she would view him in the same light. She had no intention of being intimidated. One hour later, Anthony Slako, head of the Protectorate of the Church of Life Unlimited, burst into the room.

"Welcome, Bria Delgado, I salute you in the place of J. Louis Comfort."

Bria took the small, smooth hand extended to her.

"It was very fortunate that I was just landing in Houston when I got your message. I rerouted immediately. This matter is top priority. I understand that you've been thoroughly briefed."

Bria nodded affirmatively. Slako's presence, in spite of her resolve, seemed to shove her words down her throat.

"Good. You're absolutely correct. We must act swiftly. I understand that you have a copy of the list Rienstahl's agent stole and that you feel we should turn it over to the press."

Bria made herself reclaim the psychic territory she had
lost when Slako had entered the room. "Yes. It's the only
way to stop the killings. No matter who is behind them. I
know a top investigative reporter at the *Chronicle*, Todd
Samuels. He's done a couple of investigative pieces on the
victims of IRS harassment. He'll believe me."

"Not," Slako said, holding up a cautionary finger,
"when you're associated with Life Unlimited. The media,
Miss Delgado, have systematically distorted every piece of
information they have ever published or televised about
us. Only a few months ago *Newsweek,* a supposedly reputa-
ble publication, put out a story about LU. A portion of it
was devoted to myself. I barely recognized the person
portrayed in that section. The media are controlled by
those who would see Life Unlimited destroyed."

"Mr. Slako, I can guarantee you that all it would take to
disabuse you of the notion that newspapers, at any rate,
are under anyone's control, is one day's employment with
any large metropolitan daily. There is simply not enough
time for a newspaper to go into these elaborate conspiracy
caucuses you're talking about, to slant a piece of news so
that it fits in with the vague ends of some diabolical
scheme. After it's decided whether or not readers will be
interested in a piece of news, or whether it's important
enough to print, there's barely enough time to make sure
the spelling is correct. Most of the time, papers aren't even
under the control of their own editors and publishers. All
you conspiracy theorists give us a lot more credit than we
deserve. We're just not that powerful or efficient."

Slako turned to George, who was standing beside him,
and raised his eyebrows in surprised acknowledgment of
Bria's firm rebuttal. "I apologize," Slako said in an oddly
courtly way, "for attacking your profession. I have been
overwhelmed by the treachery I have encountered lately.
It colors my thinking. I, and Lou, are deeply grateful for
your offer of help. I think it may be the only possible way
left to save the Church."

"Mr. Slako, we had better clarify one thing before we go
any further. I don't care about the Church. I care about
Dominic Cavanagh and what happened to him. And I care
about what might happen to me now that I've gotten
mixed up in this craziness. But that is all. Not a 'Church.'

Not a spiritual movement. Dom Cavanagh. He's why I will turn the government's file over to the *Chronicle* and support your story. In return, I'm going to ask two small favors. One, I want protection. Two, I want to see Dom's file, all of it, for the whole time he was here."

"See his file." Slako repeated Bria's request as if he were having difficulty making out the words. "You don't understand. Church files are absolutely confidential. They can't be violated. They're like a confessional."

"The file I am prepared to turn over to you is absolutely confidential as well. It too will remain inviolate if I am not allowed access to Dom's file."

"There is nothing in it that would make any sense to you," Slako argued. "It's mostly Tower notes, coordinates and numerical notations."

"I'd like to see it." Bria faked a firmness she wished she felt.

Slako considered for a moment, then gestured to George, who had been standing mute next to his superior. "Get Cavanagh's file."

George stepped over to his desk and pulled from the clutter a form titled File Request. As he moved closer to Bria, she caught an unmistakable odor exuding from him—the acrid scent of fear. The smell, like an atavistic warning from one herd animal to another, said, "Beware." It brought Bria's own slow-cooking fear to an abrupt, churning boil. She tried to cool it off by focusing on the form George was filling out in front of her.

She watched the long fingers fill in Dom's name and grade level. In the space for Vault Number he wrote Five. The last blank was labeled Combination. Hurriedly, as if he'd just become conscious of her watching, George filled in three numbers—26-18-46. Mentally, Bria repeated them. They were easy to memorize. She planned on stashing every stray bit of information that came her way. She might have been forced to ally herself with LU, but she wasn't passing up any opportunities to probe further, particularly into Dom's records. George walked to the wooden-paned window at the back of the room, hoisted it up, and hauled on the set of ropes that were revealed behind it. Bria had noticed the former asylum's old dumbwaiters, but she'd never actually seen one in operation before. George continued yanking on the ropes until a platform reached him, drawn up from the bowels of the building. He placed the form beneath a limestone brick, and lowered it down.

A couple of minutes later, the platform returned with a manila folder beneath the limestone brick. Bria arched her foot over the key in her shoe and weighed the dangers of driving into Houston to fetch the file herself. They, whoever "they" were, knew she had the government file and were undoubtedly watching her. If they thought she was going to expose the contents of that file, this ominous "they" would be forced to take desperate action. There wouldn't be time for a carefully planned accident. The embargo on witnesses would surely be lifted. They'd run her over as she left the airport, stab her in the elevator, ram her car off a freeway overpass. No, if she risked leaving the Academy before the story was in print, she would only be multiplying the killer's opportunities to strike. Her best bet would be to sit tight with as much protection as she could get. Unlike Leonard, she had absolutely no desire to flush out a faceless assassin.

She fished the locker key out of her shoe. Closing her hand over it, she said to Slako, "Before I turn this over to you, I want you to assign a guard to watch me around the clock. I want a room on the fifth floor. It must have a double cylinder dead bolt on the door, bars over the windows, and a private bath."

"Certainly," Slako agreed eagerly. "Most of what you want is already built into the Academy. Back when it was constructed, they made insane asylums as escape-proof as prisons." He stamped on the floor. "Reinforced with steel bars. So are the walls. Most of the windows are inset with wire mesh. The security features here were one of the main reasons I advised Lou to purchase this compound. Now you can appreciate our need for a fortress that our enemies could not easily penetrate."

Slako turned to George. "See to it that all of Miss Delgado's wishes are carried out. The file."

George handed Slako a bedraggled folder. Along the upper edge, in bold marker letters, was written: Cavanagh, Dominic. Grade: 18, Expanded. Slako passed the file to Bria. She stared into his face. He reminded her of someone, of something, but she couldn't place the impression. It had to do with his uniform, made from a shiny black material; it was clearly intended to be menacing. There was also something about the way Slako's shoulders dropped away from his neck, sloping precipitously down to the arms that hung limply at his sides. And the way his hair cut away at the sides into two steep ravines of baldness that left a widow's peak cresting over his forehead like a misplaced beak.

Bria stretched out her hand, desperately wishing for another option and seeing none. At the moment she relinquished the key, her eyes locked with Slako's. His eyes were too round, too much space surrounded the irises. In contrast to that void, the violent yellow irises practically leaped out at her. The eyes blinked. It was like no human blink Bria had ever seen. The lids shot back up in almost the same instant they dropped, as if Slako would not allow himself to be vulnerable for even the length of a blink.

As Slako's hand closed around the key, Bria's impression crystallized with a fearsome clarity. She knew what the man reminded her of: a crow, a big, black crow.

CHAPTER 17

Slako passed the key to George. "Kirby," he ordered the Tower, "dispatch a Grade Eight, Security Certified to procure the file at the airport. Have him deliver it directly to Todd Samuels. Bria, do you have Samuels's home address?"

Bria gave it to him.

"I must return to Houston. Protectorate Division Heads from all over the country are waiting for me." As Anthony Slako swept out of the room, George Kirby roused himself. "Yuh-yuh-yessir." Bria was startled by his halting response, surprised to learn that George stuttered.

George's office seemed to expand after Slako left, as if his presence had gobbled up more than its share of space.

"Where did they get him?" Bria asked, forcing a light jocularity into her voice. "Central Casting?"

George's laugh was sudden and shrill, stopping as abruptly as it had begun. "His job is to be scary. You've got to admit, he's effective. Go ahead and call Samuels. I'll arrange for a guard."

She dialed. Samuels cut the second ring in half. By the time Bria finished her story the reporter was riveted.

"Good Christ, the first six Louies on that list are dead?" he whispered hoarsely. "I can hardly believe this, but in a way it makes sense. I know that the Louies aren't exactly above reproach, but my sympathies automatically go to *anyone* who gets on the wrong side of Rienstahl and his boys or any of those other government spooks. After all the shit I've waded through during the past five years, you start recognizing patterns. Like, anytime IRS Intelligence expends the amount of energy they've expended trying to

140

nail the Louies, there's something big brewing and only the tip of the iceberg is showing. But, Jesus, six murders! You think you're safe there? Given the way the Washington grapevine works, they're sure to know that you've got the file. They've probably got a list of everyone you called from the airport too."

"I'm safer here than I would be driving through a deserted pine forest and trying to survive Houston's freeways."

"Yeah, I see what you mean. You'd give this government creep too many chances to make his hit. I'd do the same thing. Just stay under cover until this breaks."

"When do you think you could get it out?"

"Bria, even though you, of course, fall into the impeccable-source category, my editor isn't going to touch this until I can get some verification. That could delay a preliminary story, depending on who is and isn't talking. You say someone is on their way over here now with this file?"

"Right. I stashed it at the airport. A Louie cadet will be bringing it to you."

"I'll shoot for the A. M. edition." There was a silence before Samuels spoke again. "You really think you'll be okay there?"

Bria glanced at George, the man Dom would have entrusted his deepest secret to. He looked paler and more drawn than he had before his encounter with Life Unlimited's enforcer. "Yes," she answered, cupping her hand over the receiver and her mouth. "I've got someone here who isn't a total gung-ho Louie. I think I'll be all right."

After a few unneeded warnings about being careful, Samuels hung up. Holding the dead receiver in her hand, Bria felt a bit like a passenger on the *Titanic* watching the last lifeboat pull away. She prayed that in the choice between the lesser of two evils she'd been forced to make that LU was the right answer.

Sturdy knuckles rapped at the door. George opened it. A man in his early twenties filled the doorframe.

"Bria Delgado," George said, "may I present your own personal bodyguard, Travis Pulver."

Travis Pulver. Bria had the nagging feeling that she had heard that name before. Pulver made a teasing bow. Bria had to smile. Catching the muscleman in such a dandified posture was like seeing the Michelin Man executing a *pas de deux*.

"Looks like I'm your blind date for the evening." He held out his arm. Bria was reassured by the feel of bulky biceps at her side as Pulver escorted her down the shadowy hall.

Bria's room met her security specifications admirably. It was on the fifth floor, just around the corner from George's office, with its own bathroom. The windows were reinforced with steel mesh, just as Slako had promised they would be. With a good lock on the door, like the dead bolt Pulver was busily installing, an old mental hospital *was* as secure as a jail. At least for one night. On the bed was the stolen powder-blue suitcase she had abandoned in the lobby. Bria wished they had brought up her own overnight case. But she was too tired to bother with it. This would all be over tomorrow anyway.

Pulver stood up and bundled his tools. "Okay, the lock's in. You've got a double key with a two-inch throw. I promise, it would be lots easier to try and get the hinges off that door than it would be to get past that lock. Here are both sets of keys. I'll post myself right outside the door. Good enough?"

"Great." Bria felt reasonably safe as she threw the bolt behind her bodyguard. She pulled out Dom's pocket watch and his LU file. It was nearly nine. She settled down on the king-size bed. Fifteen minutes later, she was finished with the file and she didn't know anything more about Life Unlimited, or why Dom had pledged his life to it, than she had before. As Slako had warned, it was mostly numerical notations, a code of coordinates that she couldn't come close to cracking. She wondered why Slako had cared whether she saw it. There had to be more. She fished the three numbers that made up the combination to the vault out of her memory: 26-18-46. Somewhere in this labyrinth of a building was a vault with the number five on it and all of Dom's secrets locked inside. She had absolutely no intention of going out searching for it, no intention of budging from the safety of her room. But, one day, if she returned—preferably under the protection of the proper authorities—and if she did happen to run into a vault with the number five on it, she would be ready.

She rolled onto her back and the fantasy settled away like the flakes in a bottled snowstorm. Fatigue numbed her, but her mind clicked relentlessly on. She thought about George's drug-trafficking story and Slako's media-conspiracy theory. They reminded her of Carl Hayes, a friend of Dom's. Hayes was a true product of the late sixties. He would cry conspiracy if his copy of *High Times* magazine were a day late in the mail. The "United States mail," Hayes would say knowingly, emphasizing the "United States" as if that explained everything. He was forever breaking off phone conversations and calling back on a "clean" phone. With Hayes it had been amusing. Bria wondered if she could afford to laugh now. She reviewed the paltry collection of facts she had managed to gather and wished for more.

After scraping away the mossy overgrowth of assumption and innuendo, she came up with precious few bona-fide truths. The first was that LU was in deep legal trouble with the government. Another was that government did not always function the way she'd learned it did in Civics class.

Bria ransacked her brain for more bits of information about LU. Their problems with the government had started in 1956, with the FDA raid. For the past nine years they had been battling with the IRS for tax exemption. In self-defense, the Protectorate had been formed and sent its agents to penetrate government offices and steal documents.

This countersleuthing had won for LU a charge of criminal conspiracy and two and a half years under grand-jury investigation, culminating in the federal hearing that was to end tomorrow. The six indictees were to be sentenced Monday. In return, Church lawyers had pledged to tie up the courts in perpetual litigation.

Bria knew that the IRS had somehow broken through to LU's inner circle, the Protectorate, and stolen the Recon Squad list. Now the first six squad members were dead. Whether or not the deaths were a vendetta to retaliate for LU's meddling in a drug network, or a warning not to leave muddy footprints along the corridors of power, didn't matter. She had more proof than she'd ever wanted of Leonard's death. The web of motives that lay behind the murder was immaterial for, in the end, that was what all of Bria's probing came to: the memory of his corpse in that sad, narrow room and the savage compulsion of the living—herself included—to run from it, in whatever direction they thought was the safest.

CHAPTER 18

Bria pleaded with Dom to make the demanding voices stop, to ignore them and stay with her in the misty gray orchard that stretched for miles across a barren valley. But, somehow, Dom became confused and misunderstood her plea. He thought she wanted him, not the voices, to leave. An instant later he was gone. The voices continued.

"Go away." The sound of her sleep-roughened voice awoke her.

"Bria, it's me, George," he called from outside the door. "George Kirby."

Bria jerked up fully awake. Her head thudded with dull pain. She had been asleep for less than two hours, not long enough to soothe her raveled nerves. She poured her sodden body out from under the covers and oozed her feet into her shoes. Her right foot snagged on something and she remembered dimly that that had been the shoe she'd stuck the locker key in. It all seemed so long ago and so unimportant now. She didn't even bother to check what it was digging into the bottom of her foot. When she went to the door and released the bolt, she found George outside holding a tray. It reminded Bria how long it had been since she'd eaten. Travis grinned up at her from his position on a chair tipped against the wall by her door.

"He's the only one I'd allow in."

Bria struggled to return the grin. "Thanks."

Pulver tapped two fingers to his forehead in a mock salute. Bria let George in and relocked the door behind him.

"Did your cadet get the file?"

"It's already been dropped off at Samuels's apartment."

George set the tray on Bria's bedside table and pulled the dome off to expose a plate of the same gummy dressing Bria had eaten in the Mess Hall. It was accompanied by a handful of peas, some grayish creamed onions, and two celery sticks. A cup of coffee the color and consistency of motor oil after fifty thousand miles opalesced in a thick white mug next to a piece of cake with a globby mountain of spackling-paste frosting.

Bria felt her appetite nose-dive through her lower intestine. "Everyday is Thanksgiving around here, isn't it," she waved at the gummy dressing, "minus the turkey. LU certainly isn't going bankrupt providing you devotees with haute cuisine."

"I know it doesn't look like much," George apologized, "but Lou has researched the nutritional composition of every food on earth and, from that research, derived the perfect diet for Exteriorization. He tested it right here at the Academy, and the cadets at this installation went Exterior sixty-seven percent faster than those anywhere else in the world. It's a standard diet now."

"I take it protein is not supposed to enhance Exteriorization." Bria dryly appraised the mound of carbohydrates on her plate.

"No, it's not. Listen, would you like some company?" George asked, changing the subject.

"Are you volunteering yourself?"

"No, sorry, I've got a session at twenty-three-hundred hours with the cadet you interrupted."

"Pulver isn't going anywhere, is he?" Bria was startled to hear the frantic tone that crept into her voice.

"No, of course not. He's posted here through the night. I thought you might want someone to talk to. Another woman."

"I imagine this offer comes complete with all the Louie propaganda I can absorb."

"I suppose that Gretchen could be persuaded to answer any questions you might have about the Church."

"Gretchen? Sounds like some Alpine type who's going to make me do vigorous calisthenics. What kind of a name is that, Gretchen?"

"The kind my mother decided to give her. Gretch is my sister. What do you say?"

"Why not?" Bria figured it would be a good idea to have as much company as possible around. "Sure, send Gretch up." Even as she put the name together for the first time, Gretchen Kirby, Bria knew that she'd heard it before.

After George left, a sudden and extreme hunger drove Bria to consume every bite of the Louie "Exteriorization" fodder on her tray. She washed the mess down with the crankcase coffee. By the time she heard a knock on the door, she was almost pleased at the prospect of having someone to talk with. So far she had successfully avoided allowing herself to dwell on the potential dangers that waited for her. She didn't know whether to attribute the sudden palpitations within her chest to the caffeine in the coffee or to a final realization of her situation.

"Yes." Her voice was tight, constricted. Pulver's answered.

"Gretchen is out here."

She opened the door to a female Amazon. If Bria's secret self-image could have taken human form, it would have appeared as the woman in front of her. Six feet tall, Gretchen's body exuded a vitality that could only have been expressed in her broad shoulders and the thigh muscles that bulged beneath her tight pants. Still, there was something supremely and confidently feminine about her, as if she knew that hers was the perfect female shape, not the tubercular look propagated by the fashion mavens.

"Come on in." Bria locked the door behind her guest. "Gretchen, isn't it?"

"Right, and you're Bria." She had the childishly husky voice of a precocious ten-year-old. "First off, I want to tell you that I think what you're doing for LU is incredible. I personally feel like I owe you a great debt." Gretchen relaxed after she finished delivering her little speech.

Bria shrugged, uncomfortable with such earnest gratitude. She motioned toward the couch and overstuffed chair in the suite's living area. Gretchen curled up on the chair and tucked her feet under her as if she were nesting. She might have been a college co-ed preparing for a cozy chat with her dorm mate, except that she stared openly at Bria seated opposite her on the couch, for a long, silent moment. Finally, Gretchen spoke.

"You know, I totally relate to a lot of what you've been through." Quietly, she added, "With Dom."

"What do you mean?" Bria sensed a gushy self-revelation coming. "Well, because I went through a lot of the same stuff with my brother for a long time. That's why I came down here from Idaho two years ago. I wanted to 'rescue' him. He'd gotten involved in LU back in Boise and come down to the Academy to do his Upper Levels. My parents were all upset. So was I. We called. Wrote letters. Nothing came back. No response. It was awful. Worse in some ways than if we'd known he'd died. You know what I mean, don't you?"

Bria nodded; indeed she did. It was wonderful to have that feeling acknowledged by someone inside LU.

"Well, finally I just couldn't stand it anymore, the not knowing. I left school and hitched down here. Security was a lot looser then, before the indictments, and I got in downstairs at the lobby. I couldn't believe it! The way everyone acted, all the procedures, the airport talk. It was too weird for words."

Bria had never thought she'd hear a Louie utter such blasphemies. She was delighted.

"I was incredibly lucky, George was on duty in the lobby when I walked in. I immediately went up to him and started screaming and pleading and begging for him to come home, telling him how what he was doing was killing Mom and Dad." Gretchen stopped and cocked her head slightly to the side.

"George let me rant on as long as I had to. Then we went off and talked, really talked, for the first time in our lives. And he made me listen to what he was saying."

Bria found that she too was listening. Gretchen's manner was so open, so free of guile and the standard Louie jargon, that it was impossible to be put off.

"Anyway, the more I listened to George, the clearer what I was really doing became. I had come storming in and just unloaded about a ton of Drag Factors on him, guilt mostly. It didn't take me too long to see that *I* was the one who needed the help. George's life was working; mine had never really gotten started.

"I'm not saying I was some adolescent basket case with nowhere to turn but drugs. You know how the papers make it sound like everyone who enlists is some lost youth searching for answers and somewhere to belong. That wasn't me—that's hardly any of us, actually. I was in training for the Olympic trials in the women's pentathlon."

"Gretchen Kirby!" Bria interrupted. "Of course, now I remember where I heard that name. It was in all the papers when you left. They played it up like one of our athletes had defected to Russia. And Travis is your boyfriend, right? He went with you, leaving the men's team."

"Yeah, a lot of people thought I was crazy, a traitor to the country, turning down a four-year scholarship, a ticket to the Olympics, a future full of endorsements. But, after a few hours with George, I knew that, in reality, I didn't have anything. Suddenly, I wanted nothing more than to be like George, to know what it was like to build your life around your own determination—not for your coaches, or school, or even your country. Naturally, there was a huge furor when I dropped out of the trials. You read the press stuff, 'Olympics Hopeful Drawn into Cult.' It was funny, that was the first time in my life that I did something completely on a conscious level, and they made it sound like I'd been hauled off by white slavers.

"I wasn't really, truly committed, though, until I Exteriorized." Gretchen paused and stared at Bria, gauging the impact of her words. Her plain face had taken on a vibrant luminosity that transcended any mundane tag like pretty or ugly.

"It was so dramatic, Bria. After Exteriorization my life came so much more sharply into focus." Her voice rose and increased in timbre. "Suddenly each moment became precious when I found out how little time I had in this life to accomplish everything I wanted to accomplish. I got that 'robot drive' I had found so offensive when I first came to 'rescue' George."

Gretchen's words pulled Bria out of the lethargy that had been crushing her. She found everything about Gretchen appealing but, above all, Bria was stirred by the sense of purpose that guided her.

"Why," Bria asked, "if Exteriorization is such a liberating experience, freeing all of you from the control of others, why do you free spirits end up enslaved to LU?"

"Enslaved?" Gretchen asked calmly.

"Yes, isn't J. Louis Comfort dictating your life now?"

"He helped me immensely, that's true, Bria. He helped me to see my life clearly and to decide what I want to do with it."

"How do you know that you weren't programmed during these 'Exteriorizations'?" Bria asked.

Gretchen answered evenly. "It would be impossible to 'program' anyone to do anything while they are On the Grid. You've seen a Grid Screen, right? What do you know about guided soul flight?"

"Not a lot."

"I'll try to explain it without using too many technical terms." Gretchen drew in a deep breath. "When the trainee sits down and grabs the wheel on his side of the Grid, coordinates materialize on the Screen on the Tower's side. These coordinates indicate the location of the cadet's psychic mass, his soul, entity, whatever you want to call it. From them the Tower plots a Flight Path for Exteriorization. But it all comes out of the cadet's own individual experience. Do you follow me?"

Bria's face fell into a maze of perplexed wrinkles.

"Even though I'm vastly oversimplifying this, I know that it's still hard to understand. The important thing is that each cadet defines his or her own path to enlightenment through their own individual set of experiences. On the Grid, every person plots their own path to salvation."

Bria nodded thoughtfully. Gretchen's version of Life Unlimited certainly differed sharply from the popular conception. "Why," she had to ask, "am I being made privy to all this confidential information?"

"Because, like it or not, when that story comes out in the *Chronicle,* you are going to become Life Unlimited's chief representative."

"But I'm not even one of you," Bria said, knowing that, of course, she was going to be asked, and at great length, what she thought of LU. And what exactly was that? Gretchen's version, and Leonard's, and Dom's, were so far from her own. She was still no closer to comprehending why so many bright, promising young people were devoting their lives to LU. There had to be a reason. Undoubtedly, it was based on LU's own cornerstone—the Grid.

"I suppose," Bria began, in no hurry to get the words out, "that the only way I can judge whether all you've been telling me is true or not is to try the Grid out for myself."

"Do you want to?"

Want to? Of course I don't *want* to. But Gretchen's leaden question continued dropping through the rippling layers of Bria's mind. Finally it struck bottom, the basis of all her interest in Life Unlimited: Dom. That is where Bria found her answer. Dom, who was so much brighter and purer than she. Dom had traded everything, their relationship, his future, everything, to stay "Airborne," to stay On the Grid. Perhaps she would finally understand the magnetism that had drawn Dom away from her if she herself experienced it.

"Who would my Tower be?"

"How about my brother?"

"My first choice."

Gretchen rapped on the inside of the door.

"Yes." Pulver's answer was muffled.

"Get George, will you, Trav?"

"Travis Pulver," Bria repeated the name, anxious to get her mind off the step she was taking. "An Olympic bodyguard."

"We're not LU's only 'celebrity cadets.' " Gretchen's tone was lightly self-mocking. "Haven't you recognized the film stars and rock and roll idols? I'm a lot more impressed, though, by the physicists and scientists. LU tends to attract true searchers, people who have driven themselves to be the best and still aren't satisfied. People like Dom and Travis. They find what they've really always been looking for here, a way to extend themselves to the fullest."

Bria didn't comment. At George's knock Gretchen went to the door and opened it after hearing her brother's voice.

"She wants to get On the Grid." There wasn't the slightest hint of gloating in her voice. And no victorious elation in George's response, either.

"I'll have to radio the Captain to get his authorization."

"Who's the Captain?" Bria asked. George gave a whimsical, lopsided smile.

"That's the rank Lou goes by. Kind of a holdover from

his RAF days. He's the Captain and all the rest of us are cadets, except for Slako. He's the Lieutenant."

Bria returned the smile. LU's military affectations had stopped bothering her somewhere between Leonard's murder and her chat with Gretchen. After all, even the Boy Scouts had their ranking system.

CHAPTER 19

The bisected steering wheel projecting from the back of the Grid made Bria think of the games prepubescent boys play in arcades for a quarter. The metal of the Wheel was slick in her hands with the accumulation of body oil deposited by previous occupants of the chair Bria now sat in.

"Okay, just get comfortable," George instructed. He stared at the Screen in front of him and adjusted a few dials. "Good. Now, relax your wrists."

Bria attempted to loosen the tension holding them rigid.

"Let them hang limp," George reiterated. She finally managed to comply. "Good. We're just about set."

"What exactly is this?" Bria asked with the nervous loquacity of a patient who begins questioning the dentist about his drill. "Some kind of galvanometer, right? One of those instruments psychologists use to measure stress by how much you sweat."

"It's a galvanometer," George answered with a thin smile, "in the same way that a Model T is a car. The Grid incorporates the galvanic-skin-response concept along with a whole list of others that psychologists don't even have in their books because they're not clear about the true nature of man. I'll give you the complete technical rundown on the Grid later. Want to get started?"

"I guess so," Bria replied, unable to work up to an unqualified yes.

"Fine, then look closely and directly into my eyes. Concentrate on nothing but my eyes."

Without breaking the connection of their two-way gaze, Bria asked, "Are you going to hypnotize me?"

"No. This step will merely facilitate your Exteriorization. It's not usually necessary with cadets who have completed their training. Think of it as a mild anesthetic during delivery, although we would have preferred natural childbirth."

Bria started to say something, but the comeback died on her lips. A sound like the low roar of a jet engine filled the room. The tremor of sound originated in the Grid. Bria felt it resonate throughout her body. At a certain pitch, all the extraneous thoughts crowding her mind fell away. Bria nestled greedily into the carefree, floating feeling that washed over her.

"Listen to my words, Bria." George's soothing voice blended seamlessly into the jet hum. "Don't think about them. Just listen to the sound." Without breaking eye contact, George monitored the blips on his Screen and twisted a dial. "When I tell you to, you will close your eyes. You will find the instructions that I give simple and easily followed. Exteriorization will come as a full and vivid experience for you. Are you ready?"

With an effort, Bria nodded her head a fraction of an inch.

"Good. Close your eyes."

Bria complied gratefully. She sank immediately into a midnight sea. Not a glimmer of light or of thought disturbed her. The sound of her breathing was her only companion. She luxuriated in the peace that engulfed her, free from doubts and fears and emptiness. George's voice, however, drew her back to the surface. It sounded infinitely distant. His command rolled toward her from far out in the dark, warm, comforting sea, like a great wave gaining power as it approached the beach. Suddenly, it billowed under her and she was caught in its swell.

"Imagine the most peaceful place you have ever been."

Gently, the wave put her down and receded. Bria looked around. She was at the top of Truchas Peak in New Mexico. To the north was Jicarita Peak, its gulleys inlaid with snow all year round. To the east was the Pecos Wilderness. Below her the Española Valley stretched to the rust of the Jemez Mountains. An eagle soared past her, riding the currents. Bria felt she could do the same if she tried.

"Describe where you are." George's voice wasn't an intrusion. It was almost as if it had come from within Bria's own head.

She opened her mouth and experimented with speaking. After a few tries she got it right. "At the top of Truchas Peak." She didn't want to take time from watching the eagle soar, from learning how to do it herself, to elaborate on her answer.

"Fine. Experience it. Imprint the feeling of that place on your memory."

Bria was happy to oblige. She let the soul-stretching majesty of it fill her as she had never allowed it to in reality, not in all the times Dom had taken her there. She had always been focused on him, on them, on their future, on how she thought he wanted her to be reacting.

Obliquely, she thought that being On the Grid seemed awfully innocuous. More like one of those pop-psychology exercises than any earth-shattering spiritual experience. Except that she had never liked the smarmy psych games and she wanted this one to go on forever.

"Now, Bria." George's voice was low and deliberate. "Relive the most ecstatic moment of your life."

With no transition, Bria went effortlessly from the eagle's home into Dom's bed. She was suffocated by the smell, her own mingled with his, and felt the rivulets of sweat channeling down their bodies. Then that clean, clear, unexpected moment a second later, when tears had run with the sweat. Tears that had come from a part of her no one had ever touched before. Just as quickly as the image came, Bria edited it. She reminded herself that this was supposed to be a spiritual quest, so she leafed through her collection of Catholic remembrances for one even remotely ecstatic.

"Go back to the first picture that came into your mind." George's command was quiet and unwavering. Bria felt relieved; she wasn't going to have to pretend. She felt again the tears that had run straight out of her eyes to pool in the hollow of her throat where Dom licked them away, laughing with her, knowing her joy as his own.

"Describe the picture you are looking at."

This time Bria resented George. Then she remembered that he had been the one to summon up and insist upon the memory.

"I'm with Dom." The admission seemed almost super-fluous, as if George already knew the mental image in its most intimate detail.

"Good. Imprint the feeling of that moment on your memory."

It already was. No sensation in Bria's life had been imprinted as deeply. A minute passed. Two minutes. Bria wallowed in the memory.

"Now, visualize yourself preparing for a trip. A short trip. Pack light. Imagine yourself at the airport. Buying a ticket. Checking your luggage. You are excited about this trip. You are going to see your favorite person in the world and you are this person's favorite as well!"

Bria imagined a rendezvous with Dom back in the days when she was his "favorite."

"All right, you are boarding the plane. You are fastening your seat belt. The takeoff is smooth and effortless."

Bria dutifully imagined the scene George was suggesting. As the deep hum again reverberated through her, the sketch he'd drawn began to fill in. She felt her middle strain against the tight seat belt, felt her shoulders hunch awkwardly as her hands grasped the upholstered armrests barricading her from her seatmate. The drone picked up in pitch, and they took off. Her ears congested. She swallowed hard and they cleared with a squeaking pop. Below her, beneath the chair and the surface her feet rested on, she sensed the thousands of feet between her and earth.

"We've reached Cruising Altitude." George confirmed Bria's sensations. "Look out the window on your right, Bria."

Mentally, Bria obeyed. She peered down on a kingdom of sun-drenched clouds, valleys and castles, and airy wisps that made up the kingdom's citizenry. Bria wished she had always known this magical place had been waiting for her in her own mind. She would have visited often. She planned to in the future.

"Now, bring the feeling you had on Truchas Peak up here with you."

Instantly she was filled with a sense of soaring majesty.

"Feel the solidness of the mountain beneath you."

The emptiness of the thousands of feet beneath her

melted away and was replaced by the mountain. The plane had stopped moving.

"Bria," the voice commanded, "you are as solid on that experience as you were standing on the mountain. That feeling is as real as the ground you stand on. The plane is no longer needed. Gradually let the vehicle that transported you fade away. It is no longer needed."

Bria looked away from the window into the pressurized cabin. The bright oranges and pinks of the plane's interior dulled to twilight gray. The forward cabin grew translucent as if it were being worn smoothly away by a vastly accelerated aging process. In tiny bits, the plane's body chipped away. Bria's pulse leaped wildly as a polar cold stream of air seared her cheek.

"Let the plane dissolve. It is warm and still outside. Recall the firm peace at Truchas Peak and step out on to it."

Bria replaced the panic with peace as easily as changing an album on the stereo. She let the remainder of the plane fall away. The clouds tickled her toes. They were warm and soft and covered whatever it was she was standing on. Bria wished she had known a long time ago how easy this was. The eagle had known.

The immensity of creation unfolded beneath her, awesome and invigorating. Her spirit swelled to encompass what she surveyed.

"Bria, you're doing very, very well. You're scanning perfectly."

She was amused that George had bothered to state something so obvious.

"Are you ready to begin Full Exteriorization?"

Begin? Bria didn't understand. How much more fully could she be removed from earthly cares and petty concerns? She already felt so grandly detached.

"Maintain your base coordinates—I mean, stay in the same place you are now, Bria, but begin to replace the solid feeling of peace beneath you with the experience of ecstasy with Dom. Let that moment surround you."

The airy brightness dimmed. Wisps of clouds grew dense and dark. A tropical infinity, heavy, moist, and smelling of sweat began to weigh down upon her. It grew darker. She no longer knew where she was.

"No, Bria, you're losing altitude. You're falling into your Corporeal Quadrant."

The moist air cloyed. It began beading on Bria's skin like an evil rain.

"Bria," the Tower's voice was sharp, "you're drag-loading, you're . . . Bria, go beyond the physical experience. Go to the ecstasy."

The dank fog dissolved. It left her shaken, disoriented. The Tower repeated his command several times. Slowly she translated it. She retraced the tears that had run down her face that night with Dom and followed them back into her own head, searching for their source. She found it under the word "communion." Not First Holy, but the only time she had ever fully shared herself with another human being, had experienced the rapture of total mutual understanding and acceptance. She had, for a few brief seconds, fused with another being. The atmosphere around her became light again, so light that it ceased to have substance.

"Excellent, excellent." George sounded relieved. "We can move on again. You have successfully located within that emotion. You will now use it to realize your true being." With a burst of decisiveness, he ordered, "Bria, you no longer need your physical body. Let it go."

Bria was utterly unaffected as she watched her body fade just as the plane, another redundant vehicle, had. It was like taking off an itchy, crumbling cast. She was eager to be rid of it. She had never realized what a hindrance those hundred-odd pounds were, or how much of her identity she had invested in them. She saw now what a cumbersome accessory they had always been, like trying to run a footrace in a hoop skirt. "You can begin your flight now, Bria." George's voice was proud. "Follow your own course to the center of all that you desire most."

His command was like the starting gun at a track meet, except that Bria had no competitors and complete assurance that she would capture the prize. Her course was as clear as a running track though it led through unfathomable distances of galactic emptiness. Her soul was propelled by a longing that grew more intense the closer she came to the object of her yearning. Then she entered into a brilliance beyond description, and all desire ceased. All struggle and tension ceased. She was in perfect balance and became part of the light. Then she began to create the light. Bria Delgado had been but a step in a long journey that was now, thankfully, ended. That person, being a person, was becoming an insignificant memory. Intense relief was the last emotion Bria registered on George Kirby's Grid Screen.

CHAPTER 20

George watched in horror as the blip tracking Bria's progress steadily climbed. Suddenly it shot straight up and off the Screen. Frantically the Tower twisted knobs and dials from one end of their range to the other. For the first time in his experience, he picked up nothing. He reached over and touched Bria's hand. It was icy, but still in firm contact with the metal half-circle.

"Bria. Bria!" He called her name sharply. Nothing appeared on his Screen and not the tiniest flicker of emotion showed on the face opposite him. Only her eyes. The lids trembled like those of a sleeping dreamer locked in the throes of a hideous nightmare. Other than that movement, it was like staring at a breathing corpse. George corrected himself. Bria wasn't "like" a corpse; the force that animated her body, had made her Bria, that force had fled.

George swallowed hard. He'd read about losing a cadet like this, his trainers had drilled a fear of it into all the Towers. It had happened only a handful of times since the early days of Lou's research. He'd read about the results, the minds turned to pablum; now it was happening right in front of him.

"Bria," he pleaded. His years of training were useless. Maybe he could do something with a cadet who had come up through all the Levels, but a Limited? "Bria, you must come back. Are you listening to me? Bria. You cannot abandon your physical materialization. You must return. It's too early for you to leave. Bria!"

The bathroom door at the back of the Control Room opened. Lieutenant Anthony Slako stepped out. "What have you done? What's happened?"

160

"What do you think has happened?" George felt himself teeter at the edge of panic. "She's gone Off Grid. I warned you that this would happen if you Exteriorized a Limited."

"The situation is severe, Kirby. It required a severe response. Rienstahl is trying to crush us. You bungled it. Don't look for excuses for your failure. Now I'll have to bail you out. Move away from that Screen."

"What are you p-p-planning to do?"

"Move. That's an order, cadet."

Fifteen months of Discipline Drills spent responding unquestioningly to commands moved George Kirby out of the chair opposite Bria, who had sat still as a mannequin throughout the heated exchange.

Slako slid into the Tower's position. His hands played over the dials like a pilot in the cockpit preparing for take-off. He too failed to make the blinking dot that represented Bria's consciousness reappear on the Screen. Abruptly he pulled his hands away from the dials and splayed them out like a concert pianist warming up over the keyboard. He reached into his pocket and dug out a penknife and a box of matches.

"What are you g-g-going to do?"

"You still haven't mastered that stutter, Kirby? You'd better check in with your Tower for a session on it. It's probably rooted in counter-LU impulses that you had better gain some Altitude on." He flicked open the knife, leaned over the top of the Grid, and brought the blade close to Bria's neck.

"What are you doing?" George stepped forward. Slako froze him with a glance and moved the blade closer to Bria's neck.

"You can't do that!" George shoved Slako's shoulder. The knife flew from his hand.

"Tower Eleven, you are manifesting some highly subversive indicators."

"No." George shook his head. "I know what you're p-p-planning to do. You can't. You're going to Crash her, aren't you? You know what will happen. In Training they told us that it was like pulling a diver up from two hundred feet underwater without letting him decompress." George's eyes were bright, and he spoke rapidly. "What that does to a diver is explode his lungs like an overinflated balloon. By the time he gets to the surface they're useless, bloody shreds. Except you're going to do the mental equivalent of that to her brain, aren't you, Lieutenant?''

Slako pulled the walkie-talkie off his belt. "Send a provost marshal to Control Room Eleven."

When George moved he was like a man waking up. His lunge toward the knife on the floor was sluggish. His hand and Slako's black boot landed on the blade almost simultaneously, the boot crushing Kirby's hand, grinding it into the knife. It was more a stylized ritual of degradation than any serious threat.

"Consider yourself in Traitor Condition, Kirby."

The gangly Tower looked up. "You're the Traitor, Slako. You're undermining Lou and the Mission. Lou would never authorize what you're going to do; you're going to hurt her so that the guardian soul will return."

Two burly guards from the Protectorate broke in.

"Put this man in Thermal Detention."

"Isn't that what you're going to do, Slako?" George screamed the words, his stutter gone.

"And what would you have me do, Traitor?" Slako lashed out at his underling. "Present a zombie to the world's press tomorrow? Is that the kind of tribute you would have me pay to Lou's technology? Are you that degraded? Have you forgotten the allegiances you pledged to vouchsafe the Church?"

"No, Slako, but you obviously have." Slako flicked his hand and the two guards stepped forward, each one gripping one of George's forearms. "He's going to Crash her," George's voice splintered as he turned to the guards. "Do you know what that will do to her?" The guards yanked him to his feet. "You've got to stop him. It's spiritual murder. She won't want to live after he brings her back. Will she, Slako? Tell them. . . ." His shouts died as the guards dragged him out of the Control Room and down the hall.

Anthony Slako was alone with Bria. He picked up his knife off the floor and brought it close to her face. With his free hand, he pulled out a wave of black hair and sliced it off neatly with the razor-sharp blade. He wiped the blade shut against his thigh and replaced the knife in his pocket, then dug a match out. Still holding the lock of hair, he struck the match. He brought the burning match and the hair together, moving them both toward Bria. The smell of her own hair being charred was driven up her nostrils. A tiny quiver as she breathed was the only sign of life she betrayed. Slako drew the smoldering clump of hair closer until it singed the fuzz on her cheek. The muscle beneath the burning hair twitched. Slako ground the hair into the burn. Bria pulled away. The twitch in her cheek spread. Slako sat back. It was happening now.

Arbitrarily, parts of Bria's body were seized by spasms as if a current had been activated within her. Then a rippling shudder, like a horse flicking away a fly, left her trembling. As suddenly as it had begun, the spasms stopped and Bria was again as still as the dead. Five minutes passed. She opened her eyes.

Bria stared at her hands and wondered why they were gripping a greasy metal half-circle. Her hands fell away from it. She watched them land softly in her lap. After a few seconds, the palms, upturned on her thighs, caught a drop of water, then another, until they became small pools in her lap. The water ran now sliding off the tip of her nose.

"What you are feeling, Bria, is entirely normal." She did not even glance up at the voice. It was like a radio in another room playing a program she wasn't interested in.

"Everyone who goes Unlimited feels exactly the way you do now when they are forced back into the corporeal prison. We come to measure our days by how many hours there are between Exteriorizations, like a prisoner behind bars, waiting for release."

Bria watched her hands fill with tears. She did not have the words to describe how she was feeling. She had never experienced anything remotely like it. She stared at the folds in her palms as if they were being projected on a screen. In a far corner of the darkened theater of her mind, a miniature television set switched on and played an incident from her past that vaguely approximated what she was feeling now. It had taken place during her last set of finals at the university. She had tried to cram too many courses into that last semester, so that she could graduate early. Dom had already found the house in Santa Fe and was waiting for her. When Closed Week started, she realized that she would have to cut something out if she planned on passing her exams. She chose sleep. For one solid week she existed on amphetamines. The crash at the end of that week held a hint of the desolation she felt now. A very mild hint.

". . . cadets become reenergized as they realize that, every moment, they are working toward getting back On Grid. A purpose they had never known before is introduced into their lives—Staying Airborne. It is a purpose they keep strictly to themselves. . . ."

The words sifted into Bria's consciousness, and she began to reconstruct why she was sitting where she was and what she had been through. It took an effort she didn't want to make. She returned her attention to the pools in the palms of her hand. The tears had stopped. She tilted her hands and the wetness ran onto a checked, polyester fabric. She never wore polyester, she despised it. Alarmed, she surveyed the pantsuit. These weren't her clothes. This wasn't her body! That was it. That was what was wrong. She couldn't feel such a sense of alienation in her own body. But it was. The panic quieted, and it all started coming back—why she was here, why she had come. What she could no longer make any sense of was, why it had ever mattered. But, if she did have to be here, leaden with this body, there was only one thing that did matter anymore. Still without lifting her head, she asked, "When can I get back On the Grid again?"

The answer came as fast and as eager as Bria's question had been slow and labored. "Soon, Bria, soon. You do remember about the file from your father and the reporter at the *Chronicle?*"

Bria nodded her head. Talking was too much of an effort to waste on such trivialities.

"Well, certain steps, actions, must be taken to safeguard Life Unlimited, to ensure the safety of the Grid. Threats must be neutralized. Do you understand?"

Bria nodded. The assassin. Yes, she remembered. It was too insignificant to think about. She understood now. Understood everything. About Leonard and Dom. Why Dom had left and why Leonard had been so uncaring about being stalked by a killer. Bria knew how he felt. The prospect of a killer out there, waiting to murder her, elicited no emotion.

"As you have learned, Bria, the Grid is the most powerful force for good on Earth. It must be protected from the forces of evil that seek to chain its power."

Slako's words filled her head, tumbled into the void there to explain an experience she didn't even have a vocabulary for. Like a tornado victim left stunned and homeless, Bria eagerly grabbed at Slako's words, using them as timber to construct a new psychic home to replace the one she had been ripped from.

"These forces are frightened by the power of the Grid. Life Unlimited threatens their dirty little games, their attempts to addict the Limited world to drugs and materialism. They are frightened. You have seen the tragic consequences of their fear, haven't you, Bria? You've seen the tears of Dominic Cavanagh's mother, felt your own. You've seen Leonard Davila, murdered in his own bed by the agent of this evil. You've seen the grotesque face death put on him."

Bria nodded. She didn't consider it worth the effort to tell Slako that she no longer found anything grotesque about death. She thought of Leonard's dusky blue face and the single emotion that struck her was envy. Perhaps there was still time for the assassin to strike her.

"Bria." Slako tried to capture her attention. She still hadn't looked up. "It is now two-thirty in the morning. Our story will come out in the morning paper. The wire services will pick it up at oh-eight-hundred hours. Reporters from all over the world will begin converging here in a matter of hours." Slako's voice became progressively more impassioned. "They will come, for the first time, not to have the lies they already believe confirmed, but to learn the truth about Life Unlimited.

"Bria, you now know that truth and it is your urgent mission to share it with the world. To tell them what you have seen our enemies do, how the government has persecuted us. But, most of all, you must share with these reporters the incalculable change that going On Grid has made in your life. That is vital, Bria. Planet Earth must turn to the Grid before the power-hungry overlords gain total control. Will you help us defeat them, Bria?"

Help? She still did not look up.

"Will you do it for Lou, for yourself, to save the Grid? Will you help us for Dom?"

Dom, communion, Exteriorization, certainty, Life Unlimited, god, soul, the Grid, help. Bria ran through the words like beads on a rosary. "Yes." Her answer seemed to come from another person, another room.

"Altitudinal. The reporters will be here in less than seven hours. You must be rested, briefed, ready. Gretchen will work with you." He paused. "Dom was right to have loved you. You must be one of the rare, natural Unlimiteds."

At last, Bria raised her head. Anthony Slako slid his lips back over his teeth, imitating a smile.

"Where is George?" Bria's question was flat, toneless.

"George has been temporarily relieved of his duties."

Bria questioned no further. Slako flicked on his walkie-talkie and summoned Gretchen, then leaned over the Grid and gave Bria's damp hand a comradely clasp. For one second something disturbed Bria. But then Gretchen came, and, by the time they were out the door, she had ceased to think about the X-shaped medallion that had fallen out of the black shirt as Slako leaned forward.

CHAPTER 21

Bria lay on her bed, her arm crooked over her eyes. The walk from the Control Room, down the hall, and around the corner to her room had left her weak and trembly. Gretchen had supported her with an arm around her slender shoulders as Bria shuffled down the hall, head lowered like a mental patient returning from shock treatment.

She escaped into sleep only to jerk awake, gasping, heart thudding an hour later. Her neck and back were damp with sweat. Gretchen was gone. An uncomfortable pressure in her bladder forced her to shove her body to a sitting position and slide her legs out from under the covers. As she put on her shoe, the sole of her right foot slid over a ragged edge that grated the tender skin. Instead of checking to find the source of the pain, Bria shuffled into the bathroom. Sitting on the toilet, she felt a wetness on her cheek and wondered if she were crying again. Pain sliced up through her skull when she put her hand to the oozing burn. The tiny stab in the bottom of her foot returned as she stood, and Bria decided that she could deal with that annoyance better than she could the wound on her cheek. She pulled off her shoe.

Inside, a small plastic label adhered to the sole. It was the kind pumped out by label guns that emboss letters and numbers on thick plastic tape. One corner was sticking up. That was what had been poking into her foot. Bria pulled the label off and was about to flick it into the wastebasket when she saw what had been printed in white on the red plastic: "#1328."

It was the label from the airport locker key. A key that

had no other identifying marks on it. How could they have retrieved the file without knowing which of the hundreds of lockers it was in? Her numbed mind struggled with the question for a few seconds before abandoning the exhausting effort. None of it mattered anymore.

She threw the label away. If she started thinking, she would have to think about all of it. About what she had discovered during Exteriorization, after she'd gone Off Grid.

"I'm nothing," she whispered. That had been her "Fit," her revelation. "I am only the compilation of the desires of everyone who has ever mattered to me. My mother's good, obedient little girl. My teachers' best, brightest, quietest pupil. Dom's . . ." Since the day he had come into her life, Dom had ruled it as no one else ever had, certainly as she herself never had. She had looked into his eyes and transformed herself into whatever she thought he had wanted to see. She had continued trying to win him, his love, even after he'd left. She had become the gutsy girl photographer for him. Bria Delgado didn't exist. She was a phantom who sucked life from others' visions of herself. She had no power to give her own self life. Only to take it away. That was her only power, and there was someone waiting outside to take even that from her.

"No, not here." Gretchen's voice came, muffled, from the other side of the door.

"Why not? Who do you think is going to be up at four in the morning?" Pulver hissed.

"Bria might be. I should go back in and stay with her. She might wake up, and Lieutenant Slako wants me to start briefing her immediately."

"Stay out here with me," the deep voice ordered. "The way she looked, she needs all the sleep she can get. I know I would. Even with all my Levels in, I was out for almost a day after my first Solo and it was a completely guided flight, no turbulence. Come here, Gretch." The argument ended.

Bria turned from the excruciatingly mundane conversation outside her door. It exhausted her to listen to such banalities and kept her from what she really wanted to do—relive her time on the Grid, at least the wonderful, soaring part. The part before the nightmare started, the nightmare in which she was still alive, still welded to a body.

Bria's thoughts and emotions ricocheted like a steel ball in a pachinko machine, shooting up, reaching again for the bliss she had experienced On the Grid, and, inevitably, plummeting downward, funneled back into a depression so crushing it made breathing hard.

In the deepest trough of that depression she found the question she'd attempted to evade lying in wait for her: How did Slako get the file without knowing the locker number? She was certain that she hadn't told him the number on the plastic label that had come off in her shoe.

What does it matter? was again her instantaneous response. LU had gotten the file. They had turned it over to the *Chronicle.* The story would come out. The killings would stop. Exteriorization would continue. That was all that was important now. If she could only hang on until the next session, everything would be all right. Why did I resist all those years? she wondered. It was so clear why Dom had to leave, to break contact. Now, though, we can share everything, just like before. Now there will be no barriers between us. The warmth of that notion brought back the ineluctable joy of total unity she had experienced during the session. She couldn't wait to talk it out with Dom. At last they would be sharing again. She floated in that pool of thought, buffered like a fetus in a sac of amniotic fluid until that awful moment when it drained away as abruptly as it had during her Exteriorization. Hurled back down into a paralyzing depression, only one thought rose again to prick her: How did they get the file?

This time her answer was: Maybe they didn't. Maybe I misunderstood. Probably Slako is waiting right now to ask me for the number. Even in her emotionally shattered state, Bria realized that there was a simple way to test out that theory. She glanced around the room, reorienting herself, and found the telephone sitting on the low-slung credenza opposite the bed. Just looking at it triggered the conditioning she had ingrained into her personality, the personality she had constructed for Dom, the one in which *bria* meant "brave." Whatever it is you want to do last in all the world is the very thing you must do first—that was how she had survived in the newsroom, how she had gotten her reputation for daring, how she had created the Bria Delgado that the world knew. Phones and newsrooms and assignments she didn't want to cover had all elicited the one Pavlovian response: do it; whatever it is you don't want to do, do it.

She dragged herself from the bed.

"What." Samuels answered on the twelfth ring and didn't bother to hide his annoyance at being awakened at four in the morning.

"It's Bria. Did you get the file?"

"Yeah, didn't they tell you? Some Hitler Youth–type guy in a black uniform brought it to me this evening."

"Well, uh, yes. I just wanted to check." Bria's voice sounded spiritless, even to her own ears. It was hard stringing words together. She felt like someone who had been out of the country for several years, trying to remember how to speak English again.

"Thatta girl. Always best to double-check. Never know who to trust, do you. Listen, the stuff in that file is beyond belief. That list. Those deaths. You dropped page one in my lap. I was up until two checking it out, and so far everything has been verified. I mean, of course Rienstahl didn't come out and say it was all true, but enough other people have that my editor okayed the story. It'll break tomorrow in the A. M. edition. Just a preliminary. Then we'll do a follow-up, in-depth, piece. The boys from every paper in the country will be out there at that Academy as soon as this hits the wires. I know you can't promise me an exclusive, Bria, but the *Chronicle* would really appreciate it if you would give us first crack at the follow-up story. What do you think? Since you didn't want him involved, I didn't mention your father, but Rienstahl and the IRS really get scorched. You'll be perfectly safe. How about it?"

The question rattled hollowly in Bria's mind. She thought of the golden X's and started to tell Todd about them, about what she had been through, then she heard the sound of a moist palm sliding over another receiver on an extension somewhere in the dark asylum.

Todd must have heard it too. For suddenly he asked, "Are you in danger? Just tell me that."

"Yes." The answer sprang from an instinct buried deep within Bria that had been struggling for her preservation.

"Jesus, the infiltrator has identified you. Okay, listen, get someone you trust in there with you. A good Louie, get a couple. That IRS bastard isn't going to do anything with a witness around. Not now. We don't have the whole story yet, but Rienstahl's already got too much to explain. You hear that, whoever's on the line, you hear?"

The reporter's words resonated in Bria's confused mind. Depression oozed over her like warm tar, clogging her brain. The phone in her hand was growing too heavy to hold on to much longer. She wanted to lie down again, to stop thinking all thoughts except one, Exteriorization.

"Bria? You still there? Can you hold on out there? I really doubt that anything will happen now, and I'll be out tomorrow to pick you up. You probably need sleep more than anything. Try to relax." Suddenly Samuels raised his voice menacingly. "If any of you government intelligence bastards are still on the line, you'd be stupider than you already have been to hurt Bria Delgado. It's all coming out about you. It's too late to stop. Bria, you'll be okay, I promise. You're too precious to the Louies for them to let anyone near you. After tomorrow, nobody will be able to touch LU again. We nailed them. See you tomorrow around nine."

The phone buzzed in her hand, but Bria waited until she heard the second click to hang up.

Rest, that was what she needed. "After tomorrow, nobody will be able to touch LU." She clung to that thought the way a child clings to a stuffed toy, hanging on to it in the dark to ward off thoughts of bogeymen and monsters. Thoughts of files and lockers and monitored phone calls. Thoughts of golden X's. Thoughts of Bria Delgado. After tomorrow her Exteriorizations would be safe. She would be safe. She would be part of Life Unlimited.

CHAPTER 22

She awoke a few minutes later, aware that someone was standing over her, watching her.

"Altitudinal, Bria. I didn't even have to touch you. You're already operating on a megaphysical plane." Bria stared into Gretchen's beaming face.

"How did you get in?"

"You gave me the extra key to the dead-bolt lock Trav put on your door. Don't you remember?"

Bria didn't remember.

"I thought you'd probably want to start working through the basic Training Levels. Exteriorization can get pretty turbulent when a cadet doesn't have that stabilizing data base. Anyway, authorization came through for you to run the High Compression Series. You're really lucky. You'll get to zoom through in a few hours what takes the rest of us months. I haven't heard of another authorization like this ever being granted. You must really be a naturally high-altitude being."

Bria tried to understand exactly what Gretchen was saying, but her mind was still choked in black sludge. "I need more sleep before I do anything, Gretchen. I'm totally wrung out."

"But Bria," Gretchen said, her voice a mixture of surprise and disappointment. "You could be officially Unlimited in only a few hours if we work hard enough. Isn't that what you want? Didn't you discover that while you were On the Grid? No one who's gotten Exterior of the physical plane has ever wanted anything other than Life Unlimited."

Wasn't that what she wanted? The thought had lulled

her to sleep just a few minutes ago. Even as she considered it, her heart ached forlornly. Of course she wanted to go Unlimited. But even more she wanted time, if only to adjust to the 180-degree change in her life. She had to have time to think, time alone. She didn't want to be prodded. Gretchen continued to beam at her with the radiant joy of one able to help another throw off the shackles of ignorance. Bria knew that in her demoralized state, she would be no match for Gretchen's zeal. She couldn't muster the energy for a no forceful enough to deter the megawatt determination of an Unlimited.

"Come on, get dressed," Gretchen chided like a mother with a sleepy child. "Slako is waiting to start your Compression Series."

"Slako?" Bria touched the burn on her cheek and a thrum of fear beat through her gut. She was absolutely certain that if she went with Gretchen now to Lieutenant Anthony Slako she would return a Louie.

"But I'd like George to conduct my training," Bria protested limply.

Gretchen's kindergarten-teacher enthusiasm dimmed at the mention of her brother's name. She answered tightly, "Not only is George unqualified to conduct a Compression Series, he may never regain the right to sit behind a Grid again."

"Why?"

"We don't have time to discuss it now." Like a light with a dimmer switch, Gretchen's brightness faded, then glowed again. "Let's go, let's go!" She clapped her hands. Her energetic heartiness bludgeoned Bria's devastated psyche. Bria gathered up her borrowed clothes, grabbed mechanically at a cosmetics case she found in the powder-blue suitcase, and retreated to the bathroom. She closed the door and sank down on the commode. She had to be alone. That one desperate need overrode all others. Even her need to get back On the Grid.

For two minutes she simply sat, willing her mental resources to resurface. She dragged herself up in front of the mirror and splashed several handfuls of cold water onto her face. Still dripping, she examined the small, dark woman in the mirror. Grandmother Delgado's startling green eyes examined her in return. *Abuela* was not pleased by what she saw. Neither was Bria when she looked with the old woman's eyes at the defeated, mousy creature in the mirror.

"No." The defiant syllable galvanized her. She surveyed the bathroom. It had been added onto the old asylum like all the private bathrooms had been, the plumbing appended to the ancient system.

Bria ripped open the "borrowed" cosmetics case and took a brisk inventory. Maybelline mascara, iridescent blue eyeshadow, tawny beige foundation, frosted pink lipstick. In keeping with the out-of-date assortment was a steel comb with a long tail. The rest of the case was filled up by a supply of superabsorbent tampons.

"Come on, slowpoke." Gretchen pounded on the door.

Bria stuck her head around the corner of the bathroom. "Could you give me some privacy to get dressed?"

"All yours." Gretchen smiled and closed the door to the bedroom behind her.

Bria looked around the room and quickly retired any thought of escape. As Slako had said, a prison cell couldn't be any more secure. Six-gauge steel mesh covered the windows. She pulled up the rug. Concrete reinforced with steel lay beneath it. The walls were a foot and a half of limestone. There was no way out.

"Bria, come on, we've got to go. No one keeps the Lieutenant waiting."

"Be right there." Her own words kept Bria from hearing the first gurgle coming from the makeshift plumbing in the bathroom. But the second one caught her attention. By the third she was smiling.

She raced back into the bathroom, unzipped the cosmetics case again, and pulled out the tampons. Fumbling with nervousness, she ripped their wrappers off, carefully disposed of their plastic plungers, then dropped all twelve tightly packed wads of cotton and cellulose into the commode.

"Bria." Gretchen's call was shrill and impatient. The earlier exuberance was gone.

"One minute," Bria shouted around the bathroom door. The tampons were swelling with water. She flushed the toilet. For a second the plumbing made a valiant effort to ingest the sodden wad. Bria's stomach sank as she watched the white mass disappear. Halfway down, though, it stuck in the toilet's craw. A whining gurgle signaled its surrender. Bria rattled the handle. The bowl began filling with trapped water. With no drainage, it sloshed over the rim.

"Gretchen," Bria called, "I've got a problem here."

The lock twisted back from the outside, and Gretchen stood at the door's opening, with Travis Pulver looming behind her. Their intimidating size and strength no longer comforted Bria; it now menaced her, frightening her as much as the thought of the faceless killer.

"What's wrong?" Gretchen was irritated. "We should be in the Control Room right now."

"My toilet is backing up."

Gretchen entered the room, Pulver following like a bear on a leash. Bria took the pair to the bathroom to show them the overflowing toilet. She picked up the cosmetics case with the makeup and the steel comb in it and awaited their decision.

"So, what are we supposed to do?" Pulver asked crossly. "Gretchen told you, the Lieutenant is waiting. Maintenance Division doesn't report back on duty until oh-eight-hundred hours."

"I'm really sorry," Bria apologized, "but I have to use a toilet. Isn't there another one on this floor?" She spoke, not according to any finely honed plan, but simply with the hope of creating a delay, a place for an opportunity to appear. Maybe she could trip on her way down the hall and sprain her ankle, somehow stall for time until Todd and the other reporters arrived. Then she would be free. Free of the fear of some unidentified assassin leaping out of the shadows and plunging a knife between her ribs. Free of the seductive power of the Grid until she could make a calm decision in its favor.

"Sure, there are other bathrooms on this floor," Pulver answered testily, "but I have no intention of barging into a Tower's room at four-thirty in the morning so that you can avail yourself of the facilities."

"Trav," Gretchen cut in, "get a little Altitude. There's no reason to drag-load about this. Bria can use that old bathroom down the hall."

"Gretchen," Pulver's voice carried a note of questioning and of warning, "that's the bathroom where—"

"Yes, I know," Gretchen cut in crisply, "that's where the mental patients used to bathe. Well, there are also some toilets in there too. It was never converted and everything still works. Shall we escort Bria down the hall?"

"I don't know." Pulver hesitated.

"The Lieutenant is waiting, Trav."

The mention of the head of the Protectorate was enough to cancel any further debate. Pulver whirled around and led the way to the door. As they stepped out into the dim hall, each of her bodyguards clamped an arm around one of Bria's. She was secured on both sides.

"You're precious cargo," Gretchen said in a voice straining for lightness. "We couldn't let anything happen to you after the great service you've done for Lou."

But Bria felt more restrained than protected and wondered what this pair, unarmed, planned to do if a desperate assassin jumped out and waved a gun in their faces.

They marched Bria down the hall and halted in front of a large swinging door. Gretchen pushed it open, snaked her hand inside, and found the switch. A bank of incandescent lights, set eighteen feet up, blinked on, to reveal a large room tiled in white from six feet above the floor right down to the six drains set into the floor of the communal bathroom. Opposite the door was a line of seven old-fashioned tubs perched on claw feet. Along the left wall was a line of commodes exposed to each other and the rest of the bathroom.

"This room hasn't been used since long before the asylum closed down," Gretchen said. "But the plumbing still works." She nudged Bria onto the tiled expanse. "We'll wait here by the door for you, to make sure no one appears unannounced."

Bria walked in and wondered where in this porcelain-and-tile wilderness opportunity might be lurking. On the right wall was an old radiator. The ancient heating device triggered vague memories of Dom's enthusiastic lectures about heating systems. She wished now she had really paid attention to what he had told her instead of just listening for the right spots to make approving, interested noises. Next to the radiator was a ventilator grill, an ornately decorated model from the thirties. She did remember Dom explaining how elaborate systems of shafts ran through old buildings pumping heat and fresh air. She decided to investigate the rusted grating.

A queasiness rocked the pit of her stomach as she approached the line of tubs and thought of the mental patients who'd had to endure unspeakable atrocities in them, subjected to alternately freezing and skin-searing water temperatures. The feeling intensified and a disturbing presentiment, triggered by Pulver's hesitancy to let her use this bathroom, rose in her as she neared the middle, the fourth tub from the right. She checked, and wasn't surprised to find that there was an electrical outlet located closer to that tub than to any of the others. It wasn't even too much of a surprise for Bria to note that, unlike the other tubs, the center one was not coated with fine brown dust—a fact that belied Gretchen's assertion that the bathroom had not been used since before the mental patients left. She bent over and plucked from the gleaming whiteness one curly hair that glinted gold in the harsh lighting.

"He died here." She whispered what she had felt even before finding the evidence.

A noise in the hall caused her to whirl around, suddenly remembering that she was being stalked, hunted by whoever had murdered Dom in this lunatic bathroom. In the glaring white emptiness, she waited for her heart to stop pounding. The instant it did, another thought, equally menacing, sent her pulse soaring again. They were waiting for her, waiting to take her to Slako. The two opposing threats were more than Bria could emotionally handle. She needed time to find the answers to her questions. For one second she considered simply poking her head out of the door and telling Gretchen everything, explaining how she felt and why she would have to wait. In the same instant she dismissed the notion. That would take true courage, not her anemic imitation brand. Exteriorization had made Bria painfully aware of how infirm her own will really was. She didn't have the courage to say no, and to keep saying no. She knew that she would be swept away both by a desire to be realigned with Dom and by the lure of the Grid.

"Bria, what's holding you up now?" Gretchen's voice was ragged with impatience.

"Could both of you please leave the door for a few minutes. I'm inhibited knowing that you're right outside. You can guard it from down the hall."

"Please hurry, Bria." Gretchen's plea dimmed as she left her post outside the door and walked down the hall, with Pulver muttering at her side.

Bria turned to the old grating. If it did open into a ventilator shaft like the ones Dom had spoken of, it would be a conduit throughout the whole building. At least, she might find a place to hide from both the Louies and the assassin until the story came out tomorrow. Then the pressure would be off. She would have time to make up her mind.

The metal grillwork was curved and embellished in the style of the early thirties. The intervening decades had ulcerated the copper with a flaky green corrosion. Bria ripped open the cosmetics bag and fished out the steel comb. With the teeth digging into the palm of her hand, she attacked the grating with the spiked end. The grating was embedded directly in the limestone. A century of humidity had softened the porous stone so that it crumbled under the bite of the steel comb. Bria gouged frantically at the points where the fifty-year-old screws anchored the grating to the wall. When she had dug away a good bit of the screw's moorings, she braced her feet against the wall and pulled on the corroded grating. It began to give way.

"Bria, let's go. I'm coming in." Pulver announced the end of her efforts.

"No, stay out there. I'm coming." Working with sharp, rapid movements, Bria pressed the loosened grating back into place. Leaving the cosmetics case and comb behind, she got to her feet, turned out the light, and pulled back the swinging door.

Gretchen's face betrayed emotion beyond impatience. The young Amazon was scared. Bria smelled her fear and heard it in the trembling of her voice.

"The Lieutenant called. He's not happy about this delay." Pulver took Bria's other arm and, together, they rushed her forward.

CHAPTER 23

"Altitudinal, you're here!" J. Louis Comfort's right-hand man stepped forward to greet her as she entered the Control Room. He put a small, moist hand on each of her forearms and squeezed them as if he were greeting a heroine of the republic. His smile worked too hard at the corners of his mouth, drawing his lips tight over his front teeth and making the sides gape like a thick rubber band collapsed in the middle.

"Where is George?"

Bria's question wiped away Slako's taut smile. "Kirby has been temporarily relieved of duty."

"I want him," Bria stated flatly.

"I am fully qualified to conduct the Compression Series authorized by the Captain," Slako said, his lips creeping into the tight smile again.

"But I want George."

Slako issued a brief command to Pulver, who left and, a few minutes later, returned with George Kirby. Bria was shocked. George looked like a man who had spent several days on the desert without water. His clothes were rumpled and damp with sweat, his lips swollen and cracked. Gretchen made an involuntary lunge forward before checking herself.

"Go to your Tower," Slako ordered her. "Have him run you through the Response to Traitors series until you gain the necessary Altitude. Ack?"

"Acknowledged," Gretchen answered, pivoted sharply, and left.

"My God, George, what happened?" Bria asked quietly.

Kirby held up his hand in a subdued greeting. "I'm fine," he mumbled.

"That's good, Kirby," Slako said. "Miss Delgado is affording you the opportunity to redeem yourself. You will conduct a Compression Series *explicitly* authorized by the Captain." He turned to Pulver: "That will be all. Remain on duty immediately outside the door. Allow no one entrance." With a curt nod, he dismissed the Olympian.

"Won't you be seated." He gestured toward the chair tucked in front of the Grid Wheel with the unctuous servility of a headwaiter. Bria sat and faced the same half-wheel she had clung to that evening. It evoked a complicated mixture of intense longing and panic.

"Kirby, if you will join us." Slako swept the Tower into his seat behind the Grid Screen. George caught her eye as he seated himself. "You doing all right?" he asked in a reedy voice. Bria nodded, answering the intensity in his question, which went far beyond his polite words. He knew what she'd been through! The revelation exulted Bria. If only Slako would leave, she could talk everything over with him.

Bria forced herself to face Slako. "Isn't this going to be a private session?" she asked.

"Normally, of course, all sessions are absolutely confidential between the cadet and his Tower. But we received a rare clearance to run a special series with you, Bria, because of your remarkable contributions to Life Unlimited combined with the amazing aptitude for Exteriorization you displayed at your first session. As it turns out, however, there are only two Towers on this planet who are Academy-qualified to run a solo session of this nature: myself and Lou. Of course, the Captain has to stay Airborne. Since you have insisted upon having George as your Tower, and we are eager to comply with your wishes, he will conduct the session under my guidance. Kind of a co-pilot situation." He paused and looked from Bria to George, then back again, like a game-show host explaining the rules to two new contestants.

"Ack'd, Kirby?"

"A-a-acknowledged," George answered, closing his eyes tightly. Bria saw the lids jerk with a spastic tension.

"Good. Start with an Amplified Preflight, Kirby. Establish that and I'll code you from there. Bria, respond as if I weren't here."

Bria knew that an open protest would be stupid, would only serve to crystallize Slako's determination. What was at stake was her mind. It was still her choice whether or not she wanted to surrender it. At some point, there was a strong likelihood that she would; but not now. For now, she simply was not going to comply, at least not where it counted, not in her head. If she had read George correctly, he wouldn't betray her.

The lights dimmed. "Please look into my eyes." The exhaustion in George's voice made it soothing, intimate. It totally excluded the man in black and wrapped Bria in a thickly insulated contact with only her Tower. The low, bass hum was switched on. It caught her in the viscera before her ears had even defined it as a sound. It required a conscious struggle for her not to abandon herself to its resonant urging.

"Go where the chant takes you." Bria made herself resist George's command.

"Place your hands on the Grid Wheel. Let your muscles relax. Maintain a firm, yet gentle, contact at all times with the Wheel." Bria complied. A barely discernible buzz enlivened the sensitive skin of her palms as they closed around the metal wheel.

George's hands flew over the console in front of him, monitoring the blips on the screen and twisting dials, his eyes never leaving Bria's.

"Listen to my words." George's voice was as seductively soothing as the deep hum. "Don't think about them. Just listen to their sound. When I tell you to, you will close your eyes. You will find the instructions I give you simple and easy to follow. And you *will* follow them. Exteriorization will come as a full and vivid experience for you that you will be able to control completely." Bria noticed that the last part of the rote invocation was new. George had added it. Slako tensed, started toward them, then stopped.

"Are you ready?" George continued, studiously ignoring his superior.

Bria nodded.

"Good, close your eyes." The session had started much like the other one, except that, when Bria shut her eyes, she filled the darkness behind them with images of claw-footed bathtubs. She wasn't going to be caught off guard by the Tower's compelling commands.

"Imagine the most peaceful place you have ever been. Imagine Truchas Peak."

Like two slides jammed in a projector, the grandeur of the New Mexican mountain tried to force out the memory of the bathtub with the single strand of curly blond hair. She ignored her yearning to surrender and concentrated on the mildewed spaces between the tiles.

"Let the image come, Bria," George coaxed. "This session will be totally under your control." Unlike the last? thought Bria. Still, his soothing voice made her aware of how played-out she was, how, more than anything, she wanted a good meal, a shower, and sleep. Sleep Unlimited.

"Good, Bria, you're locating now."

George's approval pricked her back into alertness. She swept out the image of Truchas Peak that had been nibbling at the edge of her mind and clung instead to the most disturbing image she could conjure up: Leonard's dead face. She had to remain alert. She hoped that George would realize what she was doing and cover for her. Only silence and the grating of turning knobs came from the other side of the Grid. Then she felt Slako approach, felt him opposite her, hovering over George.

"S-s-sir," George tried to whisper, "she's too exhausted to run a session now, especially a Compression."

Slako's voice was tight and low, the headwaiter again, furious with an underling and trying to hide it in front of a patron. "Under normal circumstances, Kirby, I would agree with you. However, these are far from normal circumstances. Begin again."

Bria heard George take several shallow breaths. "All right, Bria, let's start over. You will allow yourself to return to that peaceful scene, to experience it to the fullest."

It was easier to disobey this time. She felt that, in spite of his words, George was on her side. He agreed that now was not the time to push another Exteriorization. She would insist that he be her Tower when she did decide that the moment was right again.

"Let the image, the peace, come." His words sounded overrehearsed. They were easy to ignore even without summoning up thoughts of death and murder. "Leave present reality, present concerns behind," George urged monotonously. Bria's back prickled as Slako approached again. His footsteps paused behind her, then moved swiftly to the other side of the Grid.

"Kirby," the forced cordiality was dropped, "you've got a negative elevation reading there and you haven't taken one damned corrective."

Bria jerked open her eyes in alarm. George's face was white and wrapped in a grim rigor that made his jaw muscles twitch in rebellion. Slako was hunched forward, pouring his venomous words directly into George's ear.

"That's it, Kirby. You will never Tower again, no matter what the circumstances. Institute a Grid Shift, then get out of that chair."

George turned to Slako, stunned horror drawing down his elongated face even further. He shook his head as if trying to rattle loose the words he'd just heard. "You can't do that."

"Only one man on earth can tell me what I can't do." The mask was ripped completely away from Slako's tone. "My orders come straight from the Captain."

"Slako, don't." The pleading in George's voice frightened Bria. She backed away from the Grid. "First the Crash, now a Grid Shift. I trained for three years before I was ready. She'll—"

"That's enough, Kirby. Haven't you drag-loaded our cadet enough? I told you, you're off the case."

"Please." George looked across the table at Bria. There was desperation in his eyes. Abruptly he shifted his gaze to Slako. "Let me have one more chance, Lieutenant. I have another pattern I'd like to try." Without waiting for an answer, George's hand moved across the dials. He stared at Bria intently, his eyes begging her. But for what? In a strained voice, he asked her to return her hands to the Wheel, and to close her eyes. This time, however, George did not make suggestions of peace and surrender.

"Bria, place yourself in the downstairs lobby. Visualize it as it was the first time you saw it." George's voice was demanding, sure, just as it had been the first time. Bria tensed. She thought he had understood, that he was on her side.

"Bria, you must bring that scene to mind and contrast it

with the second time you entered. Remember? Remember the lobby the second time, Bria?" George's voice was charged with an urgency Bria could not decipher.

"Stop right there," Slako ordered. But George didn't stop.

"And the file, Bria . . ."

"Stop immediately, Kirby."

George was silent. Bria snapped open her eyes and turned around. Three feet from George's head was a thirty-two-caliber revolver. Slako had it aimed straight at the space between his eyes.

"Move away from that Screen, Traitor, you're not fit to touch it. Bria," Slako said, "we've found the killer."

George's mouth dropped.

"One word, assassin," Slako hissed, "and I'll perform a thirty-two-caliber lobotomy on that twisted brain of yours."

Bria's mind whirred. George? Could he have murdered Dom with a jolt of electricity after forcing him at gunpoint into a tub of water? Had he slipped into Leonard's room to unleash the lethal gas? Bria could barely make herself consider the possibility. She trusted him. Dom had trusted him. But wouldn't that have been the essential element: trust?

George spoke quietly. "You've overstepped your authority, Slako. Lou would never have approved a Grid Shift for an Unlimited."

Slako hammered his fist against the door. "Get in here." He lowered the gun into his pocket, making sure that George was still aware that it was trained on him. Pulver burst into the room in response to Slako's command.

"Take him back to Detention, same confinement. He has officially been declared Traitor. Do you understand what that means, Pulver?"

Pulver stared at George as if Slako had just announced he had leprosy. "Yessir." The memorized sanctions tumbled out. "A Traitor is not to be communicated with. He is to be held in utter contempt by all Church members. He is to be regarded as a threat to the integrity of Life Unlimited. He is to be treated as an enemy and a traitor to the cause of spiritual advancement on the planet Earth. He is to be kept under lock and key in such confinement as the ranking officer of the Protectorate shall deem fit and deprived of food, water, clean clothing, and the company of the morally fit for howsoever long the officer shall deem fit. Said penalties will continue until the Traitor is rehabilitated through the demonstration of repentance as prescribed in Code Four-Eleven. If such a demonstration is not forthcoming, or not truly sincere, the Traitor's survival is no longer to be a matter of concern to Unlimiteds."

"Correct. I will expect your strict compliance with the conditions laid down. If you, Pulver, *do* communicate with the Traitor, you will be subject to the same penalties. And, Kirby, do not forget that your sister is only a few doors away." George stared at the gun hidden in Slako's pocket. The threat was clear.

"You do understand your position now, don't you, Traitor?"

George's shoulders slumped. "Yuh-yuh-yuh . . ." he started out, but finished by shaking his head. Pulver clamped George's spindly arm in his massive hand and pulled him toward the door, eager to demonstrate his unquestioning loyalty to Lou's chief of security. At the door, George resisted the iron grip for one second and glanced back at Bria. His eyes implored her once more. Bria felt panic push a wave of nausea up her gorge. Her mind covered miles of treacherous terrain in the few milliseconds it took her to look from the door, now slammed shut behind George Kirby, to the bulge in Slako's pocket. It ran a maze that started with Dom's words, "Tower 11. . . . All can be trusted with him," through the fact that such trust would only have made killing Dom that much easier. Her mental gymkhana came to a dead end at the pleading in George's eyes and left her exactly where she had started—trapped.

CHAPTER 24

"That pained me, that really did." Slako slid into the chair he had ordered George to vacate. "What hurts me is, I trusted that boy so completely. I was grooming him to be my second-in-command. I talked to Lou quite a bit about him, his progress. This betrayal will hurt the Captain too. When the first reports came in a few weeks ago, I couldn't believe them. Not George Kirby." He stopped and shook his head. "If only I'd taken action sooner, Leonard, maybe even Dom, would still be with us."

"Why George? What makes you think he was the killer?"

"Either George or a confederate. We don't know. This session with George as Tower provided the telling evidence. I got the proof I needed; unfortunately, it wasn't the proof I wanted."

"I didn't see any proof of anything," Bria said.

"No, of course you wouldn't. You would have to be an adept at the highest levels of LU to fully understand. Apparently, George didn't think that even I was advanced enough to know what he was attempting. What he tried to do was to use a technique that Lou outlawed several years ago to 'restructure' your memory."

Bria stared blankly.

"You have proven yourself to be a bright, resourceful being, Bria, who has performed a great service to Lou. In deference to your contributions to the safety of the Church, I am going to go outside of classification channels and tell you this: In a few hours a new era will begin for Life Unlimited. It will be heralded by the story in the *Houston Chronicle*, a story that your courage made possible. Of course, the government would have done anything to stop that story. However, it is too late now, so they had one chance left, to discredit you, your story. That was what George was making a desperate attempt to do. To rearrange some significant facts in your mind through the abuse of a highly sophisticated LU technique. The Justice Department would have been able to tear you to shreds if he had succeeded."

Confusion churned inside Bria.

"I know, Bria, that this is a lot for someone who hasn't had extensive LU training to absorb. But you know how much was made clear to you during your first time On the Grid? Well, all this will become equally transparent when you are better versed in our operating procedures."

"Yes, but George *was* right about one thing, the file. How *were* you able to get it without knowing the locker number? It was stuck inside my shoe."

"You were followed," Slako answered abruptly. "Kirby himself ordered it. Leonard was reporting to him and Kirby passed the word that you were to be kept under surveillance as a possible agent. I don't know what he was planning to do, probably throw the Protectorate off his trail by producing evidence that you were somehow involved with the government."

Bria felt as if she were trying to fight off an octopus as all the different versions of what had happened twined around her.

"But George was the one who alerted you when I told him about the file," she protested.

"By then he'd realized he couldn't shut you up. He had, undoubtedly, already notified Rienstahl and his other buddies at the IRS, who are probably busily shredding incriminating papers and constructing a defense at this very minute.

"It was immediately clear to me," Slako continued, "that you were no government agent. What it took me longer to realize was that Kirby was. He had misdirected our attention to you, and, while we were diverted, tracking you at the airport and noting which locker you put the file in, Kirby completed his assignment. As a trusted friend and fellow member of the Recon Squad, he had no trouble slipping through Leonard's defenses."

It was too much to sort out. More than ever, Bria just wanted to leave it all behind. She didn't want to have to think this all through. To decide. She was worn out. She had done enough.

"I'm going to go now," Bria announced, uncertain even if she should still be afraid to step out into the dark hall.

"I know you're exhausted, Bria," Slako said, his voice a soft caress. "But I do have authorization for an extraordinary procedure that, I'm sure, will be revoked tomorrow."

"You mean this Grid Shift? George seemed to think it was dangerous."

"That alone should recommend it to you. Kirby was opposed because it has an infallible ability to evoke truth. You will emerge from this session with a clear grasp of what LU is. The one person most able to guide you to a complete understanding of your true nature and mission on this planet will be your Tower. He is a person who knows you better than you know yourself."

Bria was repulsed at Slako's apparent insinuation that he was that person.

"Not me, Bria," he said, responding to her look of distaste. "I would never presume such intimacy. Your Tower will be Dominic Xavier Cavanagh."

Bria's heart pounded with a violent stroke that wrenched her entire body.

"Dom," she faltered. "He's here?"

"Dom never left." Slako's voice had the sanctimonious intonations of a funeral director. "I mean, of course, the real Dom, Bria. What it was you loved about Dominic Cavanagh wasn't confined to a mere earthly husk, the shell he has been freed of. As much of a burden as the physical husk is," Slako went on, ignoring Bria's expression, which was crumbling into disappointment, "and as happy as we Unlimiteds are to be rid of it when we decorporealize, death used to present a problem. Once we had dismissed the physical body, we could no longer communicate with those still trapped on the material plane. That was all changed, however, by the crowning achievement of J. Louis Comfort's metaphysical investigations, by the discovery of the Grid Shift."

As he intoned those two words, Slako pushed a button that triggered a hydraulic system. With a low rumble, the

Screen began to tilt inside the metal cabinet that housed it. The crosshatched Screen was revolved 45 degrees so that the crossed axes that divided it into quadrants were turned on their sides until they formed a giant X on the Screen in front of Anthony Slako.

"By shifting the Grid to this precise angle, as I have done," Slako explained, "a compensating factor is introduced. What it compensates for is death.

"Lou discovered the Grid Shift in 1975. It is rarely used. It enables a Tower to monitor a being without the encumbrance of a physical body. Likewise, it makes it possible for a dematerialized entity to Tower for an entity still trapped on the physical plane. That is what we will be doing."

Bria was caught between leaden disappointment and another surge of rising hope. As much as she wanted to believe, though, she could not. It all sounded like some overelaborate seance with electronic trappings thrown in as a sop to the twentieth century.

"Bria, I understand your skepticism." Slako's words cut to the core of Bria's unexpressed feelings. "No one was more skeptical than I when Lou announced the Grid Shift. I had to see it, experience it, work with it before I believed, and I don't expect you will be satisfied with anything less than a demonstration either. Let me explain, very basically, how we're going to be using the Shift.

"I have tilted the Screen so that the axes are shifted to a forty-five-degree angle. You may think of it as Dom's Screen, where his responses, as transmitted through you, will be read. Over the Screen, I have superimposed the normal axes. You will be monitored upon it in the normal way. You have the advantage in this plane of a body so that you can respond biophysiologically to my inputs. Lou gave our Unlimiteds in the spiritual realm a medium of communication with the Grid Shift. Using the file notations they amassed during Grid Time completed before their physical deaths, we can translate their extraphysical responses by interpreting their manifestations on the Screen. Do you understand?"

Bria understood so little that she didn't even know where to begin asking questions. The one thing that was clear was that Slako was offering her the chance to communicate with Dom.

"Whether or not you understand now *how* the Grid Shift operates, Bria, I can guarantee that, by the time we've finished, you will be absolutely certain that it *does* work. Shall we begin?"

Bria held up her hand in acquiescence, a gesture that encompassed confusion, exhaustion, hope, and fear.

"All right. All I ask is that you not resist, Bria. You do not have to believe in the process; simply don't render it inoperative. It will work because you and Dom were so close and because you have remained in touch with him emotionally. You will now learn that he has remained just as concerned about you. Please place your hands gently, yet firmly, on the Wheel and close your eyes."

Bria's eyelids settled fitfully down. It took an effort to keep them shut. She was wary and would rather have been able to view what was about to happen.

The low-pitched roar started softly. Then it built. Before she was aware of it, her eyelids had relaxed and were content to be closed. When Slako spoke, his voice had a new quality to it. It seemed more like an extension of the drone in the background than a human voice. It wasn't pleasant or unpleasant. Bria had difficulty imputing any human characteristics to it.

"Think back to the first time you ever saw Dom."

It was a well-worn memory. Before she could decide against it, Bria had slipped back more than a dozen years to when she was a skinny twelve-year-old with breadstick legs that could barely hold up the knee socks she had to wear with her Catholic-school uniform. Her father's political aspirations were beginning to blossom and he had made the decision that their old parish, where his family had attended Mass for generations, was no longer good enough. He wasn't meeting the right people. Francisco Delgado wanted to pray with the Governor. No matter who might officiate in the Capitol Building, "the Governor" would always be William Cavanagh. So they switched to St. Francis Cathedral. That was where she had first seen him, in the front pew with his father on one side and his mother on the other. Like the Holy Family. The hour-long service that had always before seemed interminable, began to slide past in a dreamy haze. It turned into an excruciating ordeal, however, when her father took to waylay-

ing the Governor on the Cathedral steps after Mass. Bria
wanted to be wiped from the face of the earth as she stood
mute next to her mother while her father toadied up to the
Governor. She and Dom never spoke. The next fall he
stopped coming to Mass. The Governor had sent him away
to a military school in the south of the state famous for
ramrodding discipline into rich men's sons, then off to an
Eastern university.

"Fine, Bria. You're locating nicely. Now recall the first
time you and Dom spoke."

Bria was lost in the memory before Slako even suggested it. She was on the plaza. Labor Day weekend, 1974.
She had just turned twenty and finished her second year at
the university. It was the last night of Santa Fe fiesta. The
locals disdained the plaza during the three days of fiesta,
saying that it was overrun by tourists and hoodlums from
Albuquerque. Which is precisely why Bria had come that
final night, to see new faces. Faces she wouldn't have to
play the Senator's daughter to. It was nearly midnight and
the bodies that jammed the plaza were young and rowdy. A
mariachi band played and the crowd swayed against her
like one enormous bear of a dance partner. It was more in-
toxicating than the margaritas in plastic cups being sold
from booths lining the street leading to the plaza where
the huge drunken beast danced. Bria abandoned herself to
it. For a moment she escaped, escaped her mother's voice
telling her to behave herself, to act like a lady, escaped the
nuns telling her about St. Bridget of Ireland who cut off
her beautiful long hair so that she would not tempt the
lusts of men, escaped from her own damnable timidity. She
danced from the arms of one strange man to the arms of another. Never mind age or appearance. She wanted to dance
with the bear. Then she was pulled against a tan corduroy
jacket that smelled of fresh bread and musk and looked up
into a face she hadn't seen for seven years. A streetlight
shone over his head, turning his blond curls into a halo.

"Bria Delgado." He knew her name. "Slumming?" He'd
laughed, and so had she. There were no preliminaries,
there was no awkwardness. They danced until the band
went home and the margaritas dried up. Then she took
Dom to the Homestead, where Polonia and Balthasar had
settled nearly three hundred years ago, and they spent

their first night together, she more frightened than she would admit. He was her guide that night and for the next six years.

"Good, Bria." The colorless voice seemed to come out of the mechanical box. "We are On-Line now. Dom is with us. Please, don't open your eyes, you won't see anything. He is manifesting on the Screen. I'll decode."

Bria opened her mouth. She needed more air. Her hands grew slick on the metal wheel. She was meddling in something she didn't understand. She swallowed hard. This was unnatural. Somehow she had to stop it. Already it had gone too far. At best it was a sham, at worst a sacrilege and a desecration of the dead.

"Dom suggests that you focus now on your most perfect moment of communion."

The suggestion alarmed Bria. How did Slako know that she had stored that memory in her own mind under the word "communion"? Could it have come from the notes George made during her first session?

"Dom suggests that you think back to the day of his father's funeral."

Yes, that was when it had been. But she hadn't told George. Hadn't even thought about the funeral. About how Dom and his mother had stood beside the freshly dug grave in the Cavanagh family plot and watched the Governor being settled in next to his illustrious relatives. How Dom's hands had twisted around themselves in an agony of unexpressed emotion. How that night in bed he had ridden her until their sweat and tears ran together.

But Slako couldn't know any of that. He couldn't. Only she and Dom had, ever. The cadence of Bria's thoughts fell into a dead heat, racing with the pounding of her heart. Each one beat faster, more mercilessly, against her brain. Then, suddenly, both were calm, stilled by a quiet inner certainty that opened up deep within her.

Dom had indeed never left. She was as close to him now as she had been that night. How or why no longer mattered. Whether it was the perverse little man across from her twisting dials, or her own desperate need to communicate with Dom again, became irrelevant. Dom's presence was more palpable than the metal she clutched in her hands. They had transcended the grave.

"Good contact, Bria. I knew this would go well with Kirby off the case. Dom is now co-Towering. Prepare to gain total understanding of Life Unlimited."

At that moment, Bria could not have cared less about Life Unlimited. She had waited two years for this. "Tell Dom—" She stopped. She no longer felt she needed to give voice to her thoughts. Dom knew them already.

"Yes?" Slako prompted her.

"Does Dom know," she began again, "how much I've always loved him?"

She didn't need Slako's answer. Dom's formed within her a second before she asked the question.

"Of course. He's always known."

Bria was elated. She had communicated with Dom again, and he with her. A wave of warmth welled up from the cradle of her stomach and rose, sweeping away the years of loneliness. She wondered how she could have stood the emptiness. Tears pooled in her eyes. She wept not only for the loneliness, but for all the joy that could have been theirs, all the moments like this one that they hadn't shared. Bria cried for what she was experiencing, what she thought she had lost forever—complete communion with another human being.

Slako went on speaking, but Bria was no longer listening. She had turned her heart and soul back to Dom. She was filled with the steady, sure knowledge that he had never stopped loving her, even during the long silences, even in death.

"Bria, Dom has a message for you. He wants you to know that, outside of the encumbrances of the physical plane, he has found that all of Lou's teachings are fully verified. He wants you to know that as absolute, undeniable truth. He wants you to share it with the world. They need that truth. Do you understand Dom's message?"

Bria heard the words as a distant buzz. Inside, she listened and was calmed by communications she would never be able to put into any earthly language. She twirled in a slow-moving waltz across green meadows, beside sparkling rivers, over wisps of clouds. They danced a rapture of reunion. Then the music faded and Bria understood that, together, she and Dom had crucial work to do.

"Bria, do you understand Dom's message? He wants you

to know that Life Unlimited has full and absolute truth which planet Earth must have in order to survive the madness of our enemies."

Confusion was Bria's strongest reaction when Slako's words penetrated. They directly contradicted what she knew Dom's real message was. She had felt it, not heard it, but it had nothing to do with Life Unlimited or any other group possessing absolute truth. Bria struggled to translate the feeling into a thought. The closest she could come to consciously expressing it was: Truth cannot be dictated. It is different for everyone who seeks it.

"Bria, you're not focusing." Slako's monotone had become harried. "Dom suggests that you need to focus on absorbing his revelations about Life Unlimited. It has been revealed to him in the etheric realms that you are to play a pivotal role in the history of mankind's spiritual evolution. Bria, you have been chosen as the prophetess who will lead humanity out of the spiritual void and onto the Grid!"

Bria tuned Slako out. Her pulse quickened. One image flooded her mind—George's face. His eyes pleaded with her anew. Dom wanted her to understand what they were imploring her to do. She concentrated on the task Dom and George had guided her to: contrasting the two times she had been in the lobby. Quickly, she threaded the two scenes through her mind. She relived the anxiety she had experienced as she edged toward the counter marked Verifications for the first time.

"Bria, you're not cooperating to your fullest anymore." Bria thought briefly of the gun in Slako's pocket. Her hands slipped on the Wheel and she gripped it more tightly.

"Good, you're reading again. Let's get down to business, shall we?"

Bria nodded and replayed her second entrance into the Academy. The instant she made the mental step back into the lobby, she had the unmistakable feeling that she was staring at the clue that would put all the others into perspective. It was like the annoying presentiment that would come over her when she would be on assignment, have a picture framed up, and know in her gut that something was wrong with the shot. Then, when she was in the arkroom, trying to beat a deadline, she'd come up with a print where a council member's toupee was askew or some ociety matron's bra strap was hanging out. She had that ame nagging feeling now that she was looking at a flawed image. She studied her memory of the lobby, searching it or the betraying element.

"Bria, this is not working. Your readings are erratic. They're skipping from one quadrant to another." Slako's tone chilled Bria. She sensed that he was a man for whom the distances between irritation and anger and violence were quite short. And he was irritated now. "Why are you resisting, Bria?"

She was afraid he already knew. That even now he had the answer she was searching for. That it would be dangerous if he knew she were searching. She forced a blankness over her eyes before she dared to open them.

"I'm not," she said petulantly. "I'm upset. Things have happened very suddenly."

Slako looked at his watch, webbed his fingers together, and rested his head on them. When he looked up again, a mask of tranquillity veiled his features.

"You're right, you've been pushed. But this has to be done. I, we, can't let Lou down. Not tomorrow, of all days. Let's try again. I promise you, Bria, for so little effort you will be rewarded magnificently. It is beyond your power to comprehend the richness of your reward." Slako jutted his head forward until veins and cartilage stood out in taut, ropy bunches on his thin neck. Bria gave a tight nod. "All right, close your eyes again."

Instantly, Bria was back in the lobby, replaying her second entrance, the garish fall of hair she'd stolen perched on her head. Her nervousness was accelerated by the memory of approaching the Verifications Counter wondering how she would get upstairs to warn Leonard that his name was on a hit list. She saw the two Louies collide, the bouncy young girl knocked to the floor. Even as she reframed the collision scene, her mental Geiger counter started clicking.

Slako's commands buzzed. Bria had to ignore him, to tempt his rage for a few more seconds. She was getting closer, she felt it. Sweat beaded on her upper lip. She pulled her hand from the Wheel to wipe it away. Accidentally, she brushed against the burn on her cheek. The pain was accompanied by the memory of a smell of burning, which prompted an earlier olfactory memory to surface: the smell of gas. That was when it all fell into place: No one in the lobby had been smoking.

That was what had made the collision scene seem so odd. The lobby, usually choked with cigarette smoke, had been as untainted as an Alpine mountainside. No one had been smoking. Instinctively, Bria twitched, recoiling in her chair from the implications of that realization. They hatched out like so many snakes and slithered toward her. Every damned Louie in that lobby must have known that a gas jet was leaking death only one floor above the lobby. That a lit match would have blown them all into the "etheric realm." That's why no one was smoking. They were all in on Leonard's death.

Bria replaced her hand on the Wheel to stop it from trembling. Only one man could have orchestrated the grisly compliance of all those Louies—the head of Life Unlimited's security force, Lieutenant Anthony Slako. Bria was frightened, afraid to open her eyes, afraid that what she now knew would show when she looked at the man across from her. She was more frightened, though, that her new knowledge was already being betrayed as blips on the Grid Screen. Blips that Slako could translate. There was no question that a man who had ordered, perhaps even personally carried out, the deaths of six loyal Unlimiteds, members of his own intelligence team, would not hesitate to eliminate anyone who posed a threat to Life Unlimited.

"Bria." Her heart pounded a dozen times before he continued. "I've found in my thirty years with Lou that, whenever I hit a snag like this one in a session, ninety-five percent of the time it's because the cadet is holding something back, something that might be harmful to Life Unlimited. We both always feel a lot better when we get whatever misunderstanding has arisen out into the open. Then we invariably go on to have a highly successful session. So let's find out, right now, what it is that you're holding back. Tell me precisely what you're thinking about at this moment. Remember, in order to help you get to the true root of this problem, I will be monitoring the accuracy of your statement on the Grid."

Bria was thinking how perfectly she'd set herself up. First, she'd turned over her passport out of this place, the key to the locker she'd put the file in. Then she'd called Todd Samuels that second time. No doubt Slako, if he hadn't actually been the one listening in, had a complete transcript of that call. He knew that she had told the reporter she feared for her life. And that Samuels had assumed she meant she was afraid of becoming the next victim of the secret government assassin. Only there *was* no government assassin. God, Slako must have been pleased with that stupid call. Now he had his choice. If she saw the true light of Life Unlimited during the Compression Series, she would extol it tomorrow to the world's press and usher in a new age for LU. If, on the other hand, the light failed to dawn on her, she could meet with a convenient end. She had already supplied Slako with a perfect alibi. Todd Samuels would eulogize her as the seventh martyr slain by a power-crazed government agency. Either way, LU would come out ahead and Bria Delgado, the whole Bria Delgado, wouldn't come out at all.

"Open your eyes, Bria." Slako's command jolted her. Time had run out. She slowly pulled back her lids and stared straight into the predatory amber eyes.

CHAPTER 25

"What is it you're not telling me?" The flat black pupils ringed in yellow bored into her. They tracked Bria, her face, her eyes, the signals she was transmitting on the Screen.

Bria felt naked. A few deft questions and everything would be exposed. The Grid had become a remorseless lie detector.

"That thought, Bria, what was it?"

"Nothing, I was just thinking how tired I am."

"No, Bria, that doesn't read. Tell me the real thought. It was in a negative quadrant cluster aligned with your Life Unlimited readouts. It was about LU. What was it, Bria?"

His voice had become sharper. A trickle of sweat ran down between Bria's breasts. In a few seconds he would know everything. Unbidden, Leonard's face appeared. Like a subtitle in a foreign movie, the name "Agent Wilkers" ticked across the bottom of that image.

"Bria, I would prefer to have you tell me what your negative indicators mean, but I can simply chart them in for myself. We already have enough baseline data on you from your first session to decode all future readings. Should I do that?"

"No." Bria bit the inside of her mouth. She had answered too quickly, too firmly. "No, I'm getting myself back together again. I just need to use the bathroom."

"Gretchen reported that she took you immediately prior to coming here."

"I'm sorry," Bria injected her apology with a dose of prissy indignation, "but that doesn't eliminate my need for a second trip."

"All right. There's one attached here. It's the door behind you."

Bria deflected the quavery note of despair that wanted to dissolve her voice into a whimper. Instead, she demanded, "No, I have to use the one in the hall. I'm having my period and I left my sanitary supplies in there."

Slako rapped his knuckles on the table in front of him, then turned to bawl in the direction of the closed door: "Pulver!"

The door flew open.

"Escort Miss Delgado to the hall bathroom. And, Pulver, remember, you are guarding her life. Don't leave her side for a second until you get to the bathroom, then wait immediately outside the door. Listen for any suspicious sounds. Escort Miss Delgado directly back to this room. For additional protection, grip Miss Delgado's arm securely with your own. Acknowledged?"

"Ack'd," Pulver responded, tucking his chin into his throat.

With her arm locked in his, Pulver marched Bria to her destination. His unquestioning zealotry made Bria aware that Pulver could easily have been the one who carried out Slako's orders. With an athlete's pride in his strength and speed, Pulver probably saw himself as some invincible vanquisher making the world safe for Life Unlimited. Yes, Pulver would kill her if the order came down.

"I'll be right here." They stopped in front of the bathroom door. His tone and manner made it clear that he had understood Slako's unspoken command to tighten security, the security that would keep her tightly snared in LU's net.

As Bria pushed open the swinging door, she committed herself. The commitment was to a plan for escape that had a minute chance for success and that required more courage than she had. The plan did, however, have two compelling recommendations—it was the only one Bria had, and the one alternative more foolish than trying to escape was not to try. There was no time to reconsider. She made straight for the loosened grating, squatted on the cold tiled floor, braced her feet against the wall, and pulled.

The corroded grating clung to the wall for a few seconds; then it gave way like a rotted tooth, the screws ripping out of their worn sockets. The ventilator shaft was a damp and utterly black maw that dropped straight down, plunging to the basement's concrete floor five stories below. Light gleamed back from a few faint points. Bria could just barely make out a thick cluster of pipes, bound together with thin metal straps, running through the center of the hundred-foot vertical tunnel.

She couldn't allow herself to balk. She stuck the steel comb into the waistband of her pants. If she had remembered enough of Dom's lecture, there would be yet another grill to pry loose at the shaft's bottom, one that opened to the outside, to escape. Feeling as if she were tossing herself into a bottomless well, Bria stretched a foot over the edge of the hole where the grill had been. Like the rest of the asylum, the shaft was constructed of limestone. Unlike the inside walls, however, it had never been plastered over. Deep, jagged seams cut through the spaces where the blocks of stone were laid together, leaving ridges wide enough to wedge a foot into. Bria got a toehold and inched her way into the dank opening.

Afraid to hope for much, she extended her legs into the shaft. Three feet below, her toes discovered a limestone block protruding from the wall. She sank her weight onto it. Three feet further, she encountered another block jutting out. A series of steps had been built into the shaft. She tested the step beneath her foot. It wobbled. She remembered how crumbly the limestone at the opening had been.

"You about done?" Pulver's question cannonaded through the tiled bathroom down into the shaft. Bria lowered her weight onto the step. It teetered dangerously but held. She stretched down for the next step. In the bathroom above, the door swung open. Her foot dangled in midair. She couldn't find the next step.

"Bria? Bria!" She pulled her foot back up, searching for the step. It had to be there. "Bria!" The voice was too loud. Too close. Her foot found an indentation instead of a protrusion. The step had fallen out. Bria rammed her foot into the unoccupied niche and lowered her weight. She had to put distance between herself and the Louies. She was their prey now. She scrambled for the next step down.

"What the fuck?" Pulver had spotted the gaping shaft opening, the pried-away grating lying beside it. His footsteps thundered on the floor above Bria's head. She found the next step and lowered herself onto it quickly. Too quickly. The block shuddered in protest at being disturbed from a century of slumber. Bria grabbed at the pipes to steady herself. They clanged hideously as her hand slammed against them. With the step wobbling precariously beneath her foot, Bria hung paralyzed. The footsteps stopped. She breathed deeply, pulling in all the musty odors trapped in the moldering shaft. It smelled of mold and fungus, like mushrooms. It smelled of things dark and long dead.

"You down there." It was a statement, not a question. "Come on up now, Bria. I can't protect you down there. You're out of my line of vision. That agent could be anywhere. Ventilator shaft would be a likely hiding place for him. Bria?"

Bria gently lifted her foot off the wobbly step and wrapped it and her other leg around the cluster of pipes. She clung to them like a terrified koala bear.

"Bria, I'm really worried about you down there. Come on up."

Bria chanced an upward glance. Pulver's massive head blocked out the thin drizzle of light. Suddenly the head disappeared and the walkie-talkie flicked on with a static crackle.

"Code Twenty-five. Sir, could you proceed immediately to the bathroom?"

Bria couldn't hear the reply, but she had no doubt who he was speaking to—Slako was coming. Bria investigated the wall opposite the steps, searching for a ridge to wedge her foot into. She was not in the best of physical condition and her arms were already starting to ache. She brushed her foot against the far wall. It skidded across a slimy moistness. She tried to brace herself against the wall, but her foot kept slipping. She wrapped her leg back around the vertical pipes again and felt with her hand. There were no footholds. Worse, the entire wall was worn smooth and coated in slime from the ceaseless dripping of a pipe leaking somewhere.

The door to the bathroom exploded, and staccato footsteps ground into the floor above her. "Where is she?" Slako's fury found her instantly. Bria knew that Pulver was indicating her hiding place. There was an angry buzz. "I thought I ordered you to stay with her."

"I did sir," Pulver said defensively.

A body blocked out the trickle of light from above. "Bria." It was Slako. She tried to control the panic that choked her. "I know we pushed you, probably too hard. I can totally understand your adopting this defensive posture. It's pro-survival, Bria, and that is what Life Unlimited is all about. I'm more convinced than ever now that you're a natural Unlimited. We're allies, Bria. What you want, I want. So come on up and we can start working together to accomplish your goals. You'll be safe up here now, I promise you that. No one's going to push you anymore."

Was this how he had tricked Dom? Made him feel safe until it was too late?

"Look, Bria, we don't have time to play out this entire scenario. Let's just say that you've made your point and we understand. Now come on up, okay?"

A moment of silence ticked by. Bria heard the scratch of cockroaches scuttling past her head. She hoped she wouldn't scream if they crawled on her. Another moment passed. Then Slako gave the order.

"Go down there and get her. I'll go get House Security myself."

The big pipes running through the shaft's center shuddered and clanged as Pulver knocked against them, grunting his way into the opening. He kicked loose a piece of rusted metal. It glanced off Bria's forearm, which was wrapped around the pipes, before crashing to the concrete floor of the basement five stories below. Pulver's feet pedaled in the air ten feet above Bria's head, then landed securely on the first step. Bria had worked her way around to the other side of the pipes as far from the steps and Travis Pulver as she could get. There was the sliver of a chance that he might miss her in the darkness, that he wouldn't feel her hands and legs wrapped around the pipes at his back. He dropped to the next step, three feet closer. Bria wanted to scream with tension, give herself up; but she didn't breathe.

Pulver's heavy boots thudded against the wall beneath the second step.

The quivers started. First in her hands, then her arms where they gripped the pipes, then her thighs began to tremble with fear and exhaustion.

Pulver's next step brought his foot down to the level of her head on the other side of the pipes.

The sound of his boot banging into the indentation where the block was missing thundered in Bria's ears. She could have almost stretched out a hand and touched the waffled sole. Still Pulver hadn't felt behind himself, along the pipes her arms and legs were wrapped around. Bria took a small breath. She might have a chance. In one blaze of light, that chance vanished.

Pulver's flashlight flicked on. It caught Bria in the eyes and blinded her. "So there you are."

She couldn't see anything but darkness beyond the light that exposed her.

Pulver extended a mitt-sized hand and clamped it onto Bria's arm. He tugged gently. It was enough to loosen her grip on the pipes. Bria felt herself being hauled upward, back to Slako, back to the room where Dom was murdered, back to the Grid. She locked her hands. Pulver would have to break her arms to pry her loose.

"Fuck it." Pulver hissed the impatient curse. "Game time is over, Bria." He rested the flashlight beside his foot. Pulver now had both hands free. Bria knew it was all over. She had barely been able to resist his one-handed grip. She dug into the waistband of her pants and pulled out the rat-tail steel comb. At least she wouldn't go easy.

Pulver's right hand crushed her forearm. He shifted around, maneuvering himself into a better position to extricate her. He brought his right foot down, searching for the next step. He found it and rested his foot lightly on it, his arms still supporting most of his weight. In that same instant, Bria swung the steel comb around, its spiked tail sticking out from her fist like a dagger. She dug it as deeply as she could into the back of the hand crushing her forearm.

A shriek of pain reverberated off the limestone walls. Pulver ripped his hand away suddenly, shifting his weight onto the fourth step, the step that had teetered beneath Bria's slim hundred pounds. When Pulver dropped two hundred pounds of Olympic muscle onto it, the block, without breaking loose entirely, tilted downward. It was enough to topple Pulver backward, his hands windmilling in the air. Bria felt his body slam against the pipes beneath her. Bloody hunks of Pulver's palms, nose, and lips were scraped off as he lunged for the pipes, twisting in midair, to stop his fall only a few yards beneath Bria's feet.

"You stupid cunt!" Pulver started to shimmy up the pipes. Bria closed her eyes, waiting for the manacle of Pulver's grip to close around her ankle. It never came.

With an implacable scrape, the 250-pound block that Pulver's weighty tread had loosened inched downward. Freed from the burrow it had occupied for so long, the block slid out. Reverberations thudded through Bria's stomach as the block clanked against the pipes she clung to. It lightly grazed her foot as it toppled out, then plummeted straight down, skidding along the pipes like a freight train on a rail. The one-eighth-ton block swept Pulver from his perch on the pipes beneath Bria as easily as if he'd been a spider on a web strung across the dusty shaft.

The crash as the block landed on the concrete basement floor five stories down wasn't as loud as it might have been. Pulver landed first.

CHAPTER 26

The horror of what she had done crept toward Bria, sending evil tendrils up from the bottom of the dark shaft where the man she had killed lay soaked in his own blood. She clung to the cold pipes, her feet resting on the metal sleeve that girdled them. Precious minutes were wasted as her mind reeled in revulsion. Abruptly it fastened upon the immediate consequence of her act: she had declared herself. She was irrevocably marked now as an enemy of Life Unlimited. All subtlety and charade would stop. Slako would openly hunt her. If he found her, he would kill her.

Bria forced her feet into the indentation left by the block Pulver had knocked loose. She grabbed Pulver's flashlight, which still lay on the step above, and stretched for the next step, then the next. The beam of the flashlight reflected off of the greenish slime that coated the opposite wall. She lowered the beam. Before she had a chance to orient herself, she was staring down four and a half stories into the bulging eyes of Travis Pulver. Blood frothed from his mouth. Bria jerked the beam up. In its rapid course upward, it revealed a square opening off the shaft. Bria clambered down to it. She couldn't let Slako trap her in this shaft.

The opening led to a smaller horizontal shaft branching off of the main one. Bria swung her arms and legs back around the center pipes. From there she reached out a leg to the opening. It was slick with the slime that covered that entire wall. Above her, footsteps rang on the tile floor. Below her were four floors of emptiness shooting straight down to a slab of concrete next to Pulver's body.

Overhead, something heavy and metallic clattered as it

was dragged across the tile floor. A cluster of voices grew louder as they approached the ventilator-shaft opening in the fifth-floor bathroom. Bria shoved herself into the lateral shaft. The instant that she pushed off from the pipes, a powerful spotlight illuminated the shaft. The cushion of slime beneath her helped Bria to slide far back into the dark tunnel before Slako could crowd his head into the opening next to the light.

"Pulver," he called down, "have you got . . ." His question died when he saw the answer lying five floors below him.

Bria shoved herself farther down the slimy tunnel. She craned her neck to look back. As the lighted opening behind her shrank in size, the last thing she saw was a rope dropping in front of it. She tried to turn around, but the horizontal shaft was only large enough for her to roll over, pull her feet under her, and crawl backward. Bria figured she was in a connecting shaft that cut across the front of the building. The bathroom was at one corner of the U-shaped building. With any luck there would be another shaft at the corner she was backing toward. Then what?

Bria forced herself to blank out the question and to keep moving. Her only choice was to keep using whatever opportunities presented themselves. If there were another shaft, she might be able to find where it opened to the outside, provided that the Louies weren't already guarding all the outside openings. In that very likely event, Bria decided, she would find some niche to hole up in for the next few hours. If she could stay hidden for that long, she would be safe. There would be reporters swarming all over the Academy demanding to see her. Slako wouldn't dare try anything with so many outsiders within screaming distance. Bria refused to let herself refute that thought, although logic pointed out that she had already given Slako an ironclad cover for her death and that he wasn't the type that would hesitate to hide behind it.

She continued scuttling backward. The slime had ended and the limestone she was crawling on was merely damp. Minutes ticked by as she made her laborious way through the tunnel. Finally, she drove her feet over an edge and they hung in midair. She dropped her legs, then her pelvis over the edge and scooted cautiously back. The ledge was grinding into her belly before her foot hit a step. Bria tapped it with her toe, remembering how Pulver's death had been signaled by the wrenching scrape of a moldy chunk of limestone toppling loose. But there was no sound. She lowered herself over the edge and onto the protruding block. It held. She was out of the horizontal shaft. She pivoted, switched on the flashlight, and found she was buried within another large, vertical shaft. It was identical to the one she had just crawled out of, five feet square with a tangle of pipes jutting up and down through the middle. She switched off the flashlight. The shaft was as dark and silent as a tomb. Bria reckoned it would stay that way for only a few minutes longer, just long enough for the Louies to map out a strategy and issue commands. If she moved fast, she could make her way to the basement opening. Somehow she'd pound out whatever grating covered it and head for the magnolias outside.

The next step seemed a long way down. Bria strained for it. With her leg extended as far as it reached, all she could feel was air. Pulver's grotesquely distended face flickered across her mind. Her leg froze. Below her were eighty empty feet straight down to the concrete basement. Panic hit the pit of Bria's stomach and steamrolled its way up. By the time it reached her brain, she was flashing uncontrollably between images of Pulver and Leonard, of their faces in death. Then she began splicing in her own. Panic was stealing the few minutes that stood between her and capture.

Bria forced her leg through one more exploratory arc. The top corner of a block of limestone rasped against her Achilles tendon. She didn't stop to test it. She dropped her weight on it and stretched down for the next step. Fear strummed in her head like an annoying tune she couldn't shut off. She scrambled for the next step, scuttling closer and closer to the shaft bottom, to escape. She felt the dampness exhaled from the basement and thought of the pines, fragrant in a predawn coolness far beyond this madhouse. She just might make it.

Then she heard the voices. High above her and indistinct, she knew they were the hard, determined voices of Slako and his Protectorate thugs. And they were nearing her hiding place. The panic pulsed faster. A light came on, seeping down from the fifth floor. Bria drove her foot down to the next step. She was so intent upon finding it that, at first, she didn't notice the smell. It was the dry singed odor that comes when a gas heater is relighted after a summer of disuse. Except that this smell was much stronger. It filled the shaft with the odor of dozens of summers' dust being burned off. As Bria caught the smell, she heard and felt a strangled gurgle come from the pipes at her back. They were coming to life. Bria didn't have time to figure out what that could mean. The voices above were growing louder.

She glanced down and saw a faint light. It was broken into bars by the pipes. It could have been moonlight or the first glimpse of a diffuse dawn. She decided it was the latter. It was the ventilator shaft outlet. Bria felt as if she'd found the source of the Nile.

Abruptly the cool vapors rising from the basement ceased. Bria thought she was overheating from the exertion as each movement sent another, more intense, flush of heat coursing through her body. The drops of nervous perspiration beading her forehead turned to rivulets of sweat running down her face. But it was her back that was beginning to broil. The heat seemed to emanate from her spine. Sweat collected in it like rain in an arroyo during a flash flood.

She fought the terror that steadily mounted with the temperature in the shaft. Both her fear and the heat broke loose as a screeching hiss ripped open valves that had been rusted shut for decades.

The radiator pipes were on.

One awful image blocked out all others—the striped scar a childhood playmate had carried on the back of her legs. The girl had bumped against one of the few steam radiators still operating in Santa Fe twenty years ago, and was marked for the rest of her life. Bria had been awed by the damage that water, heated under pressure to temperatures higher than its boiling point, could inflict on a human body.

"Move, move." Bria beat the words through her brain.

Mechanically, the command was relayed to her reluctant legs. Even as she hesitated, a boiler somewhere was being stoked to heat water to the scalding temperatures that would force it as steam through the pipes that lay inches from her back. No matter what waited for her beyond, she had to get out of this shaft. The only certainty here was death. Bria's foot hit the next step. For a second, she thought it was loose, then she realized that the shaking she felt originated in the quivering muscles of her own exhausted legs. She was only twenty feet from the light. Each inch she descended wrapped her in more intense waves of heat. Sweat now ran from the tip of her chin in a steady stream. The pipes grew hotter. She hugged the limestone wall, pulling her body in as far as she could from the pipes. Heat and fear exacted their physical due. Bria was panting, sucking in overheated air like a marathon runner. In the darkness she began seeing a constellation of tiny lights.

"You cannot pass out," Bria ordered herself. She straightened her leg and jammed it down. Pain shuddered through the extended limb as it pounded into a metal grating. She had reached the juncture that cut off from the shaft and led to the world outside. She had made it.

Bria turned toward the light. It leaked in from the opening and striped her face like that of a prisoner looking out of a barred window. Bria tested the cluster of pipes splayed out wickedly in front of the opening. Even before she pulled her hand away, she knew that the tip of her finger was blistered. She had as much chance of squeezing through the narrow spaces between the pipes as she had of crawling through the heated coils of a radiator. Sweat, running off tendrils of hair, dripped into her eyes. She wondered how long it would take for her to die of dehydration; or would heart failure end things first? She hunkered down on the grating, too exhausted to mind that the thick steel strips were beginning to burn her thighs through the material of her pants.

Overhead, she heard the same scraping noise she'd heard before, the one that meant a high-powered spotlight was being dragged across a tile floor and would soon illuminate the shaft. There was no way left but down. The basement below the grating she sat on was dark. Bria switched on the flashlight. Eighteen feet below her, the light she shone through the grating cast a checkerboard pattern on the basement floor. She swung the beam of light around. The basement was immense. The light picked out only one wall. It was flush with the shaft wall at her back. An ancient metal ladder was built into it. It led up to the grating. Bria swung the light over the grating. One section was hinged, a maintenance hatch that opened directly above the metal ladder.

The scraping sound stopped. The light was in place. Bria crammed her hand through the grating and felt for a latch on the other side. Dizziness rolled over her when she lowered her head to hunt for the latch. Muffled commands were barked overhead. She found the latch and pushed against it. Like every other piece of metal in the neglected ventilation system, it was rusted. She pushed harder. The trapdoor in front of her knees dropped with a screech. Too late, Bria realized that she had rested the flashlight on the swinging grate. It landed with a crack on the cement floor, and the beam died. Bria found the metal ladder in darkness.

The basement, buried beneath the earth, welcomed her with a soothing dampness. She stumbled down the ladder and collapsed on the concrete floor, soaking up the subterranean coolness.

Five floors above, the light blinked on. She scurried out of the crosshatched square of light like a cockroach caught on a midnight kitchen floor.

"She's not in the shaft, sir."

"What do you mean?" Slako's voice raged, becoming louder as he stuck his head in to check the shaft himself.

"No, she's not, is she?" The voice was almost subdued. Then it lashed again. "Get back over to the north shaft."

The light snapped off and the voices disappeared. It was quiet, cool, and totally dark on the basement floor. Bria lay there until her breathing returned to normal. She'd won a reprieve, but knew it wouldn't last long. There had to be another outlet, and she had to find it.

She staggered to her feet and crept forward in the darkness, her hands extended in front of her like antennae. She walked for what seemed to be an interminable length before she ran into a wall. The wall intersected with a wide expanse of steel that jutted out across the basement. Bria slid her hand along the cold metal and made out the solid forms of eight bank-type vaults ranged in a row along the middle of the basement. As she came to the end of the eighth vault, she caught the first glimmer of light she'd seen in the basement. It came from the area behind the row of vaults, from what appeared to be a door lit from within. When she neared the door, she found it was attached to a brick enclosure the size of a small room. Heat and pipes radiated from it. The light leaking out from around the door was bright enough for Bria to read the curlicued words on the brass plaque screwed into the bricks above the door: "Le Bosquet's High Pressure Steam Heating Apparatus, 1877."

She'd found the source of the infernal heat that had come close to baking her alive: the brick enclosure surrounded the building's furnace. Maybe, if she could open the door, she'd have enough light to search for another outlet. Bria twisted the warm knob and yanked open the door. The blast of heat and light that met her was so intense that, for a moment, she didn't notice the tall, knobby body that rolled out at her feet.

George was naked, his hands bound behind him. A gag pinched his cheeks together. Bria untied George's hands and the gag knotted behind his head, and rolled him to a cool spot. She now knew what "Thermal Detention" meant.

"George, George," she whispered urgently. He had to regain consciousness. They would escape together. He'd die if she left him behind.

"George."

A low moan got past his swollen tongue. "Wah . . ." The monosyllabic demand died. Bria tried to imagine how she could fulfill it. Where was she going to find water in this dark cave? She surveyed the basement. The glow from the boiler furnace seemed to have grown brighter. It cast a pale light on the farthest wall. When she saw the big, fat-bellied barrel with the long-handled tin dipper depending from it, Bria was almost afraid she was hallucinating the too-perfect realization of her desire. She expected the barrel to disappear like a mirage as she drew closer. It didn't. It remained, solid and moist to the touch in front of a padlocked door. The disappointment came when she lifted off the lid. The liquid within was a slime-ridden cesspool.

As Bria debated whether to risk the near certainty of

contagion, she heard a slight scuffling from behind the door next to the barrel. In the dim light, she examined the sturdy door more closely. A ring of keys hung beside it on a nail. She stopped breathing and attuned her ear to the faint noises within. When she heard a muffled cough, she grabbed the keys and found the one that fitted the lock.

The stench that greeted her when she pulled back the heavy door caused her to gag. A dozen human figures scurried away from the door, retreating into a windowless cell with nothing in it other than some filthy straw on the floor and two buckets filled with a foul accumulation. Even before the trickle of light hit their faces, Bria knew these were the Traitors she had seen in the Mess Hall. They looked emaciated, feral, frightened, as if the opening of the door signaled horrors worse than those they were living among.

"Don't be scared. I'm not a Louie." Bria's words tumbled out in a frantic jumble. "I'm trying to escape. We can all escape. Come on." She motioned the cowering figures out of their captivity. Not one of them moved or spoke. "Come on," she repeated herself. "We've got to hurry. They'll be coming soon. If we all work together, we can find some way out of here." Bria held the ring of keys aloft. "These keys, maybe you know what they unlock. Come on." She raised her voice, hoping to wake them from the somnolent stupor they seemed to be in. There was no response. Behind her George moaned.

She whirled away from the Louie-designated Traitors and ripped the tin dipper away from its perch. She plunged it past the furry scum on the surface. George gulped the water as if it had been ladled from a mountain stream. Bria went for another dipper. When she returned, the twelve Traitors came out of their stinking hole and followed her like fearful trolls trapped in the wicked giant's dark forest. George's eyes were open when she got to him. He drank the second dipper with less relish.

Bria listened to her heart pound, aware that, with each beat, she had lost approximately one more second of the indeterminate time before Slako would find her.

"Listen," she began earnestly, trying to spark a flicker of animation in the sunken eyes staring at her, "if we all fan out we can cover this basement. Find some way out."

Bria was the only one who moved. She clapped her hands. "Let's go. The Protectorate is searching for me. They'll be down here in minutes. Don't you want to get out of this madhouse? What's the matter with all of you?"

A bitter laugh threaded its way through the silence that followed Bria's impassioned inquiries. It was George. His voice was little more than a croak, but his words were clear enough.

"No. No, they don't want to leave. If you opened the front door, they wouldn't leave." Again the laugh.

Bria felt her heart beating away the seconds. She had wasted too much time. She had no allies. No one was going to help her. She raced around the basement.

"Stairs!" She cried out her discovery from the darkness to the silent Traitors in their dirty rags clustered in the tiny pool of light beside the boiler room. The only response Bria received came from the door at the head of the stairs she'd just found. Someone on the other side was unlocking it.

CHAPTER 27

Bria's principal emotion when the basement lights came on was resignation.

Slako came down the stairs, followed by Gretchen and a Louie as overdeveloped as Pulver had been. They flanked Slako on either side. Both had guns. Bria didn't know which was more frightening—the guns or the inhuman look in Slako's eyes.

In the light, Bria saw that the metal expanses she had felt were indeed the steel doors of concrete vaults. Eight of them, each one eight feet tall, marched in a line across the basement, a row of thick-bodied bullies, their feet sunk in concrete. Each one had a number. The number five caught Bria's eye—Dom's vault. Beyond the vaults, in the far corner next to the Traitors' cells, was the crumpled heap of Pulver's body. Bria's glance skittered away from the corpse and landed on Gretchen's face. Bria was startled by the change in the young woman. Gretchen had been transformed from the college coed who drops by for a slumber party into a hardened commando. Bria wanted to say something consoling about Pulver, to explain what had happened, but the hard lines of hatred rutting the girl's long face told Bria that Gretchen had already tried and convicted her of murder and that she wouldn't flinch at personally carrying out a sentence of death.

Slako turned to the twelve Traitors, who had begun to tremble visibly when he entered. "You're all to be commended for resisting the propositions of a Degraded Being. I was monitoring the responses each one of you made to this demonstration and was quite pleased by your show of loyalty. I hereby officially upgrade all of you from Traitor to Out of Favor status." For the first time, the twelve displayed an emotion other than fear. They grinned with delight at their promotions. "Elevate to the second floor and present yourselves for suitable confinement." They stood, unmoving, for a second. "Go!" Slako ordered, and they rattled past him like a band of phantoms.

Bria, stunned by their timorous obedience, felt herself slump into a posture of defeat.

"Futility is exhausting, isn't it, Bria?" Slako asked. "Lou taught me that. Lou taught me not to resist what will be. Why can't all of you Limiteds recognize that Life Unlimited is a force that cannot be deterred?"

"I never wanted to 'deter' Life Unlimited." Bria's voice sounded as defeated as she felt. "All I ever cared about was Dom."

"You cared enough when you were On the Grid, though, didn't you? You all start caring then. You smart-assed college kids, you rich bitches who were born holding all the aces in the deck, that's when you start caring. Not me, I cared about the man, about J. Louis Comfort first. I've always cared about him first. He is my master for all of eternity."

Bria looked away. The private demons that drove Slako were slithering out of their hiding places, and she did not care to see them.

"You cared enough to decorporealize Pulver, didn't you? To squash the life from his physical entity."

"He was going to kill me or bring me to you to kill or brainwash. It was self-defense." Bria's words echoed back to her with a hollow ring; a concept like self-defense was illogical in this madhouse where "self" was the enemy Comfort fought to conquer.

"He was a Grade Sixteen." Slako spit out the numbers. "You are nothing, a drag-loaded Limited with no Ceiling Potential. It wouldn't have mattered if Pulver *had* killed you. But it is a great loss to Lou that Pulver's years of corporeal operation were cut short." Slako's faced stopped squirming and his voice went flat. He sounded now like a bored pedant instructing a particularly dull student. "For that alone, your current existence must be terminated. As an enemy of Life Unlimited your punishment will be even more severe. All future cycles of existence that you might initiate are hereby nullified. Your potential for being is nullified."

George struggled to sit up and groaned involuntarily with the pain the slight movement caused him.

"He has to have a doctor," Bria stated. Neither Slako nor Gretchen responded. "He's going to die," she said, addressing her plea to Gretchen. "Your brother is going to die."

Slako answered. "I think that Gretchen knows far better than you the condition her brother is in, don't you, Gretch?"

Gretchen, never taking her eyes off of the whimpering form, spoke. "Yes, I saw it all clearly while On the Grid. With any luck, this Soul Parasite who scavenged my brother's body will die. Then George, the real George, not this degraded entity who has stolen his body, can recorporeate and return to us." To demonstrate the virulence of her feelings toward the "Soul Parasite" inhabiting her brother's battered body, Gretchen gave the crumpled figure at her feet a solid kick in the ribs. She glanced at Slako, who nodded approval.

Bria choked back the cry rising in her throat. George's muffled moaning became a sharp cry in answer to the kick.

"Good, Body Snatcher," Slako said, "you are able to make it up to our realm. Pay attention and you will learn the penalty for stealing the material essence of an Unlimited before he has finished with it. As for you," Slako turned to Bria, "you have caused the decorporealization of one of Lou's finest." Bria glanced at Gretchen. Tears were spilling down the young woman's cheeks. It was like seeing rain run off one of the figures carved into Mount Rushmore. Her face was set hard as granite.

"Your sentence, Bria Delgado, is death. And the manner of execution, fire."

This isn't how I want to die, where I want to die! The thoughts screamed through Bria's mind. Not in some dank basement, at the hands of a punk psychotic turned demagogue. What lies will they tell? Will my father know the truth? Will Dom's mother? Bria fastened her gaze on the vault with the large "5" painted on the front in gold. Dom's vault. She'd never have the chance now to unlock it, to set free all the secrets within. The numbers to the combination that George had written on the File Request form ran through her mind like a chant to ward off evil. 26-18-46. The numbers blocked out Slako, his voice reading off a litany of her "crimes" against Life Unlimited. She looked at George. He had regained enough consciousness to comprehend what Slako was saying. His face told her that he knew the sentence was meant for him as well.

"All right," Slako went on briskly. "Bria has already provided the explanation for her death to that reporter. It has also been established that she came here to snoop. That will explain why she will be found in the Vault Room. She suspected George of being the agent and followed him down here to find him burning the incriminating papers he had collected."

Slako stopped and held an index finger aloft. He tapped it to his head like the director of a play guided by inspiration as he blocks out a scene. "Our intrepid heroine surprises the despicable double agent trying to destroy the evidence of his culpability before the story breaks in the papers and the inevitable investigation reveals him. But what—"

"You're ruining it." George was still curled in a fetal position, but his voice was strong. "You've twisted everything that Lou created. He couldn't know what you're doing, what you have been doing. He would never . . ." The sob that stopped George's heartbroken words sounded as if his brittle throat had cracked. It broke something in Gretchen as well.

"George? George, is that still you? The real you?"

"Of course it is, Gretch." George's answer held more sadness than anger.

"They're tricky, aren't they?" Slako asked Gretchen. "I do believe that our old friend Agent Wilkers is the Parasite Entity that has taken George's body. I've never encountered any being so devoted to obliterating the force of good on the planet. I'm sure Wilkers was enlisted on the other side for a couple of millennia at least. Don't listen to Wilkers, Gretchen. We'll get George—the real George—back, I promise. He's probably already hunting up a suitable physical vehicle for recorporealization."

The concern in Gretchen's eyes snapped off, and she

nodded her head in silent agreement. Satisfied, Slako continued outlining his scenario.

"Bria then surprised Kirby/Wilkers burning his dirty secrets down here in the old boiler. There are two unfortunate aspects to this discovery, however. The first is that Bria closes the Vault Room door behind her, unaware that it is self-locking and can only be opened from the outside."

Bria glanced at the door on the opposite end of the warehouse-sized basement. There was a set of sturdy locks sunk into the door, but no knob.

"Lou himself ordered that as an extra security measure. You see, Bria, all our cadets' case files are stored down here in these vaults. The secrets of the Grid must be kept confidential. The Vault Room is fireproof. Concrete below and above. Earth on all four sides. It will be too late by the time anyone even realizes that there is a fire down here to do anything about it.

"And there *will* be a fire. That is to be the second unfortunate aspect of your discovery, Bria. George, knowing nothing about furnaces, does not realize that the boiler's safety valve is clogged by years of rust and neglect. His attention is diverted when you enter and confront him with your suspicions. He doesn't notice how dangerously high the pressure in the furnace is building. Doesn't notice anything until the deteriorated boiler furnace blows open, spewing flames and burning embers everywhere. Lots to burn down here. Enough to kill you both, but not enough to threaten the Academy. The fire will burn itself out before it can do any real damage. Pulver . . ." Slako glanced at the corpse in the far corner of the basement, an element that hadn't been accounted for. He quickly found a role for Travis Pulver to play posthumously.

"Pulver will be our gallant rescuer. He is the only one who *does* hear something, a faint scream trickling up the ventilator shaft, and, curious fellow that he is, he tracks it down. He slips on a loose block and falls to his death. A death that is tragic, but far preferable to the one you two Traitors will meet shortly." Slako surveyed the basement, then turned to the burly Louie at his side. "Verify that all the flues are closed, the metal covers placed over the basement shaft openings, and that the horizontal shaft is sealed off so that the fire can't spread. Any outside investigators will be told that the covers were put in place *after* the fire was detected."

Slako glanced around. "I have already closed the steam circulation system on the furnace. It's been years since I worked with a furnace. I spent many cold Chicago winters with them, though, down in the basement of the private school where my father worked. The only fit place for a janitor's son. But, as Lou says, 'an Unlimited uses all experiences, even the most humble, for his unique abilities make even those into powerful tools.' "

"You've perverted everything Lou ever said." George let the words fall, a flat statement of fact that needed no emotional ballast.

"Shut up, Wilkers, we know who you are, so quit spewing your filth."

"You actually believe that, don't you, Slako? Believe that I'm Wilkers reincarnated?" George looked at his former superior with an expression verging on amazement. "Of course you do." Painfully he angled his head around to face Gretchen. "So do you, you really do. So would I. That's why we did it, isn't it? Why we did all of it. Every one of us, true believers. Leonard, Dom, all of us. All of us . . ."

"Murdered," Bria finished.

Neither Slako, nor George said anything, but an odd expression passed between them. "Not exactly murdered; right, Slako? Nothing that blatant?"

Wordlessly, Slako led George's gaze with his own merciless avian stare down to the pocket where the gun was still hidden. It was pointed at Gretchen.

"Gretchen," Slako called out, "back out slowly, keeping your gun trained on them."

"Shoot him, Gretch," George rasped at his sister. "Shoot him right now and let us go. For God's sake, Gretch, don't leave us here to die. I'm your brother. This isn't human. You can't . . ." His words dissolved in tears.

For one second Gretchen Kirby hesitated. Conflict clouded her features. A moment later it cleared, to be replaced by that remorseless Louie mask of unbroachable certainty. She shook her head no, refusing to be swayed by demon cleverness. She continued to back away, joining

Slako at the basement door. Slako pulled out a ring of keys to open the double locks.

"No, you can't. No!" Bria's voice keened in a piercing wail as she watched the three Louies slip out the door, hearing it click, locking, behind them. "They're not really serious, are they?" she asked George frantically. "I mean about the furnace exploding, the fire? They wouldn't leave us here to die like that?"

George looked up. There was no question in his eyes that he believed every word Slako had spoken.

Bria's glance ricocheted wildly around the basement. To her horror she saw that the furnace was beginning to glow in the dim light.

"No," she said in fright-mad disbelief. "No!" She ran to the ventilator shaft. A thick steel lid was lowered into place to cover the meshed grating. "Help! We're in the basement! We're trapped, someone let us out!"

"Don't bother," George croaked. "Even if anyone could hear you, Academy residents are trained to ignore any communication from a Degraded condition. If the police ask later if anyone heard anything, they will be able to answer, in all honesty, that they didn't. They will even be able to pass a polygraph test."

Bria's horror broke into a full, panicked gallop.

"Can't you do anything with the furnace?" she shrieked at George. "Tell *me* what to do." Tears and sweat mixed on her face. The furnace was clearly backing up, blasting more and more heat into the basement. Each degree the temperature rose brought the rusty old boiler furnace closer to rupture. "Can't we do something? I don't want to die."

"You're right," George dragged himself to his feet. "Too many have died." He shuffled toward the boiler. "Move away," he ordered. The heat slammed against them. "I said, move away."

Bria backed away toward the row of vaults. The heat from the boiler was so intense that George had to turn away to suck in a lungful of air before he could approach the straining furnace. He was bent over, trying to grab a breath, when the boiler exploded. Bria was knocked to her knees by the blast.

Bits of molten metal and burning embers spewed out.

The tongue of flame imprisoned in the detonated furnace was set free. It lapped greedily at the piles of paper that covered the basement. It devoured the oxygen with a roar and replaced it with smoke that seared Bria's lungs. She'd been shielded from the explosion by the vaults. George hadn't.

"George!" There was no answer. She dropped to the floor and drank in the oxygen that remained there. George was a lump on the concrete floor, silhouetted by flames. Heat waves and the tears streaming out of Bria's eyes made him look like a corpse seen from a blurry distance underwater. She crawled to him. He was still breathing, but his back was a mass of charred flesh. She grabbed him under the armpits and tried to pull him toward the vaults where the flames hadn't reached. She couldn't budge his long body.

"George, you've got to help me." Bria smelled something burning close to her and realized it was her own hair being singed.

"Move, George," she screamed in his ear. A feeble hand came up from under his belly and his rickety knees bent so that he was propped up, leaning forward. Bria pulled and he collapsed forward. Like a crippled turtle racing with a ravening hare, Bria forced George to flop his way toward the vaults. The fire kept pace with them. Once they reached the vaults, there was no place left to go. With her back to the wall of steel, she was trapped.

26-18-46 . . . The numbers beat through her brain. Without thinking, she turned, found the golden "5" above her head glowing orange in the reflection of the flames, and began dialing the combination.

Bria twisted the dial to the last number, 46. Slick with sweat, the knob spun out of her hand. Pieces of paper at her feet were being gobbled by the flames. Bria couldn't think. There was no air. She didn't know if she had time left to try again.

26-18-46 . . .

Bria reached for the handle and pulled it down.

It didn't budge.

Oh, God. Had she remembered the numbers correctly? She blinked back the acid fluid pooled in her eyes and stared at the dial. It was stopped at 45. She inched it forward to 46. The handle swung down. She yanked the door

open and prodded George inside. Then she stepped over the
vault threshold. As the door clicked behind her, Bria
couldn't force back the feeling that she had just sealed her
own tomb.

CHAPTER 28

Nothing penetrated the concrete-and-steel vault J. Louis Comfort had ordered built into the basement of his Academy. When Bria swung the steel door shut she blocked out heat, noise—and escape. For, like the basement door, the vaults opened only one way, from the outside.

It was still cool inside. Bria reached behind a row of boxes that lined the vault's shelves, all of them filled with files, and put her hand against the concrete wall. It was warm. The other side was a sheet of flames. The metal-and-concrete box would heat up quickly once the fire buried it completely.

She ran her hands along the steel door. Was it airtight? Would they die of suffocation? Bria realized the question was foolish. If the vault were airtight, they would die when they had consumed all the oxygen in the small space they were trapped in. If the vault weren't airtight, then the fire would force its poisonous vapors inside and they would die of smoke inhalation. All she had accomplished by dragging herself and George into this high-security coffin was to delay their deaths by a few hours.

The more she reflected, though, the more the thought cheered her. She had sabotaged Slako and his tidy scenario for their deaths. She had chosen the way she was going to die. Death had always been a foregone conclusion; from the instant of her birth it had been inevitable. How she met it was all that she could possibly have varied. Bria was satisfied that she hadn't allowed Slako to define her end.

George moaned. The plasmic stream that coursed life

through his abused body was leaking out in a ceaseless trickle. Bria looked for something to stanch the flow. Absolutely everything in the vault was either steel or paper. She took off her top and patted it onto his oozing back to dam up some of the vital fluid, then grabbed a file out of the nearest box to tuck under his head as a pillow.

A paper slipped out of the folder and fluttered to the concrete. The words "Sex Rundown" caught Bria's eyes. She propped George's head on the thick folder and turned her attention to the provocative page. In the upper-left-hand corner, the page was number 15. Bria began readings.

Runthrough #33—Family. Still lower R quad readings. Cadet continues to resist.

Runthrough #34—Family. Breakthrough! Cadet has finally de-cogged on area of turbulence in 11th year. Immediate altitude gain. She was 11, brother, Bernard, was 13. Parents out of house. Brother displays his penile development, encourages Sheila to reveal her own precocious breast development. Bernard has erection, draws her hand onto it. Following his guidance, she masturbates him to climax.

Runthrough #35—Family. Area completely clean. Cadet has elevated to upper R quad. Runthrough complete.

Cadet reaction—"My parents never knew. I'm sure Bernard has no conscious recall of that incident. Thank Lou for clearing that drag-loader off my circuits!"

Bria stopped reading, though the file went on for many more pages, covering every aspect of the woman's sexual history. She looked at the boxes of files walling her in and thought of the other seven vaults, and the vaults around the world, all crammed with the festering secrets of ten million young people. Bria was pierced by an ineffable sadness for all the secrets that had been exchanged to "gain altitude," all the secrets that took so much energy to keep hidden, and were never any worse than those everyone else was hiding.

She knew Dom's files were in here, but she didn't want to see them, didn't want to read about him "clearing the turbulence" from his first masturbation or cheating on a college exam. Perhaps the catalogue of his sins would include a "drag-loaded" desire to see her again, to be with her. Bria chose to believe that it would.

She continued to stare at the names written on the section dividers that stood at the head of each group of files. So many of them were Irish, Italian—Catholic-sounding names—so many were Jewish. The one Spanish surname her glance fell upon was so familiar that it took a second for it to fully register: Gabriellana "Bria" Delgado.

Bria took a stunned inventory of all the dark corners in her life. How could Life Unlimited have invaded them? She reached out for the file folder behind her name, wondering how she could destroy anything she might not want discovered by whomever found her body. The contents were far more startling than any accumulation of tawdry secrets could be.

Copies of all the letters she had sent Dom since he'd left Santa Fe were inside. They had obviously been copied from those she'd found in Dom's room. All the underlinings were the same, all variations on the theme of her dogged loyalty: "I'll never give up what we had." "I'll never stop trying to find out what has happened to you, to us." "I love you now as much as I ever did."

She flipped back to the beginning of the file and found a detailed data sheet, unlike any she'd seen before, all about herself. Beneath her name, address, place of employment, age, parents' names, addresses, and occupations (her father rated three stars next to the listing "Senator") was the entry: RELATION TO RECON SQUAD MEMBER: Primary, non-Blood, Major Terminal. Bria rifled through the rest of the report. It detailed a stupefying amount of information about her life.

She found copies of her grade-school report cards and the personality evaluations that the counselor at her high school had filled out on all the students and kept in a confidential file. There were copies of her bank statements from the time she opened her first checking account. They even had a listing of all the books she'd ever checked out of the Santa Fe Public Library and statements from all her em-

ployers about her "credit reliability." Then there were
pictures—all those she had taken for the paper, plus prints
of her, obviously shot with a telephoto lens and showing
her in every phase of her daily life: climbing out of her
jeep, entering the *Sentinel* building, squatting with a camera pressed against her face, strolling across the plaza,
ducking into La Fonda for a drink. There were dozens of
photos, but the one that sent chills down her spine depicted
her standing next to Mrs. Cavanagh, just four days ago, at
Dom's memorial service.

The file dropped to her lap. The cover flipped away to reveal the front page again. A paragraph labeled COMPOSITE
SUMMARY caught her eye. She figured it must be the syn-
thesis of all the documentation they had collected on her:

> The Subject is recommended as primary candidate
> for Operation Jugular. Her access through her father,
> Senator Frank Delgado, to the Rienstahl files, com-
> bined with Subject's obsessive attachment to R.S.
> member Dominic Cavanagh, and her Predicted Pat-
> tern of Response uniquely qualify her for this opera-
> tion.

Bria read on:

> PROCLIVITIES: (Extracted from Cavanagh's file.) Sub-
> ject has manifested a high inverse need to exert
> cause. A classic example of Lou's Pendulum Axiom.
> Product of repressed Hispanic upbringing. Mother
> very much in Submission Vector, early attempts to
> mold Subject. Subject swung in last four years to op-
> posite apex of pendulum. Demonstrated aggressive-
> ness in work as photographer for *Sentinel.* Stuck on
> upward swing by disconnection from Cavanagh two
> years ago. Proclivity programmed to magnify upon
> Cavanagh's death.

> PREDICTED PATTERN OF RESPONSE: Subject will initiate
> energetic personal investigation of death. Unlikely
> to accept official report. Likely to favor direct con-
> frontation.

> SUGGESTIONS: Display initial resistance to Subject's in-

vestigation. Allow Subject to discover extent of
Rienstahl's harassment of Life Unlimited. Supply
no information. Arrange for Subject to come to se-
lected squad member with questions. Plant knowledge of the existence of government's LU file and tie
in with Cavanagh's death. Subject thus briefed is
given 85% probability of procuring file. Equally
high probability that Subject will suggest enlisting
media assistance to publicize file contents and implications. Once On Line with Lou, have Subject get
On Grid. Allow Subject to convince herself and she
will make exceptional media presentation.

At the bottom of the proposal, next to a slot marked AP-
PROVAL, was Slako's signature. It was followed by another
report, dated November 6. "Subject sighted at Verifications Counter. Subject feigned inability to speak English. I
received assignment to establish link as fellow Chicano
outsider. Contact established in Mess Hall." Bria skipped
to the end of the report and found the signature she'd expected: Leonard Davila, Recon Squad.

Next was a report on her first Exteriorization session.
George had filled out the first half of the report with codes
and numbers that had charted the flight of her soul. Slako
had completed the last half. Beside several of the codes
were notations to "see Cavanagh's file," along with a session number. Bria dug through the thick collection of files
behind Dom's name until she found the correct session
numbers.

It was all there, the entire history of their relationship
in underlined notes from Dom's sessions on the Grid. Even
the night after his father's funeral. Dom too had catego-
rized their night together as his most complete experience
of "communion" with another human being.

Only what she had lived through since first stepping
through those oak doors sixty hours ago, could have prepared Bria for the conclusion she was forced to: she had
been studied, stalked, and lured, played out and reeled in
like some prize trout with Dom's murder as the bait.

The Louies had known precisely which strings to pull,
and she had jerked in response as neatly as any mario-
nette. Her own personality kinks had built the walls of a

maze she'd run, straight to their objective, the file. She had procured it from her father, just as they'd predicted, and obligingly presented it to the media to prove the extent to which they were being harassed by an insane government. She'd lent whatever credibility she had to Slako's story of the squad members being assassinated by a government agent. Now she too would be painted as a martyr in Lou's holy war. She wouldn't be around to tell them who the real murderer was, to send Slako back to the imprisonment he deserved for plotting six murders, besides her own and George's. And what had it all been for? For those few lines in a newspaper that would shift the glare of negative publicity from the Louies to the government, turn it into the villain who had murdered the young people on the confiscated list? For a publicity coup that would offset the coverage the Louies would receive when the federal judge found the six indictees guilty of conspiracy to steal government documents? Dom had been sacrificed in a ridiculous war where the ammunition was files, stacks of paper—government files against Louie files. A war of files. Bria laughed. She had no more tears to waste on this absurdity. So much had already been wasted—Dom, the life they could have had together.

"No, Gretch, no . . ." George's sudden cry trailed off into indistinguishable, half-conscious mutterings.

Had he known? Had George been a part of the murders? It was hard to believe otherwise. Bria's thoughts acted upon George like a mental transfusion. He slowly opened his swollen eyes and, for several minutes, stared at her in blank silence. Bria didn't know whether he was seeing her or not, if he had been blinded in the explosion or knocked senseless.

"Why didn't you let me die?"

"George," Bria spoke softly, "neither of us will be living much longer. I've only postponed the moment of our deaths."

He looked at the files barricading him and squeezed his eyes shut again, as if a thought that had been hounding him in unconsciousness had caught up with him. Soundless tears poured from beneath his lids.

"I wish there was something I could do to make you more comfortable."

"You could have let me die. My body is no longer of any concern to me. I had already detached from it. I can barely feel any pain. I wish it were as easy to blank out thoughts."

Bria didn't know what to say to ease the mental torment George was undergoing.

"I was the one who got Gretch into LU. She came to save me, and I thought I was saving her. Saving us all. We could have, you know. Could have saved this planet. Except for Slako and . . ." His voice broke. "God, she left me here to die. My own sister."

"She was brainwashed, George, you all were."

"Brainwashed? What is that? I don't know anymore. Is it what makes some Alabama insurance salesman let himself be dunked in a muddy river? Or what makes a Hindu beggar starve to death while a cow chews its cud in front of him? Or is it . . ."

"George, don't talk anymore." The effort was taking a toll on George's savaged body. His voice was a parched whisper. He tried to swallow and licked his lips with a dry tongue.

"I don't know. I never knew. Lou had all the answers. Pretty soon I just stopped asking the questions."

The vault had grown suffocatingly hot. A panicked claustrophobia attacked Bria. The one thing that kept the terror of her own dying at bay was concentrating on making George's less painful. She struggled to divert him.

"George, I'm not saying that Gretchen and Dom, all of you, had water dripped on your foreheads or tape recorders planted under your pillows. There are more subtle ways to reshape minds. There was the psychological coercion you all were under, the constant group pressure. That alone is powerful enough to change the way a person looks at the world. Plus, none of you ever got enough sleep or a decent, nourishing meal. You were charged up on caffeine and your grand mission to save the planet. When you start you're overwhelmed by attention and approval. Pretty soon you're working to keep the approval of the group. You get On the Grid and it's unlike anything you've ever experienced. You try to 'gain altitude' by jettisoning a lifetime of secrets. I'm sure no one ever so much as hints at blackmail. But do they have to? All you cadets know that your secrets are enshrined in vaults that will be around when your grandchildren are dead. Maybe a few indirect threats that the vaults could spring a leak, combined with an appeal to 'the Mission,' was enough to convince you all to go along with what you did."

"What do you mean?"

"Murder. Leonard's, for sure. The whole Academy had to have been in on that one. No one was smoking while Slako or one of his Protectorate henchmen gassed Leonard in his sleep. Then Dom in that bathroom. Surely someone on that floor must have known."

"Bria, I . . ." George stopped, shaking his head wearily.

"Look, I know that my coming here was rigged from the start; I saw the file Slako had on me." She remembered the perplexing image she had seen in her rearview mirror when she hurtled out of the Academy parking lot. She saw vividly the guard, his face split by laughter. "You all must have gotten a big laugh out of my pathetic attempts at cunning. At least I didn't believe your drug-conspiracy story."

George's voice was leaden. "That part of it was true."

"You're still a believer, aren't you, George? Were you in on the cover-up of the murders, making it look like they were the work of a government assassin?"

George shook his head in a nod that was neither affirmation nor denial. "That was the object of Operation Jugular. Slako planted the Recon Squad list right after the indictments were handed down. He knew Rienstahl's agent would steal it. When our sources in his office confirmed that the list was in the government file, Slako turned the tapes over to the Senate subcommittee on drug trafficking."

"Then, a week later," Bria cut in, "to make it look like retaliation, Slako had Leslie Aaronson murdered. Right?"

George didn't answer. His expression disturbed Bria. It was like the last look he'd exchanged with Slako.

"Well, isn't that what happened?" she demanded uneasily.

"You've experienced a Grid Shift," George said, his voice a whisper. "You know that death can be transcended, that the body is only a vehicle for the inner entity. Death destroys only the vehicle. The entity then must relocate in another vehicle. That is all death is, a relocation. And, when a person has a mission, relocation is swift and sure. Do you see?"

"Sure, it sounds like a variation on reincarnation or a possible interpretation of Christianity."

"Yes, but this isn't a loose interpretation I'm talking about. I'm describing the literal basis for an elite corps in LU called Wing. Membership in Wing was a prerequisite to membership in the Recon Squad. Dom was a Wing member. So was Leonard. So was I. So was Slako. We all wore an emblem. I can't reach mine. It's on the chain around my neck."

Bria bent closer. Her stomach jackknifed at the sight and smell of George's back. She forced her hand forward and had to will it not to recoil when she found that the chain was embedded in the charred flesh at the back of George's neck. She moved her fingers along to the front of the chain until they reached a spiky medallion. It was the tilted cross. She dropped the golden X. "I don't see what that has to do with the murders."

"Hold it up," George insisted.

The medallion was balanced perfectly on the chain. It twirled first one way, then the other, seeming to gain momentum with each revolution.

"Are you starting to understand now?"

Bria shook her head no.

"It doesn't stop. The X, it matches the angle of the intersecting axes of the Grid when it is shifted. It symbolizes LU's triumph over death."

"No more symbols," Bria said quietly. "Just explain how this all fits in with Dom's murder."

"I'm trying to, but I want to put it in perspective. It's starting to seem bizarre even to me now." Several minutes passed while George took deep, rattling breaths, gathering his strength to speak again. "Look in Dom's file," he said at last. "In the last folder. The last document."

Bria found the large section divider with Dom's name on it. She leafed through a dozen folders stuffed with forms and papers and stopped at the last one. It was slim, containing only a few papers. She pulled out the final entry. It was an official-looking document on thick parchment embossed with LU's stylized jets arching across the top. Her eyes dropped to the last line, where she recognized Dom's bold signature. She began reading.

"What does this all mean?" she asked, lifting her eyes from the puzzling document. "It looks like some kind of enlistment, pledging service to Lou and the advancement of his mission for the next ten thousand lifetimes. This is insane. Dom signed on with Wing for seven hundred thousand years?"

"Given seventy years a lifetime," George answered, "that's about right."

Bria waited for him to say more, to explain. "Is this a joke? Another symbol?" She already had a chilling presentiment that it was neither.

"I signed one. So did Leonard. All of us in Wing did. It was not a joke and not symbolic either. After the indictments, which imperiled Lou and the Mission, Slako came up with Operation Jugular and the service of Wing members was required. Look at the date Dom's service was scheduled to begin."

"November first, 1980." Bria's stomach lurched. The day Dom had died. She no longer wanted to know the answer to her question. She wished she had never started asking. She didn't want to hear what George was saying.

"There were no murders, Bria. Slako didn't need to resort to that to frame Rienstahl. We all signed on willingly for an eternity of service. We felt privileged. My activation date hadn't been designated yet, but, when it came, I would have happily done what the others before me had—commit suicide."

The word shrieked savagely in Bria's mind, louder and louder, until a white hot light blew it apart. Then a silent blackness soothed her brain. Bria retreated gratefully into it.

CHAPTER 29

The long, confused night was ending. Soon morning would come. She would filter coffee and fry *chorizo* and eggs. She and Dom could eat on the patio, it was warm enough now, and watch the hummingbirds feed from the hollyhocks. Time for him to be getting up.

"Dom . . ." The small voice was a shattered croak scratching out that same dry syllable.

"Oh, Christ." Senator Frank Delgado turned away from his daughter's bed. There was nothing else to look at in the private room. Everything was so white, so sterile. He walked to the window.

"Frank, I'm sorrier than I can ever tell you." Still Mary Margaret Cavanagh had been trying, ever since they'd flown Bria up from Houston, trying to tell him how much she regretted having involved his daughter. How, if she'd had any idea . . .

Delgado could no longer stand looking at those watery gray eyes swimming in that fallen face. He almost wished for the days when they had been frozen against him.

They were on the seventh floor of St. Vincent's Hospital. He could see Rosario Cemetery, with the Delgado family plot marked off by iron spikes. Stone angels slept under mantles of snow. The tiny carved lamb that Delgado knew was in the west corner of the plot looked like a toy from this height. He thought of the heartbreakingly wistful inscription beneath the lamb's front paws: Rest in Peace, Beloved Rafaelito, 1904–1905.

The doctors had told him that they didn't know when, or if, Bria would come completely out of the coma. She had progressed from a comatose state to semicomatose, and now remained in what the doctors termed a "lethargic state." There had been some brain injury during the explosion. Sometimes, they said, the healing is rapid and total, with no complications. Other times, they would begin, then trail off into "it all depends on the individual."

"Frank," Mrs. Cavanagh whispered, "I think she's coming around."

Delgado didn't move from the window. Every few days his daughter stirred and his hopes were rekindled. It was better not to hope. The disappointment hurt too much. Bria hadn't regained consciousness yet, not in the three weeks since . . .

"Frank," her voice was urgent now, "really."

Delgado left the window. Halfway to her bed he stopped. Bria sat up and paralyzed him by opening her eyes. Those Cerrillos turquoise eyes, just like his mother's, just as green and beautiful. Except that they didn't seem to be seeing anything.

Bria looked around. The room was too bright. Her head ached ferociously. Her body felt unused, rusted. She had been awakened too early. There was still a full night's sleep waiting for her. What was Dom's mother doing here? And her father? Their expressions were so odd. Was there something wrong with her? She wanted to sleep. One question surfaced from the dark, distant pool that drowned her memory.

"Guh . . ." The name, formed perfectly in her mind, died in her throat.

Mrs. Cavanagh rushed to fill a glass from the green plastic pitcher by her bed. She held the glass to Bria's lips and water sloshed down, lubricating her dry vocal cords.

"George." The name was all she could force out. It stood for all the amorphous phantoms beginning to take shape in her mind.

Delgado and Mrs. Cavanagh looked at each other.

"Kirby." It was an effort to add the last name. They already knew anyway who she was talking about. They looked at each other, consulting, deciding.

Delgado moved to his daughter's side and took her hand. His hair had gone from gray to silver, like Cesar Romero's. When had it happened? Why hadn't she noticed? And his eyes, so tender and brown, like an old spaniel's. Had they always been like that?

"He's dead, Bria. He was dead when they got to you."

Dead. Her memory, a haze in the distance, began to shift, to come into focus, like an image in the viewfinder of her camera. The first clear memory to emerge pumped her body with a jolt of adrenaline. She was in that vault. It was getting hotter. There was no way out.

"Who got to us? How did we get out?"

"Bria," her father soothed, "you're weak. We can discuss all this after you're rested. We should tell the doctor you're awake now."

Bria's thin fingers dug into her father's arm. "How."

Delgado sighed. He hated to go into this in front of Mary Margaret. "After I sent you that damned file, I regretted it. I called Rienstahl. He had one of his agents check on you. That's when we found out what was happening. Rienstahl sent in a special team to blow open that vault." Delgado stopped and looked at his daughter, thinking of how close she had come. *"Dios,* you were smart to get in that vault. That was what saved you."

More of the picture came into focus and with it came more questions. "The file. Newspaper story. Trials."

"Bria, *hija,* we can go into all of this later. It's long, complicated. It's . . ."

"Tell me."

"Okay." She couldn't remember ever hearing her father's voice so soft, so gentle. "The story broke three weeks ago in the *Houston Chronicle.*"

Three weeks? Where had they gone?

"Of course, it created a huge uproar. People are so willing now to believe in government duplicity, in the unlimited power of government, especially the IRS. That's why it worked, why the public believed that Rienstahl had had all the Louies on that list murdered. By the time it came out that all the deaths had been . . ." He paused and shot a glance toward Dom's mother. Her face was taut and pinched, as if she were bracing herself for the blow that was to come, "suicides, instead of murders, most people still believed that where there was that much smoke, there must be at least some fire.

"The trials." Delgado stopped and sucked in a deep

breath that he let escape in a long, hissing leak. "Lawyers on both sides are gearing up. There are four grand juries investigating now. Given the issues in the case, it's sure to go all the way to the Supreme Court. It will be years before they get this mess litigated. As of this moment, though, you're the witness every lawyer wants to subpoena and the subject every reporter wants to interview."

Bria closed her eyes. Things were becoming foggy again, hard to focus on.

"We'll keep them away, *hija*, as long as we can. No one knows you're here yet and they won't until you're ready."

One sharp recollection spiked Bria on her slide into a misty warmth. "Slako."

"Ah, yes, Lieutenant Anthony Slako." Her father used the voice he reserved for those he wanted, or would try, to crush beneath his heel. "When everything came out about Operation Jugular, Slako claimed it was all his, start to finish, completely unauthorized by Church officials, completely antithetical to Church philosophy. LU spokesmen are saying now that everything underhanded the Louies have pulled for the past twenty years was masterminded by Slako."

Delgado seamed his mouth tightly shut for a moment, then burst out, "I don't believe a goddamned word of it. Slako is a scapegoat, a willing one. He gets all LU's sins hung on his back and Lou comes out clean. There's no way Comfort couldn't have known of and approved Operation Jugular. It was probably his idea. But with Slako taking the rap, there's no way to get at him. LU bigwigs are acting like Slako was some kind of rogue elephant. They're issuing all sorts of public apologies, vows never again to 'stray from the traditional role of the Church.' One of those 'traditional roles,' as it turns out, is spying. They call it 're-form action.' Seems I've had a 'reformer' working for me for the past five years; most everyone on the Hill has."

Bria prompted her father with her eyes. "Who?" she asked.

The Senator's tight mouth quivered into a slack, bewildered hole. "My secretary, you know, Jenni, been with me for five years, she's one of them. The Louies have copies of every incriminating letter, memorandum, note, that ever passed through my office. Nothing that could get me impeached, mind you, nothing that anyone on the Hill would even blink twice at, but certainly enough to keep me from being reelected if those notes and memos were spread out all over page one of the *Sentinel.* Anyway, the day after dear Jenni abruptly resigned, I started getting phone calls, usually around three in the morning. That's how I found out about the existence of all this extra paperwork Jenni had been spiriting out of the office. They've proposed a deal, an 'exchange,' our silence for theirs."

Bria ached for her father, for Mrs. Cavanagh hovering behind him, for herself, for what they all still had to face.

"You were right, Bria. All that about the First Amendment, you were right. I had no idea of the vermin hiding behind it. Anyway, I'm not going to run for reelection. They can do their worst to me because that's exactly what I intend to do to them. No one buys my silence, especially not them, especially after what they did to . . ." His anger and the words it had fueled died.

"So she's awake, and you didn't tell me. That was naughty." A frizzy-haired nurse, perky in starched peaked cap and bouncy in white, crepe-soled shoes, pushed through the door trailing an IV hookup. She shone a tiny flashlight into Bria's pupils. "Looks good in there. How long has she been awake?" The nurse cradled Bria's wrist in her hand as she took her pulse.

"Just a few minutes."

"They were supposed to tell me the minute you opened those beautiful green peepers." The nurse directed her reprimand to the Senator through Bria. "I'll bet you're exhausted. No more visitors today."

The woman's cheeriness exhausted Bria more than anything else had since she'd opened her "peepers." Her father gathered up his sheepskin jacket and helped Mrs. Cavanagh put on her coat.

"I told your mother I'd call the minute you came around. Of course Ignacio wants to visit and your friends at the *Sentinel* have all been asking about you."

Bria nodded; she was tired. There was one last thing, though. "Wait."

"Yes," Mrs. Cavanagh answered. Sometime in the weeks since Bria had last seen her, the woman had crossed the line from "older" into "old." It was an old woman who waited for her to continue.

"Dom's watch," she said, hoping she would be spared the exertion of further explanation.

"Yes, it was returned. I've put it in your drawer."

Bria shook her head against the pillow. "Yours," she said, the dozy haze already rising in her brain. "The Governor's, Dom's, yours."

Mrs. Cavanagh bobbed her head down, tears spilling over her cheeks. "Thank you," she whispered, bending close to Bria's ear. Bria felt her cheek, its fuzzy softness, felt the wetness of the tears and her own as they mingled with Dom's mother's, both of them mourning someone they had lost over two years ago.

"Now, that's enough," the nurse ordered with mock fierceness, "everyone scoot. This little lady needs her rest."

Her father ignored the nurse and clasped his daughter in an embrace that spoke of protection and pride and love. "I'll be back tomorrow." His voice was thick. "Rest. Don't think about any of this. They can't touch you, I promise."

As the door swung shut, the focus Bria had struggled to maintain slipped away. She was sliding back into sleep, the tears still wet on her face, as the nurse began expertly to attach a new bottle to the tube feeding into her arm. Even if she had been fully alert, though, Bria probably wouldn't have noticed that the new bottle had been opened and resealed, the edges of the metal stopper at the bottle's throat crimped, almost undetectably, back into place. But, if Bria had been watching, she surely would have noticed the medallion that swung out of the woman's uniform as she adjusted the stopcocks on the IV tube. It was a golden X that twirled in feverish revolutions.

The Senator and the Governor's widow walked in silence toward the swinging glass doors at the ward entrance. Outside, a thickening snow had turned the late afternoon sky a dull pewter. Mrs. Cavanagh hesitated as Delgado shouldered open the door.

"You don't suppose that that silly nurse would neglect to call Dr. Fowler, do you? He did want to know the moment Bria woke up."

Bria's father let the door sigh closed again.

Mrs. Cavanagh began fishing in her purse for coins. "I think I'll call him myself just to make sure."

Delgado nodded, looking down the hall. "Good idea. Tell him I'll meet him in Bria's room."

"Yes, we can't take chances, can we?" Mary Margaret Cavanagh asked the Senator. But he was out of earshot, already hustling back to his daughter's room. She quickly ducked her head, whispering the answer to her question to herself. "No, we can't take chances, not with our children."